THE BRIEF AND FRIGHTENING REIGN OF PHIL

and

IN PERSUASION NATION

GEORGE SAUNDERS

BLOOMSBURY

First published in Great Britain 2006
This paperback edition published 2007

The Brief and Frightening Reign of Phil
copyright © 2005 by George Saunders
In Persuasion Nation copyright © 2006 by George Saunders

Bloomsbury Publishing Plc,
36 Soho Square,
London W1D 3QY

A CIP catalogue record for this book is
available from the British Library

ISBN 9780747585961

All papers used by Bloomsbury Publishing are natural,
recyclable products made from wood grown in well-managed
forests. The manufacturing processes conform to the
environmental regulations of the country of origin.

10 9 8 7 6 5 4 3 2 1

Printed and bound in Great Britain
by Clays Ltd, St Ives plc

www.bloomsbury.com/georgesaunders

THE BRIEF AND FRIGHTENING REIGN OF PHIL

To Joe and Sheri Lindbloom,
brilliant teachers, beautiful friends.

It's one thing to be a small country, but the country of Inner Horner was so small only one Inner Hornerite at a time could fit inside, and the other six Inner Hornerites had to wait their turns to live in their own country while standing very timidly in the surrounding country of Outer Horner.

Whenever the Outer Hornerites looked at the hangdog Inner Hornerites crammed into the Short-Term Residency Zone, they felt a little sick, and also very patriotic. Inner Hornerites were pathetic and whiny and grasping, unlike them, the Outer Hornerites, who for many years had been demonstrating their tremendous generosity by allowing the Inner Hornerites to overflow into the Short-Term Residency Zone. Not that the Inner Hornerites appreciated it. No, they never wept with gratitude anymore, only stood very close together, glaring resentfully at the Outer Hornerites, who, having so much room, had no need to stand close together, and in fact could often be seen drinking coffee at the spacious Outer Horner Cafe with their legs thrown out in the aisles, causing the Inner

Hornerites to wonder: Jeez, couldn't those jerks spare us a couple hundred extra square yards of that vast unlimited country?

For their part, the Outer Hornerites felt that, yes, okay, their country was big, but it wasn't infinitely big, which meant they might someday conceivably run out of room. Besides, what if they gave more of their beloved country to Inner Horner and some other crummy little countries came around demanding bits of Outer Horner? What would happen to the Outer Horner way of life, which was so comfortable and afforded them such super dignity and required so much space? Well, those Inner Hornerites could take a flying leap if they considered Outer Hornerites selfish, it was pretty nervy to call someone selfish while standing on land they were letting you use for free.

So it went, year after year, with much mutual glowering and many murmured rude comments and the occasional angry word hissed across the border.

Then one day Inner Horner got smaller. It happened without warning; there was a loud scraping rock-on-rock sound and suddenly three-quarters of Elmer, the Inner Hornerite then in residence, was not in Inner Horner at all. That is, every part of Elmer but the octagonal shovel-like receptacle with which he scooped dirt when nervous was suddenly now located in Outer Horner.

Just then Leon, the Outer Horner Border Guard, came by on his rounds, noted the presence of three-quarters of Elmer in Outer Horner, and rang the loud buzzer that meant Invasion in Progress.

The Outer Horner Militia (Freeda, Melvin, and Larry) came rushing over and stood glaring fiercely across the green piece of string that constituted the boundary of the Short-Term Residency Zone.

"What are you people trying to pull?" said Larry. "What's that part of a guy doing in our country?"

"Our country shrunk," said Elmer, digging nervously in the dirt with his octagonal shovel-like receptacle.

"Oh please," said Freeda. "You expect us to believe that? Our country never shrinks."

"Decent countries don't shrink," said Melvin. "They either stay the same or get bigger."

"Take a look," said Elmer.

And the Outer Horner Militia (Freeda, Melvin, and Larry) looked into the deep heart of Inner Horner, by leaning over the red string that constituted the Inner Horner border, and saw that Inner Horner had, in fact, shrunk.

"Weird," said Melvin.

"Gross," said Larry.

"What do we do now?" said Freeda.

"I say we expulse the invaders," said Larry.

"That sounds pretty good," said Melvin. "How do we?"

"We just, ah, you know, expulse them," said Larry. "Watch. Something like this."

And Larry expulsed Elmer. That is, he pushed the portion of Elmer that was in Outer Horner back into Inner Horner. But since Inner Horner was now too small to accommodate all of Elmer, as the portion of Elmer in Outer Horner was expulsed into Inner Horner, a different portion of Elmer reemerged out of Inner Horner, sort of inadvertently reinvading Outer Horner.

"They're a scrappy, stubborn people," said Melvin. "You've got to give them that."

"Sneaky," said Larry. "That's what they are."

"What you need to do," said someone, with great authority, from over by the Cafe, "is tax them."

This was Phil, a middle-aged Outer Hornerite generally considered a slightly bitter nobody. Many years before, Phil had, from across the border, fallen in love with a largely vertical, left-trending Inner Hornerite named Carol. He was captivated by her glossy black filaments and transparent oscillating membranes, the delicate curve of her exposed spine, her habit of demurely scratching one bearing with a furry glovelike appendage, and spent many hours casually circling Inner Horner, hoping to catch

4

her eye, inflating and deflating his central bladder in order to look more manly and attractive. But no. Carol was in love with Cal, an Inner Hornerite who resembled a gigantic belt buckle with a blue dot affixed to it, if a gigantic belt buckle with a blue dot affixed to it had been stapled to a tuna fish can.

The day of the wedding was the worst of Phil's life.

He stood across the border, heartbroken, passing bits of machine oil from his lower strata as the Inner Hornerites performed their marriage ritual, which consisted of standing even more closely together than usual and singing sentimental songs about the enviable compactness of their country.

Over the years Phil's bitterness increased, as day after day he watched Carol polishing Cal's belt buckle and playfully opening and closing Cal's tuna fish can. When Carol and Cal's son, Little Andy, was born, Phil's bitterness was complete. He couldn't help thinking that, if only Carol had used better judgment and shown better taste, Little Andy could've been his son. Although if Little Andy had been his son, Little Andy would no doubt have been better-looking and more intelligent and certainly wouldn't have been given a dopey Inner Horner–sounding name like Little Andy.

"You tax them," Phil said again. "You charge them for every day they take up room in our beloved land."

"Wow, great idea," said Larry. "How much do we charge?"

5

"How much do they have?" said Phil.

"How much do you have?" Larry asked the Inner Hornerites.

Using his octagonal shovel-like receptacle, Elmer opened the cash box, which occupied the entire northwest region of Inner Horner.

"Four smolokas," he said.

"Then tax them four," said Phil.

"But then we'll have zero," said Cal.

"Tax them four," said Phil. "They pay us four, they can stay in the Short-Term Residency Zone the rest of the day. That's how you do it. That's fair."

"Pretty smart guy," said Larry.

"Yeah, who knew?" said Melvin.

Now, in addition to having been jilted by the love of his life, Phil had another problem, which was that the bolt holding his brain in position on his tremendous sliding rack occasionally fell out, causing his brain to slide rapidly down his rack and smash into the ground. This happened now. His brain slid down, smashed into the ground, popped off his rack, and rolled into a ditch.

"I'll tell you something else about which I've been lately thinking!" he bellowed in a suddenly stentorian voice. "I've been thinking about our beautiful country! Who gave it to us? I've been thinking about how God the Almighty gave us this beautiful sprawling land as a reward for how wonderful we are. We're big, we're energetic, we're generous, which is reflected in all our myths, which are so very populated with large high-energy folks who give away all they have! If we have a National Virtue, it is that we are generous, if we have a National Defect, it is that we are *too* generous! Is it our fault that these little jerks have such a small crappy land? I think not! God Almighty gave them that small crappy land for reasons of His own. It is not my place to start cross-examining God Almighty, asking why He gave them such a small crappy land, my place is to simply enjoy and protect the big bountiful land God Almighty gave us!"

Suddenly Phil didn't seem like quite so much of a nobody to the other Outer Hornerites. What kind of nobody was so vehement, and used so many confusing phrases with so much certainty, and was so completely accurate about how wonderful and generous and underappreciated they were?

"Boy oh boy," said Freeda.

"He just comes right out and says it," said Melvin.

"Thank goodness someone finally has," said Larry.

"As for you Inner Hornerites!" bellowed Phil. "Please take heed: You are hereby testing the limits of our legendary generosity, because of how you are, which is so very the opposite of us. Friends, take a look at these losers! If they are as good as us, why do they look so much worse than us? Look how they look! Do they look valorous and noble and huge like us, or do they look sad and weak and puny?"

The truth was, long years of timidly standing very close together in the Short-Term Residency Zone whispering complicated mathematical proofs to pass the time had made the Inner Hornerites frail and small, whereas the Outer Hornerites, with an entire huge country to roam around in, were stocky and hearty, and knew absolutely no mathematical proofs.

"Pretty darn puny," said Melvin.

"I never really noticed that before," said Leon the Border Guard.

"Collect the taxes!" shouted Phil, and Freeda reached over the border and seized the Inner Horner cash box.

Larry and Melvin rushed into the ditch, retrieved Phil's brain, and remounted it on his big sliding rack.

"Thank you, my friends," said Phil, his voice suddenly less stentorian. "What wonderful examples of our famous Outer Horner generosity."

Larry gave Melvin a proud secret look, and Melvin gave Larry a proud secret look, and Freeda, counting the contents of the cash box to verify that there were in fact four smolokas inside, felt a little sad that Phil had not cited her as a wonderful example of that famous Outer Horner generosity, and resolved that, next time Phil's brain slid off his rack, she would be the one to remount it.

Next morning, Phil and the Outer Horner Militia (Freeda, Melvin, and Larry) arrived at the border before dawn and stood watching the Inner Hornerites sleep while standing up.

"Snooze, snooze, snooze," said Phil. "Sort of lazy, aren't they?"

"Whereas us," said Larry, "we're up before dawn, diligently working."

"That's right Larry," said Phil. "Good observation."

"Doing our diligent work of collecting taxes," said Melvin.

"Super, Melvin," said Phil. "We really are a diligent people."

"Diligently collecting taxes to protect the security of our nation," said Freeda.

"You know what?" said Phil. "After spending some time with you folks, I am tempted, in terms of our most important National Virtue, to replace 'Generosity' with 'Remarkable Intelligence.' "

Larry, Melvin, and Freeda beamed.

"Now what do you say we collect some taxes?" Phil said,

and nudged Leon, who, with his Border Guard pole, gave Wanda, the nearest Inner Hornerite, a hard poke in her thermal venting apparatus.

The Inner Hornerites woke and, as on every other morning, briefly considered stretching, then remembered that, if they all stretched at once, someone would get knocked out of the Short-Term Residency Zone and would technically be invading Outer Horner.

So they began stretching, one at a time, by age, oldest first.

"Tax time, slackers," said Phil. "Stop that stupid stretching and listen up. You're late with your dang taxes."

"But we don't have any money," said Elmer. "You know we don't. You took it all yesterday."

"Oh, you people," said Phil. "What did you have in mind? Living in our beloved country for free forever? Do you know what we do? In our country? We work. We believe that time is money. Therefore, as time passes, in our land, we diligently work, which produces, guess what? Wealth. Money. Smolokas! You people! Knowing you owed us money, what did you do? You slept all night like babies! Dreaming, probably, of further taking us to the cleaners! So here you are, smolokaless, again owing your daily taxes. What else do you have? Larry, inventory their resources."

Larry looked at Phil blankly.

"Count their stuff," said Phil.

"Oh," said Larry, and inventoried the resources of the nation of Inner Horner, by examining the length and breadth of Inner Horner and carefully recording the results of his inventory on a piece of paper, which he then handed to Phil.

"Okay, let's see," said Phil. "Apple tree, very small: one. Stream, nearly dry: one. Dry cracked dirt: approximately three cubic feet. Excellent, Larry, an excellent inventory. Now, let's assess the total value of their national resources. Freeda, what do you say? Do you say four? Do you say all that junk is worth exactly four smolokas?"

Overnight, Freeda, a lonely bushlike widow, had developed a bit of a crush on authoritative, gleaming, shouting Phil, and nodded her head yes with a rapt look on her face, without even looking at the tree, the stream, or the dirt.

"Excellent job, Freeda," said Phil. "A really nice assessment. Leon: Uproot that tree and drain that stream and dig up that dirt and let's bring it all back home, to Outer Horner."

Leon stepped over the border and uprooted the apple tree and drained the stream into his see-through stomach. Then, using his spadelike tail, he dug up the dirt and added it to the stream in his stomach, making a pale red mud.

"But what will we eat?" said Carol. "What will we drink? What do you expect us to do when it's our turn to live in our country, stand in that hole?"

"That's not really my problem," said Phil. "My problem is, where am I going to store this junky tree and this boring little stream and this laughable dirt? Any suggestions?"

"How about West Distant Outer Horner?" said Larry. "It's pretty empty out there."

"Super input, Larry," said Phil. "Leon, would you do the honors?"

Carrying the tree over his shoulder and the streamwater-dirt mix in his stomach, Leon walked out to West Distant Outer Horner, a bleak area of recurring icy crevasses, and dropped the former national resources of Inner Horner into the deepest, iciest crevasse he could find.

That night in the Short-Term Residency Zone the Inner Hornerites held a whispered frantic national referendum. Years of standing with their limbs intermingled had made the Inner Hornerites extremely considerate of one another's feelings, so much so that even the simplest decision, such as whether to declare it National Bedtime, sometimes took hours.

"So how should we start?" said Elmer. "How should we proceed? What's our primary issue here?"

"Wait a minute, Elmer," said Wanda. "Aren't you getting a little ahead of things? Don't you think we should first determine if determining our primary issue is indeed our highest priority?"

"Which I suppose raises the question of whether determining our highest priority really is in fact our initial goal," said Old Gus, the oldest Inner Hornerite, who was so old and tired he was shaped something like the letter *C*, if the letter *C* was bald and had two gray withered antlers.

"I think the primary issue is, we don't have any food," said Carol.

"I agree with Carol," said Cal, who, after ten years of marriage, was still nuts about Carol.

"Although the lack of water isn't so great either," said Curtis.

"Of course we also have no dirt," said Elmer.

"Well, the lack of dirt I think is not so primary," said Curtis.

"I beg to differ," said Elmer. "I think the lack of dirt is very primary. I mean, look at our country."

And everyone looked at Inner Horner, which now looked something like an open grave.

"To be frank, I'm feeling a little left out of this discussion," said Old Gus. "My concern about whether determining our highest priority was indeed our initial goal appears to have been dismissed out of hand."

Just then Inner Horner was hit with a blinding light

from somewhere up high.

"Phil's orders, folks," said Leon the Border Guard, standing behind a spotlight he had just installed on top of his Guard Shack. "He wants me to keep a better eye on you people, because you're so sneaky, which he feels will be easier if it's not so dark at night."

"Gosh, that's bright," said Wanda.

"Leon, if we're so sneaky, how come you're always playing checkers with us?" said Cal.

"I'm not," said Leon. "I've discontinued that."

"Maybe we should draft a petition of protest," said Wanda. "After first discussing the idea among ourselves, of course."

"Maybe we should hold a straw poll to assess the level of support for the idea of drafting a petition of protest," said Cal.

"I say enough talking," said Curtis. "I say it's time we *did* something."

"Maybe we should go on a hunger strike," said Old Gus.

"Excuse me, Gus," said Carol. "Not to dismiss your idea? But aren't we sort of already on a hunger strike? Because no food? Remember, they took our apple tree? So I'm not sure how effective a hunger strike would be. I mean, they might not even notice we were on one."

"They've essentially put us on one," said Cal.

"I have an idea," said Little Andy.

Even though Little Andy was the youngest Inner Hornerite, he had an acute probing intelligence that the Inner Hornerites all respected, an intelligence probably related to the fact that he had two distinct functional brains, one on the side of his neck and the other on his hip, with a shiny yellow Decider located midway between them.

"Go ahead, son," said Cal.

"Why don't we write a letter to their President?" Little Andy said.

"Ha ha!" said Curtis. "That is so cute."

"That is cute," said Wanda. "But also it's not bad."

Actually it was good. The President of Outer Horner was an affable old man with five white mustaches and seven ample bellies, who many years before, while a student, had spent a semester abroad in Inner Horner, or at least part of him had, and so the conventional wisdom was that he had a soft spot for Inner Horner and Inner Hornerites.

So the Inner Hornerites, with virtually no debate or discussion, blinking in the blinding light, wrote a letter to the President of Outer Horner.

Dear Mr. President, the letter read. *We respectfully request that you bring your honorable several mustaches and historically righteous bellies to the border so we can discuss some taxes that have recently been levied against us by some guy named Phil who, to our knowledge, has nothing to do with your government, or at least we hope not.*

"This will work," said Elmer. "I feel confident this will work."

"The President won't stand for this," said Carol.

Wanda tiptoed out of the Short-Term Residency Zone, into Outer Horner, past the now-sleeping Leon, and slipped the letter into a mailbox outside the Outer Horner Cafe.

Then, ignoring the other Inner Hornerites, who were frantically gesturing for her to hurry home, she stood a few minutes in Outer Horner, extending her tendrils and breathing deep and walking around in wide leisurely circles.

Next afternoon, amid a tremendous fanfare of trumpets and crashing cymbals, the President of Outer Horner arrived at the Border Area, on a lavish Presidential Board carried by a team of sweating, panting Advisors. The President was a small but impressive man consisting of a jumble of bellies, white mustaches, military medals, and dignified double chins, all borne magnificently aloft on three thin wobbly legs.

"Ah, the memories," he said, gazing down into Inner Horner. "Ah, the days of my Youth. It looks quite different than I remember it, of course. Because I was looking at it through the eyes of Youth back then, whereas now I am looking at it through the eyes of Old Age. Have I said that? Lately I'm always repeating myself. It looks quite different than I remember it, of course. I remember apple trees and rushing streams. But of course I was a young buck then, in love with life, with fewer chins and bigger dreams, whereas now I'm an old fossil with my best years behind me, and several additional chins before me, and as for dreams, my only dream is to lose a few of these chins. Ha ha! One must keep one's sense of humor, yes? One must keep one's chins up! Ha ha! Strange how one's memory plays tricks though! I clearly remember apple trees and a rushing stream. And a girl named Mona. Have I said that? Have I already asked if I've already said that, that thing about Mona? I seem to re-member sitting with Mona under an apple tree, beside a rushing stream, under a lush full moon, and also some fond whispered words? Where is Mona? Was there ever a Mona, or did I make that up?"

"There was, sir," said Elmer. "She died just last year."

It was true. Mona had died last year and been buried in the portion of Inner Horner displaced when Inner Horner shrunk, so that, as they spoke, Mona was lying directly be-neath the President.

"Oh dear," the President said. "Mona dead? It seems that only yesterday she was a little cutie, kissing my then-blond mustaches, and now look at me, all white-haired and forgetful and fat, and look at her, all dead and so forth! My advice to you is: Don't get old! Have I said that? Remain young! Because once you get old you start misremembering, for example, that there were apple trees and rushing streams in your youth, when in fact the country where you spent your semester abroad was only a deep ugly gash in the earth."

"Actually, sir," said Cal, "even yesterday we had an apple tree and a stream."

"What's that?" said the President, looking confused. "Then I should've come yesterday, yes? Is that what you're saying? And Mona? Was Mona here yesterday too? Did Mona die just this morning, and I therefore barely missed her, and therefore, had I come only a few hours sooner, she could've stroked my mustaches one last time?"

"Sir," said Cal, "it was Phil who did this. Phil took our tree and our stream."

"Was it Phil who took Mona?" said the President. "Who is this Phil anyway? Is Mona being kept with your tree and your stream, by this Phil character? I wish you'd make yourselves clear. I'm not so young anymore. First you say she's dead, and then you say she's with the stream and the tree, being held hostage by this Phil fellow."

"Sir," said Cal, "Mona's dead."

"I understand that perfectly well!" thundered the President. "I'm not stupid, you know, just forgetful and shaky and cantankerous. I understand everything you've said to me. Mona is dead, killed by Phil, who then stole your tree and stream and moon, the rascal, although how the moon came to be your property, I'm not quite sure. You people are certainly proprietary. The moon, I believe, is for us all. Haven't I often said that?"

"You have, sir," said a Presidential Advisor whose face was a mirror with two shifty eyes set in it. "You have often said that the moon and the stars are for us all."

"And the stars, yes," said the President. "I forgot about the stars being for us all. Write that down. For my next speech. Moon, stars, for us all. That's good."

Just then Phil came clanking up, accompanied by the Outer Horner Militia.

"Mr. President," said Phil. "I beg your pardon, but these people are slandering me."

"Who are you?" said the President.

"I'm Phil, sir," said Phil.

"I don't see why you had to kill Mona, Phil," said the President sadly. "She was a lovely girl."

"I didn't kill anyone," said Phil.

"He didn't kill anyone," said Elmer. "Mona just died on her own."

"For the love of God, man!" the President shouted at Elmer. "Then why claim such a thing? Why accuse an innocent man of murder? That is a very serious accusation.

19

That's one thing I remember about you people, from my youth, you were always quite frivolous. Take Mona, for example, she was quite frivolous, kissing me like that, and me a stranger, and a foreigner. Kiss kiss kiss, like some sort of crazy woman. So frivolous. Not that I minded! No, I liked it, Mona's frivolousness, it was the best part about her. But this level of frivolousness is something altogether different. Kissing my mustaches is one thing, but falsely accusing Phil of murder, even Mona wasn't frivolous enough to do that, and believe me, she was plenty frivolous. Now tell the truth: Having established that Phil did not kill Mona, did he or did he not do the other things you slandered him with, that is, steal your tree and stream and moon?"

"Just the stream and the tree," said Wanda.

"So you retract your accusation regarding the moon?" said the President disgustedly. "So frivolous. I don't know what to believe anymore."

"Sir, with all due respect," said Phil. "I did take the stream and the tree, but I was only attempting to enforce your decree."

"I'm glad to see someone enforcing my decrees," said the President. "Back in the capital they're always ignoring my decrees. Tell me, which decree were you enforcing? Was it a good decree?"

"The Short-Term Residency Zone Tax Decree," said Phil. "A very good decree."

"I don't remember that one," the President said to his Advisors. "It sounds like a good one but I don't remember it. Did I decree that?"

"Well, sir, it depends," said the mirror faced Advisor. "What we need to ask ourselves is, what, in general, has been the reaction to this Tax? Have the people been in favor of the Tax? If so, then it is my recollection that you did indeed make such a decree. On the other hand, if the people have been unhappy with this Tax, then I very clearly remember you pounding the table, denouncing someone for even suggesting that you make such a lame-brained decree. It is clear, sir, that we must, to honor our democracy, go to the people, in order to determine just what it is you decreed."

"So be it," said the President grandly. "Let us see what I said."

The Advisors rushed around polling every Outer Hornerite they could find. That is, they polled the Outer Horner Militia (Freeda, Melvin, and Larry) and Leon the Border Guard and Phil himself.

When the votes were counted, it was determined that the people of Outer Horner were unanimous in their support of the Short-Term Residency Zone Tax.

"You know, sir, in light of that vote, I just remembered something," said the Advisor. "You did indeed decree that. It was a Thursday. You decreed the Short-Term Residency

Zone Tax, and I remember I congratulated you, and then you thanked me for helping you come up with that decree. For sort of laying the conceptual groundwork."

"Well, I thank you again," said the President. "Because look how popular you have made me with my people. They look so happy. They look as if they're about to burst into applause."

And Phil and Leon and the Outer Horner Militia burst into applause.

"Mr. President," Phil said when the applause had died down. "May I also just say how proud I am to have been appointed your Special Border Activities Coordinator?"

"Well of course you're proud," said the President. "Who wouldn't be? That's an important job. And I'm glad I appointed you that. If in fact I did. Did I? Did I do that in conjunction with that decree about that Tax thingie?"

"May I suggest we go to the people again?" said the Advisor.

"By all means," said the President, still very much moved by the standing ovation he had recently received.

So once again Freeda, Melvin, Larry, Leon the Border Guard, and Phil himself were polled, and it was determined that the people of Outer Horner were unanimously pleased with the idea of Phil being Special Border Activities Coordinator, and so it was determined, by the President's Advisors, that the President had, in fact, several months ago, appointed Phil to that post, and there was some concern, among the Advisors, that Phil did not appear at present to be wearing his Presidential Appointment Medal. Fortunately an extra was found, hanging over the awning of the youngest Advisor's exposed spleen, and Phil bent low, and the President hung the Presidential Appointment Medal around Phil's neck.

"Now as for you people," the President said sternly to the Inner Horncrites. "I suggest that, in the future, you refrain from all frivolity and false accusations and obey Phil, who has already done so much for you, and will, I'm sure, continue to do so much for you, including, perhaps, someday, if you remain nonfrivolous, obtaining some replacement trees and a replacement stream, to replace those you so frivolously lost."

"Thank you, sir," said Phil.

"No, thank you, Phil," said the President. "For doing such a tremendous job of enforcing my decrees and calling me out here to see what a tremendous job of enforcing my decrees you've been doing. It does me good to see a young man enforcing my decrees. Sort of a protégé!"

Then the Advisors loaded the President back on to the Presidential Board and, straining under the weight, set off for the capital.

"Goodbye, Phil, dear boy!" the President shouted. "Keep up the good work!"

Next morning Phil and the Outer Horner Militia arrived at the border to find the entire population of Inner Horner heaped up in a tremendous teetering pile of grimaces and side-paddles and Thrumton Specialty Valves and cowlicks and rear ends and receding hairlines, a pile that began in the hole that was formerly Inner Horner and rose some thirty feet in the air, leaning precariously out over Outer Horner.

"My God, look at those people," said Melvin.

"So uncouth," said Larry.

"Animals," said Melvin. "How do they live with themselves?"

"I mean, look at us," said Freeda. "You don't see us piling on like that."

"They seem sort of imprisoned by their own dark urges," said Larry.

Everyone looked at Larry, impressed.

"No wonder we treat them so unfairly," said Melvin, trying to counter Larry.

"Not that we treat them unfairly, Melvin," said Phil a little sternly.

"Oh, we treat them fairly," said Melvin. "I'm just saying, you know, think how fairly we'd treat them if they didn't behave like uncouth animals imprisoned by their dark surges."

"Urges," corrected Larry.

"What are you schmoes doing up there anyway?" shouted Leon the Border Guard.

"As long as we stay out of the Short-Term Residency Zone, we don't have to pay the Tax," shouted someone from the pile. "Isn't that right?"

The Outer Hornerites looked at Phil, the recently appointed Special Border Activities Coordinator.

"Well of course that's right," said Phil. "Why would we charge you a tax for being in our country if you weren't even in our country, you morons?"

Just then the big pile of Inner Hornerites came tumbling down into Outer Horner.

This was unprecedented. Never before had so many Inner Hornerites infiltrated so deeply into Outer Horner. Leon frantically rang the loud buzzer that meant Invasion in Progress and the Outer Horner Militia (Freeda, Melvin, and Larry) quickly outflanked and surrounded the entire population of Inner Horner.

"This is an outrage!" Phil shouted. "Halt! Advance no farther! Invade us no more! Do you surrender? Surrender at once! Drop your weapons! Does everyone see how forceful

I'm being? As Special Border Activities Coordinator, I command you!"

The Inner Hornerites had no weapons, and no desire to invade Outer Horner, and were still dizzy from their fall, although a few of the less-dizzy Inner Hornerites were, in spite of themselves, sneaking dazed, curious glances over at the Outer Horner Cafe.

"We're not invading anybody," said Elmer. "We just tipped over."

"Return to the Short-Term Residency Zone at once!" shouted Phil. "With your hands up!"

So the Inner Hornerites raised their hands and stepped back over the green string into the Short-Term Residency Zone.

"Now that we have totally subdued you," Phil shouted, "allow me to remind you that you still owe us four smolokas."

"Well, we still don't have it," said Elmer. "You know very well we don't."

"Larry," shouted Phil. "Inventory their resources!"

Larry looked at Phil blankly.

"I thought we already took everything," Larry whispered.

"Look harder, Larry," said Phil. "Exhibit more vigilance."

Larry looked harder, exhibiting more vigilance.

"Well sir," he finally said. "The only thing I could find? Other than additional dirt? And I'm not sure this counts? Is that they're wearing clothes, on their bodies, sir."

"Well done, Larry," said Phil. "An excellent observation. Clothes are indeed a resource."

"Wait a minute," said Cal. "You're not proposing to take our clothes?"

"If you take our clothes, we'll be naked," said Wanda.

"But at least you'll have your taxes paid," said Phil, and gestured to Leon, who pushed his way into the Short-Term Residency Zone and started removing Old Gus's shirt.

"Hey, stop it!" shouted Old Gus. "My scar will show!"

"He's very sensitive about his scar," said Wanda.

But Leon kept tugging on Old Gus's shirt, and soon both nations could plainly see Old Gus's scar, and hear, from his Entwhistle Slit, the whirring noise that meant he was frustrated beyond speech and would any second now burst into tears while emitting clouds of green steam from his Leftmost Vent.

"Oh, that's enough," said Wanda, taking a swat at Leon's pointy hat.

"My God, Leon's under attack!" shouted Larry, and rushed into the Short-Term Residency Zone, causing Carol and Cal to inadvertently reinvade Outer Horner and Leon to bash his right Brow Clip into his own spadelike tail. Leon sprung from the hole, hatless and terrified, with a swollen bleeding Brow Clip, having failed to collect the taxes, and dove back into Outer Horner, while Phil heroically rescued Larry by pulling him out of the Short-Term

Residency Zone by his belt loops.

Both sides stood gasping on their respective sides of the green string, shocked at this sudden outburst of violence.

Phil stamped his foot, and his brain slid down his rack and rolled across the ground, and his central bladder inflated to the bursting point, and his Phalen Extender began slapping back and forth against his secondary spout.

"Your disgraceful attitude!" he bellowed in the stentorian voice, "being the result of centuries of taking our people for granted, habitually manifests itself in arrogance, an arrogance that has as its seed the apparent belief that we are less than you and must be subjugated. But we will not be subjugated! We are a noble people, of ancient lineage, and have a right to live and thrive, whereas you, who would take away our right to live and thrive, I'm not sure about you, I'm not sure that you have not, over the long years of taking advantage of our simple generous nature, forfeited certain rights having to do with your continued existence!"

Now, Larry knew Phil from high school, and knew that the longer Phil's brain stayed off, the less sense he would make, until finally his brain-rack would spasm and he would run totally out of juice. Once, Phil had run out of juice during a swim meet and sunk to the bottom of the pool, after which he had been winched out of the pool and connected to a Farley ReMotivator. For weeks afterward, the popular kids had mocked Phil mercilessly, even inventing a dance called The Phil, which involved making an awkward desperate jerky motion with one's torso, which, apparently, was what he had done while on the Farley ReMotivator.

"Phil, sir?" Larry said now, meekly. "May I remount your brain for you?"

"This is not about my brain!" shouted Phil. "It's these idiots who've got the brain problem. They owe us taxes! And have refused via violence to pay those taxes! In light of the heinous events of this outrageous day, which shall henceforth be known as Dark Dark Thursday, but also in light of the valor we Outer Hornerites have shown on this memorable and historic day, which will henceforth also be known as Amazing Heroic Thursday, I hereby declare a Federal Tax Mercifulness Occasion. An FTMO. Yes, an FTMO of celebration. That's it. And I declare this FTMO not out of fear, not at all, but out of pride, pride in our strength! Let us return to the capital on this joyous FTMO, to celebrate our astonishing victory!"

And Phil, carrying his brain under one arm, led his flustered Militia away from the border, hissing at them now and then to stop looking back so fearfully over their shoulders.

* * *

That evening Phil stormed around the disgusting southern portion of Outer Horner City in a frenzy. His brain had been knocked out of round by its recent smashing and sat crookedly in its rack, and now and then a spark flew out of his nosehole and his Phalen Extender flipped up for no apparent reason. Those stupid Inner Hornerites! How he hated them! Wasn't it just like them to sit like inert slugs on borrowed land, then suddenly erupt into inexplicable pointless violence! Here he was, finally starting to get a little something for himself, and they dared openly mock the authority of the President's Special Border Activities Coordinator, via bloodying Leon's Brow Clip? It was so frustrating! If only there was no Inner Horner, the Border Area would look so nice, and he could move on to more substantial Border Area issues, such as making the Border Area look even nicer. And he imagined the Border Area free of Inner Hornerites, enhanced by a Museum, a Museum of Outer Horner Culture, and in front of the Museum would stand a statue of him, Phil, and around the statue he imagined a group of swooning Outer Horner girls, with that classic Outer Horner beauty, and just as he was, in his mind, about to approach them and introduce himself as Phil, founder of the Museum and President of the nation, he turned a corner and almost ran into two enormous young men with rippling biceps and cruel beautiful faces, being methodically covered in mud by a tiny old woman on a ladder.

"Forget it, I'm not hiring," the old woman said. "I've got enough. I've got two. Two is plenty."

"I'm not looking for work," Phil said. "I'm the Special Border Activities Coordinator."

"Sure you are, sure you are," said the old woman. "And I'm the Queen of Mud."

"Why are you doing that?" said Phil.

"We're testing it out," she said. "To see if it's good. Look close. See how some of it's runny and some of it's nice and firm?"

"Why do you care?" Phil said.

"Why do we care!" she said. "You'd think you'd know that, if you're really the Special Activities Border Whatever Whatever. We care because we gotta write it on the package. Either 'Runny' or 'Nice, Firm.' That's why. Now move along. I'm not hiring."

"How much do you fellows get paid for this?" Phil asked the enormous muscular young men.

"Don't talk to them," the old woman said. "They're on the clock. They don't get paid nothing. They're apprentices. When they really learn how to do it, then they get paid."

"Not much of a job," said Phil.

"Well, sir, it's a living," said the first mud-covered young man.

"Anyways, it will be," said the second. "Someday. After our apprenticeships."

31

"And it sure beats being back home," said the first.

"Back home, when Ma covered us in mud or grease or lard?" said the second. "Not only did we not get paid, she'd yell at us while she did it."

"Edna never yells at us," said the first.

"Well, I like you boys," said Edna. "You boys have potential."

"Did you hear that, Vance?" said the first boy. "Edna said we have potential."

"Wow, I am so moved by that," said Vance. "Jimmy, can you imagine Ma ever saying something that nice to us?"

"The only nice thing Ma ever said to us?" said Jimmy. "Was once she said we looked slightly better in lard than in mud."

"Guys," said Phil. "You look pretty strong. Are you pretty strong?"

"Oh, we're strong," said Vance.

"Not to brag," said Jimmy, "but we really are strong. Watch this, sir."

And Jimmy lifted Edna between two fingers and set her on top of his head.

"All right, all right, mister comedian," said Edna. "Put me down. Back to work."

Jimmy put Edna down and she climbed back up her ladder and again started applying mud to his neck.

"Maybe you guys would like to come work for me," said Phil.

"What?" said Jimmy. "Wow, I can't believe it. On the very same day, Edna says we have potential and this guy tries to hire us!"

"Pretty big day, all right," said Vance.

"What exactly would we have to do, sir?" said Jimmy.

"Well," said Phil. "You'd be sort of like special friends of mine. Like bodyguards. You'd just do whatever I told you. Out at the Inner Horner border. I do a lot of work out at the Border, national security work."

"Bodyguards, wow!" said Jimmy. "National security work, wow! No offense, Edna, but I think bodyguard sounds even more impressive than Mud-Consistency Testing Associate."

"You boys aren't smart enough," said Edna.

"You're probably right," said Vance.

"Oh, they're smart enough," said Phil. "They're exactly the level of smart I'm looking for."

"Wow, Vance, did you hear that?" said Jimmy. "We're exactly the right level of smart!"

"Edna, we have to try it," said Vance. "Don't you see? This could be our big chance. Sir, how much would you pay?"

"Vance, God, don't be pushy," said Jimmy. "We don't necessarily have to get paid."

"A smoloka each," said Phil.

"Wow, that's pretty good," said Vance. "A whole

smoloka. I mean, if we could make it last, that could be really good. Jimmy, if we wanted to make that one smoloka last the rest of our lives, how much would we be allowed to spend each day?"

"Well, that depends on how long we're going to live," said Jimmy. "And we don't know that yet."

"He's better at math than me," explained Vance.

"I don't think you understand," said Phil. "That's a smoloka a day. One smoloka for every day you work. It's a salary."

"Holy cow!" said Vance. "A smoloka a day! For every day we work! A salary! So that would be like, seven smolokas a week, if we worked seven days a week, right? Are there still seven days in a week? Anyway, wow, we'd be rich. And all we have to do is do whatever you say?"

"That would be easy for us," said Jimmy. "Ask Edna. Edna, wouldn't you say we're really good at doing whatever someone says?"

"They're excellent," said Edna. "Very obedient. Whatever you tell them to do, they immediately do it."

"That's because if we didn't do exactly what Ma said, she made us sleep in the yard with the dogs," Vance said. "And we had pretty mean dogs. And a pretty yucky yard."

"Right at the edge of a cliff," said Jimmy.

"Lost a lot of dogs that way," said Vance.

"So anyways we got excellent at obeying," said Jimmy.

"Watch this," said Vance. "Watch how obedient. Sir, tell us to do something. Anything."

"Tear down that shack," said Phil.

"This one?" said Vance. "This one here with the cute little rose garden?"

And Vance and Jimmy tore down the shack with their bare hands, with amazing speed, revealing a family sitting in their pajamas at a crooked kitchen table.

"What in the world?" said the father.

"Don't even think about mouthing off to my brother, man!" shouted Vance.

"And don't even think about mouthing off to my brother, man!" shouted Jimmy, and lifted up the father by one leg, after which the father got very quiet.

"You're hired," said Phil.

"Ha!" said Jimmy, dropping the father back in the rubble that had been his shack. "What an amazing day."

"Hang on, Jimmy," said Vance. "I have an additional request. Before we sign on."

"Vance, jeez!" whispered Jimmy. "Don't get all demanding! You'll screw it up!"

"Jimmy, don't worry, I know what I'm doing," said Vance. "What I want, sir, to, uh, request, additionally? Is that, every now and then, you say something nice about us. If that's not too much. Like you could say something about how much potential we have, or how obedient we are, it doesn't even need to be true. Just something nice to us every day."

"We didn't get much of that at home," said Jimmy. "Mostly it was just, you know, Jimmy you jerk, how did you get so dumb? That sort of thing."

"Or like: Vance, you're pathetic, why did you even have to be born," said Vance.

"Or like: Jimmy, if I had to throw either you or one of the dogs off the cliff, I'd throw you," said Jimmy.

"I'll tell you what," said Phil. "Every day, in addition to your smoloka, I'll say something nice about each of you."

"About *each* of us?" said Vance. "Oh wow, I was just thinking you'd say something nice about one of us. Like one per day? Alternating? But now you're saying you'll say something nice about each of us every single day? Plus the smoloka?"

"A smoloka each," said Phil. "Do you understand that?"

"A smoloka *each*?" said Jimmy.

"Wow," said Vance. "Wow wow wow. I'm getting dizzy here."

"You dream and you dream," said Jimmy. "And one day it all comes true."

"Well, Edna," said Vance. "I guess this is goodbye."

"We've got to do it, Edna," said Jimmy. "Don't you see? Please don't be mad."

"Don't sweat it," said Edna. "You'll be easy to replace."

"I'm sure that's true," said Jimmy.

"We're certainly nothing special," said Vance.

"Let's get you fellows cleaned up," said Phil.

"You're going to *clean us up*?" said Jimmy.

"And get you some uniforms," said Phil.

"You're going to get us *uniforms*?" said Vance.

With tears of gratitude in their eyes, Jimmy and Vance followed Phil out of the disgusting part of town.

Next morning Phil and the Outer Horner Militia arrived at the border, accompanied by Vance and Jimmy, who were now wearing tight red t-shirts that read: "Phil's Special Friends."

"Tax time, tax time," said Phil. "And don't even think of grabbing Leon's hat. The way I figure it, you owe us four smolokas for Dark Dark Thursday and four for today, which I am hereby declaring the Memorable Friday of Total Triumphant Retribution. So eight smolokas. Leon, inventory their resources."

Leon, very cautiously, bandage on his Brow Clip, holding his hat on with both hands, walked around the Short-Term Residency Zone, squinting his eyes.

"Still just the clothes," he said.

"Kindly collect the taxes," Phil said to Jimmy and

Vance, who entered the Short-Term Residency Zone like twin grinning mountains, if twin grinning mountains could crack their knuckles while flexing their pecs and chomping gum, and soon shirts and pants and shoes and socks were flying over their tremendous shoulders into Outer Horner, where they were collected into a sack by Leon.

When Jimmy and Vance stepped away, there were the Inner Hornerites, totally naked.

"Freeda," said Phil. "Assess the value of these clothes. Is the total value of these clothes exactly eight smolokas?"

"I'm not sure," said Freeda, a little taken aback by the sight of so many naked blushing ashamed Inner Hornerites scrambling to stand behind one another.

"I think what you mean to say is yes, Freeda," said Phil sternly.

"Okay," said Freeda. "Yes."

"Super," said Phil. "Taxes paid. Enjoy the rest of your day, folks."

And Phil and the Special Friends and the Outer Horner Militia walked off, sorting through the clothes as they went.

"My God, those guys were strong," said Wanda.

"They were incredibly strong," said Curtis.

"This is terrible," said Elmer. "So humiliating."

"On the other hand, you know, nakedness is completely

natural," said Carol.

"That's true, I guess, Carol," said Cal. "I mean, our naked bodies are nothing to be ashamed of. Although guys? Actually? I'd prefer you guys didn't look at my wife."

"Also?" said Wanda. "Would you guys mind not looking at me? I feel so fat."

"Why are you all staring at my scar?" said Old Gus.

"Maybe we should just agree not to look at one another," said Wanda.

"Oh, this is crazy," Curtis said. "How long are we going to take this? We've got to *do* something. We've got to start resisting."

"Oh right, Curtis, let's resist," said Wanda. "Don't you get it? If we resist, they'll crush us. Did you see the size of those guys?"

"Cal, you're the one I don't get," said Curtis. "Here's your wife, naked and being displayed to the world, here's your shivering hungry kid, and what are you doing about it? Don't you love them? Don't you care?"

"Curtis, leave Cal alone," said Carol. "He's doing the best he can."

"Carol, please don't speak harshly to Curtis," said Wanda. "He was only expressing his opinion."

"Look at us bickering," said Curtis.

"I don't consider this bickering," said Wanda.

"Well, I do," said Curtis.

"It could be worse," said Elmer.

Everyone looked at Elmer.

"I thought we agreed not to look at one another," said Elmer, and for the rest of the day the Inner Hornerites stood staring straight ahead, except for Cal, who now and then snuck a guilty ashamed look over at Carol and Little Andy.

Then it was dusk, and the bright spotlight came on.

All night a bitter wind blew, causing icicles to form around the Inner Horner exhaust ports and steam vents, which made it even more galling when the Outer Horner Militia arrived at dawn wearing articles of former Inner Horner clothing over their Militia Uniforms.

"Good morning all," said Phil, wearing what appeared to be Wanda's former stocking cap on his brain. "What time is it, Leon?"

"Tax time, sir," said Leon.

"Bingo," said Phil.

The Inner Hornerites were silent.

"Look, what the heck am I supposed to do about this?" said Phil. "You people owe us four smolokas. There's a law, you know the law, yet you insist on defying the law. I am really at a loss here."

"Maybe they could run a tab?" said Freeda.

"Freeda, I appreciate your input," said Phil. "But do you really think these people are going to pay a tab? Are these trustworthy people? Honorable people? Did they or did they not recently attack Leon, leaving him bloody? Have you already forgotten the nightmare that was Dark Dark Thursday?"

"Maybe we could sell tickets?" said Melvin. "Sell tickets to people who want to, you know, sort of stare at them? Because they're naked and all?"

"Melvin, no," said Phil. "I mean, I like the idea conceptually, but the thing is, one, people can stare at them now, for free, so why impose additional costs on our people, and two, who the heck wants to stare at them anyway? They don't look so good. Except for Carol. Carol, I have to say, looks pretty good. Carol I would possibly pay to look at. Don't you guys think Carol looks pretty good?"

And Larry and Melvin and Leon and Phil's Special Friends all took a long look at Carol and agreed that she looked pretty good, good enough that they would possibly pay to look at her.

If someone had bothered to take a look at Cal, they would have noticed that his tuna fish can was trembling and his belt buckle was starting to glow.

"Look, here's an idea," said Phil. "I don't think it's any big secret that I've always had a thing for Carol. How about you people give me Carol, for my wife or whatever, and I give you, not just four smolokas, but *twelve* smolokas? That's enough for three days' taxes. What do you say? That sounds fair, doesn't it?"

At this Cal burst out of the Short-Term Residency Zone, blatantly invading Outer Horner, and threw himself at Phil so savagely, while angrily gnashing the lid of his tuna fish can, that Phil's gasket cover flew off and his brain came sliding off his rack and it took both Special Friends to finally pry Cal off of Phil's neck/sternum assembly.

"You little creep!" bellowed Phil. "You've damaged my gasket cover! How dare you attempt a revolution! The gasket cover of the Special Border Activities Coordinator!"

Jimmy was now holding Cal high up in the air, higher than Cal had ever been in his life, while Larry and Melvin scrambled to recover Phil's brain.

"You people," Phil shouted in the stentorian voice, "via shiftlessness and inertia, have forced us, a normally gentle constituency, into the position of extracting water from the recalcitrant stone of your stubbornness, by positing us as aggressors, when in fact we are selflessly lending you precious territory, which years ago was hewed by our ancestors from a hostile forbidding wilderness! When I think of my poor, dead grandparents, how hard they hewed, and here you come, sneaking into their sacred former wilderness to murder us in our beds via stealth! But shoulder that musket we must, that musket of subduing you, and this we will, using our usual indomitable methodology and excellent creativity and spirit of love. I don't dare undertake such a huge momentous decision on my own, since we are a democracy, so I suggest we take an urgent vote. Let us vote urgently: Do we or do we not enact my momentous decision?"

"But what is it?" said Melvin. "What is your momentous decision?"

"Do you really want to quarrel with your leader at a time like this, Melvin?" said Phil. "Is this really the time for naysaying? Do we or do we not enact my momentous decision, namely, to disassemble this aggressor? Freeda, please tally the vote."

"Disassemble him?" said Freeda. "Can we do that?"

"Guys!" shouted Cal from way up high, upside down. "Now's the time! It's now or never! Join me! Join the fight!"

"Listen to that little rat!" said Phil. "Still advocating violence!"

The other Inner Hornerites, seeing Jimmy's rippling biceps and cruel expression as he dangled Cal over the Cafe, imagined themselves suspended over the Cafe, about to be disassembled, and each decided, in his or her own way, that it was not, perhaps, at this time, entirely prudent to join the fight, and opted instead to stare down mutely at the green string, except for Carol, who stared up at Cal while blinking back tears and trying to restrain Little Andy, who was desperately trying to join the fight.

"May I please have a vote?" said Phil. "Do we or do we not disassemble this aggressor, for the good of the nation, in the interest of preventing further violence?"

And the citizens of Outer Horner, casting nervous sideways glances at one another, unanimously voted to support Phil in his decision to disassemble Cal, for the good of the nation, in the interest of preventing further violence.

"Kindly enact the will of the nation!" Phil said to the Special Friends.

The Special Friends leaned down over Cal and, using a socket set and a pair of pliers, enacted the will of the nation.

Soon Cal was reduced to a limp belt buckle and a tuna fish can and the blue dot and a few connecting parts.

"I guess we were wrong when we thought they had no additional assets," Phil said. "Actually they've got plenty of additional assets. A nation's most important asset is its people, don't you think? Freeda, how much would you say this bundle of additional assets is worth? This pile of junk? Four smolokas? Would you say the tuna fish can is worth two and the belt buckle is worth one and the blue dot and various connecting parts are worth a total of one?"

"Okay," said Freeda, trying to keep from crying.

"Congratulations," said Phil to the Inner Hornerites.

"Taxes paid. Thanks so much."

Then Phil reracked his brain and directed Leon to in-
carcerate the various parts of Cal at several discrete locations across the length and breadth of Outer Horner, in the
interest of national security.

Leon, using a wheelbarrow, incarcerated Cal's tuna fish
can in Far South Distant Outer Horner, a region dotted
with thousands of tiny identical lakes, and incarcerated
Cal's belt buckle in Far East Distant Outer Horner, a lush
verdant zone where cows' heads grew out of the earth
shouting sarcastic things at anyone who passed, which,
though lush and verdant, was unpopulated because the
cows' sarcasm was so withering, and incarcerated Cal's various connecting parts in Far West Distant Outer Horner,
where pairs of trees made X shapes as far as the eye could
see.

This left only Cal's blue dot, which, per Phil, was placed
in a glass case a few hundred feet from Inner Horner, as a
warning and a reminder to the other Inner Hornerites,
who all night long, from the Short-Term Residency Zone,
watched the sad blue dot that had formerly been Cal's torso
expand and contract, as if hyperventilating, or sobbing.

*   *   *

Freeda of the Outer Horner Militia had always felt that she'd been built too wide at the bottom and thin at the top, and because of her shape and her extensive shoulder and torso foliage had, several times, when pausing in public, been mistaken for a shrub or small tree and, in fact, the Christmas she was eight, having paused to gaze up in wonder at the stars, had come home in tears, covered with lights and glass balls. So it was a great delight to her when her only child, Gertrude, grew into a tall beautiful preteen with no foliage at all, who took dance lessons and could gaze at the stars for hours without ever once coming home decorated.

That night Freeda had a dream. In her dream, Gertrude was a tall beautiful vase belonging to Phil, who kept holding Gertrude up to the light, looking for flaws. Freeda was a small furry dog, who kept leaping up, trying to bite Phil as he inspected Gertrude.

"Put her down, put her down," Freeda barked at him. "Why do you want to be so bad?"

"I am not bad," said Phil. "I am totally good. What I do, benefits all."

Then Phil found a flaw and threw Gertrude against the wall, breaking her into a thousand pieces.

Freeda woke and rushed to Gertrude's room. Relieved to find that Gertrude was not a broken vase and that her pink shelving was still intact, she gave Gertrude a kiss on the middle of her three rosy cheeks.

"Snowing on my face," Gertrude mumbled.

Then Freeda went to her desk and wrote a note to the President.

Dear Mr. President, it read. *Today Phil, whom I previously so much respected, disassembled a fellow, an Inner Horner fellow, who seemed nice enough, and even had a family. Is this what we stand for here in Outer Horner? I hope not. Our country is big, let us be big. Phil is out of control, sir, and must be stopped. Please do something. We're all counting on you.*

Then she put on a cloak with a hood, walked to the Presidential Palace, and slid her note under the huge jeweled door.

The lowliest butler read the note and passed it to a slightly less lowly butler, who passed it to the mirror-faced Advisor, who read it with grave concern and passed it on to the President.

"This is an outrage!" shouted the President. "Isn't it? Isn't it an outrage?"

"That depends, sir," said the Advisor. "Do you think it is?"

"Well, it seems to me it is," said the President. "Although I could be wrong. But we've never done that before, have we, this disassembling business?"

"Not unless you say we have," said the Advisor.

"Get me Phil!" thundered the President.

"But sir," said the Advisor, "I'm not sure, in light of your condition—"

"What condition?" thundered the President. "I don't have any condition. Are you saying I have a condition? Are you saying I'm somehow getting worse or something? Are you saying I'm so old and fat and nostalgic that I'm becoming increasingly ineffectual and am always repeating myself in a state of perpetual confusion?"

"No sir," said the mirror-faced Advisor. "I'm not saying that at all. You are no more old or fat or nostalgic or ineffectual than you were yesterday."

"Really?" said the President. "Do you really think so? Thanks. Thanks for saying that. Look, let's get this Phil fellow in here and clear this thing up before I forget how I feel about it and/or misplace this note."

So the mirror-faced Advisor passed a note to the squat greenish skulky guy in charge of delivering messages, who went skittering over to Phil's crummy apartment and slipped it under Phil's nicked-up door.

What's all this about disassembling someone? the note read. *The President will see you first thing tomorrow morning.*

*　*　*

The Presidential Palace was a gleaming gold-domed building with a vast high-ceilinged Entry Hall, decorated with paintings of various types of animals the President liked to eat, served on plates, although in the paintings the animals were still alive and had all their fur on and looked a little panicked.

As Phil entered the Intermediate Hall with the Special Friends, the mirror-faced Advisor pulled him aside.

"First of all, let me say," whispered the Advisor, "in terms of the President's condition, that I don't want to imply that there are problems, with the President, with the President's health, especially with his mental health, in terms of how nostalgic and ineffectual he's become."

"What Al is trying to say?" said a second Advisor, who had three identical smiles, one beneath the other on his perfectly round face. "Is that he is not, by pulling you aside like this and denying that the President is growing ever more batty, implying in any way that the President is in fact growing ever more batty."

"Absolutely," said the mirror-faced Advisor. "That is exactly what I am not saying. And furthermore, I am also not saying that we should work together to ensure that the entirely false news of the President's alleged recent battiness not travel beyond these walls. On the contrary, I encourage you to think and say whatever you like, once you leave here, bearing in mind, please, that a weak, infirm, half-crazed

President would not at all be the worst thing that could happen to a country that finds itself threatened by a hostile bordering power."

"If we had that sort of President," said the very smiley Advisor.

"Which we don't," said the mirror-faced Advisor.

"Unless you notice that we do," said the very smiley Advisor.

"In which case we might," said the mirror-faced Advisor.

"We could discuss that," said the very smiley Advisor.

"The President will see you now!" boomed a third Advisor, basically just a mouth wearing a wig.

Phil entered the Great Hall. The President, surrounded by tables of souvenirs from his illustrious career, looked even fatter than he had looked at the border and seemed to have sprouted several additional mustaches.

"Phil!" said the President. "So nice to see you! Isn't that your name? Oh, I remember that time at the border. What a sweet time that was! We won't see the likes of those days again, will we? Sit down, dear boy. How do I look? I bet I look fatter than ever. Plus sadder. Lately I'm so sad. Do you know what I was thinking about? Just now? I was just now thinking about that wonderful time when you walked in just now! Remember that? I was so happy to see you! I remember that time so well! We won't see the likes of those days again, will we? And you know what else I remember fondly? The time, just now, after you walked in, when I asked you to sit down, dear boy. Do you remember that? How I sort of patted the coat, the coat you are now sitting on? Oh, sweet memories! Wasn't that a time! We won't see the likes of those days again, will we? Everything passes so quickly in this life! It seems like just yesterday I was young and powerful, and now look at me, I can't even get up. Too fat, I guess. Whereas even this morning, I could get up. Remember that, Al, remember this morning when I stood right up? We won't see the likes of those days again, will we? I hopped right up, didn't I?"

"Yes you did," said the mirror-faced Advisor, giving Phil a look.

"I've been working very hard today, Phil," the President said. "What I've mainly been working on is, first, trying to remember why I called you here, and second, deciding what to feel weepy about. Because lately my weeping has become a little unfocused. In the middle of weeping about my weight, I find myself suddenly weeping about my legacy. In the middle of weeping about something I should've said fifty years ago, I suddenly find myself weeping about the rate at which my pants seem to be getting tighter. And then suddenly I pause in my weeping to sit for hours at a time, re-creating my childhood home in my mind. Nothing gets done! It's become clear that I need a weeping schedule. That way, you know, you look at your watch, you look at your schedule, you know what you're weeping about. Phil, do you remember why I called you here?"

"Yes, Mr. President," said Phil. "You called me here for a report on the situation at the border. And I'm happy to report that I was recently able to gracefully quell a disturbing outbreak of violence at the border by enacting certain physical rearrangements designed to prevent further outbreaks of violence, thus rendering the instigator of the violence incapable of instigating further violence, via separating the instigator's component parts and relocating them in discrete physical locations."

"Curt," said the President, to the Advisor who was a mouth wearing a wig. "Do you remember that time, I don't know when it was, when you came in here and said I had a visitor? And I said, Curt, show him in? Oh, those were the days. When was that? Who was that?"

"That was just now, sir," said Curt. "I said that when Phil here arrived."

"We won't see the likes of those days again, will we?" said the President. "Al, would you mind weighing me again? I'm curious. Also, let's count these mustaches again. I feel like I've sprouted a few, even since those halcyon days way back when, this morning, when I hopped right up."

So the mirror-faced Advisor lifted the President onto a

scale while the smiley Advisor counted the President's mustaches and confirmed that the President now had eighteen mustaches, whereas this morning he'd only had sixteen.

"Oh, this morning," said the President. "Blessed time of sixteen mustaches and hopping right up. What did you want to see me about, Phil? Or did I want to see you? Did I summon you?"

Phil had a sick feeling but also an excited feeling. This was his President? This man was running his beloved Outer Horner? If Inner Horner mounted a full-scale invasion, this was the man who'd be leading the fight? He'd had the vague sense, out at the Border, that the President was not quite as sharp, perhaps, as himself, Phil, but now it was suddenly obvious that he, Phil, was his floundering nation's only hope.

"Phil," said the President, looking up at the Special Friends. "Who are these lads? Makes me remember my youth, when I was big and muscular. Are they strong? They certainly are big enough."

"They are very strong," said Phil. "May I demonstrate?"

"Please," said the President.

"Jimmy," said Phil. "Lift off the dome."

And Jimmy stood up straight and lifted the Palace dome over his head with one hand.

"Ha ha!" said the President. "Bravo! Look at those birds flying in! That's really something."

"Now, Jimmy," said Phil. "Step over that wall, while still holding the dome, and take the dome over to my apartment. Then come right back."

"This I've got to see!" said the President, clapping his hands with delight.

And Jimmy stepped over the wall of the Palace, still holding the dome, and disappeared in the direction of Phil's apartment.

"Well, we certainly get a lot more sun this way, don't we?" said the President. "How about that other one? Is he strong too?"

"Vance," said Phil. "Take a wall under each arm. And carry them to my apartment."

"Ha!" said the President. "That will be hard. A wall under each arm. Ha! Did you hear that, Ed?"

"Yes sir, I did," said the smiley Advisor, looking at Phil with new respect.

Vance placed the north wall of the Palace under one arm and the south wall under the other, stepped over the east wall, and disappeared in the direction of Phil's apartment.

"Oh boy!" said the President. "All we've got left is two walls! I have to admit, I'm feeling sort of nostalgic for the time when I had not only four walls, but a roof. I could just weep! Remember that, Al, when we had all our walls? However, I'm also looking forward to the time when my ceiling and walls are brought back, which I'm sure will be soon. Won't it? Won't it be soon?"

Jimmy returned, domeless, and stepped over the east wall.

"Now watch this, Mr. President," said Phil. "You might think Jimmy here would be a little tired, but no. Watch this. Jimmy, take the other two walls, one under each arm, and sprint to my apartment."

"Sprint?" said the President. "Are you sure he's not overdoing it? We wouldn't want him to strain himself."

Jimmy tucked the east wall under one arm and the west wall under the other, and took off at a sprint in the direction of Phil's apartment.

"Well, well," said the President. "I congratulate you! Those are two very strong boys. And they work for you? My Advisors, I like them well enough, but I don't think they could do that. Do you boys think you could do that?"

The Advisors mumbled that, no, they probably couldn't exactly do that.

"Well, Mr. President," said Phil. "I'd best be going. I have to get back to the border and collect my taxes."

"Ha ha!" said the President. "You, Phil, are a real go-getter. I admire that. Just, you know, have those large boys return my Palace whenever it's convenient. When do you think it will be? In an hour or so? Sometime later today?"

"I'm pretty busy today," said Phil. "I have problems at the border, as I've said."

"Tomorrow then?" said the President.

"Tomorrow's also not good," said Phil.

"Well, Phil," said the President. "As President I, you know, sort of need my Palace, otherwise . . ."

"Actually I think I'm going to keep the Palace awhile," said Phil.

"Well, Phil," said the President. "I don't know how I feel about that. You're not the President, I'm the President, I'm the one wearing the Presidential Cravat, and so, it would seem to me that I would be the one to decide when you should bring my Palace back. Right? Am I right in that, Al?"

The mirror-faced Advisor said nothing.

"That's a nice cravat," said Phil.

"Yes, yes it is," said the President. "Would you like to see it? If I let you see it, will you think about returning my Palace?"

"I'd love to see it," said Phil, and took the Presidential Cravat off the President and put it on himself.

"Well, it looks nice on you," said the President.

"Looks very nice on him," said the mirror-faced Advisor.

"Super on him," said the very smiley Advisor.

"Oh, I remember the time when I used to wear that

Presidential Cravat," mumbled the President. "It seems like ages ago. But it was just minutes ago, wasn't it?"

"Yes it was," said Phil.

There among the President's many mustaches bloomed a slow look of understanding.

"We won't see the likes of those days again, will we?" said the President.

"No we won't," said Phil.

"Mr. President?" said the mirror-faced Advisor. "Mr. Former President? May I just say what a pleasure it's been serving you, even in this time of twilight and diminishing strength. Although I would be remiss, sir, if I didn't add that I feel it was somewhat injurious for me, in the prime of my career, to have been serving you, someone growing increasingly weak, when I could've been serving someone strong and getting stronger. Strength is, sir, and I expect always will be, a lure for the ambitious and clever. Phil here has, sir, I think you must admit, a great deal of strength. He is not only strong, but getting stronger, I think you must agree, and——"

"Are you leaving me, Al?" said the President.

"I'm afraid so," said the mirror-faced Advisor.

"And are you leaving me, Ed?" said the President to the smiley Advisor. "Leaving me for Phil? Are you all leaving me? Is Phil now the President? Is that what you boys are saying?"

The smiley Advisor lowered his eyes and one of his smiles turned sad.

"Oh," said the President. "How well I remember those distant times just this morning, when you all so reverently dressed me. I will never forget those times. I thank you for them. And Al? I'm not so sure about this Phil fellow. Careful, Al. This Phil, he's a little frightening. He gets things done, yes, but—"

"Excuse me, sir," said the mirror-faced Advisor. "I would ask you not to insult our President."

"That could be construed as treasonous," said the smiley Advisor.

"Ah," said the former President. "I see."

Then President Phil and his Advisors briskly left the former site of the Presidential Palace, which was now just a patch of extravagant flooring in the middle of a vast garden.

"Where to, Mr. President?" said the mirror-faced Advisor.

"To the Presidential Palace, of course," said Phil. "For my Inauguration, and my Inaugural Party."

"How wonderful!" said the mirror-faced Advisor. "A President who loves a good party."

"That former President?" said the smiley Advisor. "Never threw parties."

"Never once," said the mirror-faced Advisor, who had,

at one of the former President's frequent parties, gone overboard on glass cleaner and temporarily blinded himself, then bashed into the smiley-faced Advisor, sustaining a hairline crack between his eyes, about which he was still self-conscious.

"To the Presidential Palace!" shouted the Advisor who was just a mouth and a wig, throwing back his head so energetically that his wig flew off, and he therefore briefly became just a mouth.

At the new Presidential Palace, which was just the walls of the former Presidential Palace propped against Phil's apartment and crookedly capped with the golden dome, the Inaugural Party ran late into the night. The Outer Hornerites, deeply proud to be Outer Hornerites, staggered from wall to wall, overfilling their toluene receptacles and bellowing their national drinking song, "Large, Large, Large, Beloved Land (If Not the Best, Why So Very Dominant?)."

The Special Friends sat in a corner, wearing headphones, listening to personalized Tapes of Praise, made for them by Phil.

"Oh jeez," said Jimmy, too loudly. "He just said I have great biceps!"

"He just said, about me?" said Vance, also too loudly.

"That he loves the focused look I get on my face when following an order."

"He likes the way my lats flare when I pick someone up!" shouted Jimmy.

"I work well with others!" shouted Vance.

"There's a deep intelligence in me that others rarely see!" shouted Jimmy.

At the wild peak of the night, Phil mounted Jimmy's shoulders and, raising his Phalen Extender in a spastic victory salute, knocked off his own brain, which dropped into a bowl of chips.

"My people!" he shouted in the stentorian voice. "I shall speak now of us! Who are we? We are an articulate people, yet a people of few words. We feel deeply, yet refrain from embarrassing displays of emotion. Though firm, we are never too firm, though we love fun, we never have fun in a silly way that makes us appear ridiculous, unless that is our intent. Our national coloration, though varied, is consistent. Everything about us is as it should be, for example, we can be excessive, when excess is called for, and yet, even in our excess, we show good taste, although never is our taste so super-refined as to seem precious. Even the extent to which we are moderate is moderate, except when we have decided to be immoderately moderate, or even shockingly flamboyant, at which time our flamboyance is truly breathtaking in a really startling way, and when we decide to make mistakes, our mistakes are as big and grand and irrevocable as any nation's colossal errors, and when we decide to deny our mistakes, we sound just as if we were telling the truth, and when we decide to admit our errors, we do so in a way that is truly moving in its extreme frankness! Am I making sense? Am I saying this well?"

"Yes you are!" said Larry. "You're saying it very well!"

"Yes I am!" said Phil. "My saying it so well proves what I have just been saying, namely, that our ancient noble stock has, over many centuries of right living, evolved into the highest and most advanced nation there is, a nation that has, after many years of misrule by that chubby old guy, finally gotten the leader it deserves! That chubby old guy, in addition to being criminally forgetful, was recklessly flagrant. Knowing these Inner Hornerites were prone to unmotivated spasms of violence, he daily proclaimed, via that pathetic mere string of a border: Come in, invade us, feel free to commit your unmotivated violence spasms all over our sleeping innocent babies, while I obsess about my bellies and mustaches. Well, I am not flagrant or forgetful, I have one belly and no mustache, and my only obsession is the safety of my people, which is why I hereby proclaim, as my first Presidential Act, my innovative Border Area Improvement Initiative! Who is on board? Who will sign this Certificate of Total Approval, sanctioning my Initiative?"

"What does it say, sir?" said Melvin.

"Why do you care what it says, Melvin?" said Larry. "Don't you trust Phil?"

"Of course I trust Phil," said Melvin. "I trust Phil like twice as much as you trust Phil."

"Then why are you resisting signing the Certificate of Total Approval?" said Larry.

"Give me that thing, I'll sign it," said Melvin. "I'll sign it right now, without even reading it."

"I'll sign it without even looking at it," said Larry.

"I'll sign it with my eyes closed," said Leon the Border Guard.

"I'll sign it with my eyes closed, facing away from it," said Melvin.

So Larry and Melvin and Leon and the Special Friends and the Advisors lined up facing backwards, eyes closed, and signed the Certificate of Total Approval.

Even Freeda signed it, because everybody was staring at her.

"Excellent, Freeda, thanks so much!" said Phil. "All have signed. All Totally Approve of my Border Area Improvement Initiative. Although Freeda? Too bad you didn't sign it with your eyes closed while facing away from it. Not that I mind! You signed it, which is what matters, basically, I guess."

Just then from out in the street someone cleared his

throat so loudly that the bowl of chips bearing Phil's brain fell off the table, causing Phil's brain to roll under the couch.

"BUG CARRIES BREAD CRUMB!" shouted someone from outside. "OTHER BUGS LOOK ON IN AWED SILENCE!"

"WATER RUNS DOWNHILL TOWARDS SEWER!" shouted a second voice.

"AIR CONTINUES TO FLOAT AROUND, BEING BREATHED BY MANY!" shouted a third.

Looking out, Phil saw three handsome well-groomed squat little men with detachable megaphones growing out of their clavicles.

"MAN REGARDS STRANGERS IN STREET!" shouted the first little man.

"What are you guys doing?" asked Phil.

"MAN ASKS QUESTION, EXPECTS ANSWER!" said the third little man.

"MAJOR MEDIA FIGURES PREPARE TO RE-SPOND!" said the first man.

"IS THE MEDIA HELD TOO MUCH ACCOUNT-ABLE?" said the second.

"We're with the media," said the first man, in a normal tone of voice that issued not from the megaphone but from a toothy smile near his rear end.

"Not much happening out here," said the second man.

"So we're just practicing."

"In case someday something does happen," said the third little man.

"SKY REMAINS DARK AS NIGHT PROCEEDS!" said the first little man.

"Good one," said the second.

"I felt that was an important issue," said the first.

"MAJOR MEDIA FIGURE COMPLIMENTED BY SECOND MAJOR MEDIA FIGURE!" said the second little man.

"MAJOR MEDIA FIGURE ANNOUNCES COMPLIMENTING OF MAJOR MEDIA FIGURE BY SECOND MEDIA FIGURE!" shouted the third little man.

"IS THE MEDIA TOO FOCUSED ON THE MEDIA?" shouted the second little man.

"DOG PEES ON SHRUB, LOOKS ASKANCE AT OWN REAR!" shouted the first little man.

"You should come out to the Border Area tomorrow," Phil said. "Big things happening out there. We're dealing with a violent, irrational people who really hate us. The nation just Totally Approved my Border Area Improvement Initiative. So tomorrow we Implement. It won't be easy. Lots of heavy lifting. We've already accomplished a number of painful, difficult security-related tasks, but tomorrow we'll be attempting the most painful, difficult task of all. It would be super to have some skillful truth-tellers out there, encouraging the nation in its critical hour of destiny. I'd be happy to pay your expenses and a small stipend."

"Wait a minute," said the first little man. "Is that the Presidential Cravat you're wearing?"

"Oh my God," said the second little man. "Are you the President?"

"I thought the President was that little fat guy with the mustaches," said the third little man.

"That was the old President," said Phil.

The little media men were amazed and gratified that this new President possessed such a nuanced understanding of the vital role of the media, unlike the old President, who used to claim that their attempts to keep the nation informed made his bursitis worse and shattered the Presidential Cups in the Presidential Cupboard.

"NEW PRESIDENT VOWS TO ELIMINATE BORDER THREAT!" shouted the first little man.

"NEW PREZ TO NATION: YOU SHALL KNOW PEACE!" shouted the second.

"WHAT TIME SHOULD WE BE THERE?" shouted the third, who then realized he was presenting his personal views as the objective view of the media and asked his question more ethically, by asking it out the mouth near his rear.

"Things tend to start around dawn," said Phil.

"Then we'd better get practicing," said the third.

"MOON, STARS CONTINUE TO BE LOCATED IN SKY!" shouted the first little man.

"NEIGHBOR LADY DRAWS BLINDS WITH CRABBY LOOK ON FACE!" shouted the second.

"EXCLUSIVE SERIES ON BORDER AREA STRUGGLE STARTS TOMORROW!" shouted the third.

"I like the sound of that," said the first.

"I hope it's not too late to find flak jackets," said the second.

"Just save your receipts," said Phil.

The little men's voices drifted out across the farthest reaches of Outer Horner, until finally, because Outer Horner was not infinite, their voices drifted into the surrounding country of Greater Keller, which ran like a six-inch-wide circular strip of ribbon around Outer Horner.

Because Greater Keller was so thin it was almost nonexistent, it was rarely visited much less invaded, and was therefore very prosperous. The nine Greater Kellerites spent their days walking behind their President single-file, carefully placing one foot in front of the other, happy and cordial, engaged in endless energetic conversation about the appearance of the portion of Outer Horner they happened to be walking around, the nuances of the cup of coffee they were currently enjoying, and/or the enjoyable impression being made on them by the way the person in front of them looked when viewed from behind.

"Temporary Halt, please!" called President Rick, leaning into Outer Horner airspace, hand to his ear. "Someone is saying some rather loud and interesting things from Outer Horner, concerning a new President."

"I find myself wondering what happened to their old President," said the First Lady.

"Excellent point, dear!" said President Rick. "Let's discuss that. Let's have some good national conversation about that, thus increasing our National Enjoyment Level. Did he retire, one wonders? Was he forced out of office?"

"Did he pass away?" said the First Lady. "If so, were his last words inspirational?"

"Or was he perhaps bitter at the end?" said the First Daughter.

"Oh, I doubt it, dear," said the First Lady. "Remember when he visited?"

"What a sport!" said President Rick. "Such a fat little man, but did he ever give walking in a circle a good try!"

And the nation fondly remembered the former President of Outer Horner, one of its rare visitors who, finding it difficult to walk in a circle, given his three legs and multiple bellies, kept falling out of their nation and inadvertently returning to his own.

"Just who is this new President?" said Lenore, Citizen #5, meaning she was fifth in line. "Is he as good a sport as the old President? Does he like to talk? Is he sociable?"

"Can he walk in a circle?" said President Rick. "That's the main thing. Does he like to make pleasant conversation as he walks in a circle drinking coffee?"

"Does he even like coffee?" said Kevin, Citizen #8.

"Is he, perhaps, more of a tea drinker?" said the First Daughter.

The nation of Greater Keller went momentarily silent at this troubling thought.

"I think we should invite him for a Visit," said the First Lady. "For days before his Visit, we could look forward to his Visit. For days after his Visit, we could discuss how well his Visit went. Think how Enjoyable we'll find that!"

"Cliff?" said the President to Citizen #4. "How are we doing? How good, rich, and beautiful is our life at the moment? How fully are we living?"

"Well, sir," said Cliff, the National Enjoyment Assessor. "Our cups are approximately half-full, our coffee is still warm, the First Lady has just passed around some nice cookies, we've got the sudden surge of interest associated with the possible Visit of the President of Outer Horner—I'd say we're Enjoying at about an Eight of a possible Ten."

"Not bad," said President Rick. "We are really Enjoying!"

"Life for us is rich," said the First Daughter.

Suddenly Kelli, Citizen #7, blew a whistle.

"Mid-Morning Reversal!" President Rick called happily, and the population of Greater Keller lay flat on the ground so the President could take his rightful place at the front of the line, by stepping very gingerly over the prone forms of his people, after which the First Lady stepped gingerly over the prone population, after which the First Daughter and those behind her in line stepped gingerly over the prone population, until finally the President stood at the head of a line that was now a mirror-image of its former self.

"Who would like to deliver our invitation?" said the President. "Dale? Would you mind?"

"It would be an honor, sir," said Dale, and the First Daughter blushed, because, unbeknownst to her parents, she was in love with Dale, who, unfortunately for her, was Citizen #9, which meant there were five citizens between her and Dale, and therefore they never got any time alone, except briefly during Reversals, when he was lying prone and she was stepping gingerly over him.

Dale shot a quick loving glance at the First Daughter, then advanced into Far West Distant Outer Horner via a series of large arcs, which was the only way Greater

Kellerites could walk, trained as they were from youth to circular motion.

If this mission was successful, Dale felt, it would put him in an excellent position to approach the President with a Line Position Change Request.

"Shall we?" said President Rick, and Kelli, Citizen #7, blew her whistle, and the Counter-Clockwise Morning Circumambulation began.

All morning and most of the afternoon the Inner Hornerites stood shivering in the Short-Term Residency Zone, waiting for Phil to arrive, deeply ashamed about what had happened to Cal. Like anyone deeply ashamed, they looked for someone to blame, and decided to blame Cal, who they all missed tremendously.

"What was that crazy guy thinking?" said Wanda. "I mean, jeez, what a hothead."

"When I advocated resistance I certainly didn't mean that," said Curtis, looking guiltily over at the little blue dot.

"What did you mean?" said Carol.

"Well, I meant some, ah, conversational resistance," Curtis said, blinking nervously. "A period during which we would say challenging but polite things, things which might cause them to possibly consider reassessing their positions vis-à-vis us."

Just then the Inner Hornerites heard a fanfare similar to the Presidential Fanfare, and saw what appeared to be the Presidential Board, being carried by what looked like a group of Presidential Advisors, except that, sitting where the President usually sat, sat someone who resembled Phil, had Phil been wearing a smug euphoric expression and the Presidential Cravat.

"You've got to be kidding," said Elmer.

Then Phil did something he had never done before: He yanked his own bolt. He yanked his bolt, feeling that, although he was feeling quite Presidential, he would feel even more Presidential once he got the rush of confidence he always felt when his brain slid off.

But when he yanked his bolt, nothing slid off.

His hands flew up to his rack and a sudden look of panic shot across his face.

With a sense of dread he remembered his spasming rack, the slow descent to the bottom of the high-school pool, waking up senseless on the Farley ReMotivator unable to make words, his arms and legs flailing, hydraulic oil running out of his Pan and into the floor drain.

"Boys!" he shouted frantically in the stentorian voice. "Quickly now! Implement Phase I!"

From a huge backpack the Special Friends took a post-hole digger and eight stout posts and a roll of barbed wire, then dug eight quick holes around the perimeter of the Short-Term Residency Zone, dropped the posts in, nailed the barbed wire to the posts, and hung a sign reading: "Peace-Encouraging Enclosure."

"What, we're in jail?" said Elmer.

"You're putting us in jail now?" said Wanda.

"How typical of the Inner Horner mindset!" said Phil. "To be unable to distinguish a jail from a Peace-Encouraging Enclosure. Safe inside the Peace-Encouraging Enclosure, you will be protected from your innate violent tendencies, and we will be protected from you. It is a real win/win."

Just then the little media men came racing up, equipped with flak jackets and new megaphones twice the size of their former megaphones.

"Sorry we're late!" the first little man said from the mouth near his rear.

"What'd we miss?" said the second little man. "What's going on?"

"Phase I of the Border Area Improvement Initiative is complete," Phil said. "And we are rapidly moving on to Phase II."

The Special Friends disappeared behind the Outer Horner Cafe, and reemerged pushing an enormous wooden cart overflowing with soil, shovels, an apple tree, barrels of water, and what looked like an aquarium.

"Fill in that hole, boys!" Phil shouted. "Then plant the tree. And restore the stream. Make it wider than before. Also, stock it with fish! At last we are reclaiming our ancient ancestral land, and we want it to look nice!"

The Special Friends took off their shirts and put on tanning oil and in no time at all had filled in the former nation of Inner Horner, planted a new apple tree, dug a wider stream, and stocked the stream with fish.

"PREZ TRANSFORMS VIOLENT MUDDY HOLE INTO PASTORAL PARADISE!" shouted the first little man.

"PEACE FINALLY ACHIEVED AT PROBLEMATIC BORDER AREA!" shouted the second.

"VISIONARY LEADER DAZZLES NATION WITH DECISIVE GREATNESS!" shouted the third.

It was true, Phil realized. He was great. He had come so far from his humble beginnings. He remembered his pathetic childhood home, the family crammed into the little kitchen, his father sitting in the sink so his mother could open the refrigerator, his mother climbing on top of the refrigerator so his father could let down the ironing board. Then he remembered the dark days after his father left, when suddenly there was more room to get the refrigerator open but no reason to open it, since there was never anything inside. Why had Dad left? Phil knew very well why. One day they'd gone on a family picnic, to the Border Area, and Dad had been playfully throwing some rocks, small rocks, pebbles really, into Inner Horner, just for fun, when one of the Inner Hornerites, apparently unable to grasp the difficult concept of lighthearted playful joshing, claimed one of the pebbles had entered his Exhaust Port, and alerted the Border Guard, at that time a guy named Smitty, a humorless jerk with pronounced Inner Horner tendencies, who'd asked Dad to stop, since, strictly speaking, harassing Inner Hornerites was illegal. The look on poor Dad's face! He'd been so embarrassed. Phil felt certain that the humiliation of being publicly corrected in front of a bunch of smirking Inner Hornerites while his wife and child looked on had pushed Dad over the edge.

A week later Dad left, and Phil never saw him again.

Oh, if Dad could see him now! Dad had always said Inner Hornerites were the dirt of the world, and now the world was about to be cleansed of dirt, once and for all, by him, by Phil!

It was time for Phase III.

"My people!" he shouted in the stentorian voice. "As long as they are existent, they seem to keep rising up against us! Therefore, for us to be at total peace, they must be totally gone! Gone gone gone! Let us now create permanent peace, while simultaneously demonstrating good fiscal sense, by collecting the taxes in advance for the next five days, via collecting all their national assets at once, right now!"

"All of them?" said Freeda.

"The whole country?" said Melvin.

"Are we not us?" bellowed Phil. "Are they not them? Us being us, do we not, being fully good, have the right to end what, totally bad, threatens us, even in the slightest? Would it not be negligent to do otherwise?"

"Ah, here we go," muttered Old Gus, who was by now so hungry that whenever he tried to breathe he looked like he was smirking.

"What was that?" said Phil. "What are you smirking about?"

"I'm not smirking," said Gus. "I'm trying to breathe."

"Very funny!" thundered Phil, so loudly that Gus's left antler popped out.

Freeda stood frozen. Gertrude Gertrude Gertrude, she was thinking, what would Gertrude think if Gertrude learned her mother had once stood silently by while a trembling grandpa was disassembled? Freeda had nothing against this trembling grandpa, who actually looked very much like her own trembling grandpa, except her grandpa looked more like a *J* than a *C* and had branches, not antlers.

"Phil," Freeda said hoarsely, several leaves dropping off due to sudden dryness. "I'm not sure about this."

"You're not *sure* about this?" said Phil. "Freeda? Did you sign your Certificate of Total Approval? I believe you did. Although, as I recall, you signed it rather disrespect-fully, with your eyes open, while facing it. That should have been my first clue that your Loyalty was suspect. Did you even read your Certificate of Total Approval before signing it, Freeda? Especially Paragraph D, Disloyalty Conse-quences? 'When Disloyalty occurs (to be determined at the discretion of PHIL), the consequence for that Disloyalty will be determined by PHIL and PHIL alone.' Therefore, since I simply can't have someone Disloyal around me, con-taminating my nation, per my determination, will you hereby make things easier on yourself, by kneeling before the Special Friends with your primary connecting parts easily accessible?"

"Me?" gasped Freeda. "You're disassembling me?"

"You're disassembling Freeda?" said Melvin.

"Melvin!" said Phil. "Don't make me invoke Para-graph H, Nipping Probable Disloyalty in the Bud! Does anyone have a problem with this, other than Melvin? If so, please step forward. And please don't think I will necessarily consider it Disloyal for you to publicly contradict me at this critical national destiny hour. I mean, I probably will, but if you reference Paragraph N, The President's Incredible Mercy, you will see that I, and I alone, reserve the right to be as merciful as I choose about cases of Probable Disloyalty."

No one stepped forward.

"So everyone is fine with this?" said Phil. "Except Melvin?"

"No, I'm fine with it," said Melvin, a little frantically. "I'm totally fine with it."

Freeda did not kneel with her primary connecting parts easily accessible, but stood up straight, thinking of Gertrude, while the Special Friends trimmed back her Sternum Foliage, then removed her Personal Boundary Sensor and her Hat-Holding Pin System and her bulbous Left Foot.

Soon Jimmy was down to the last step, which involved removing Freeda's third arm, which flailed around frantically, as if trying to put out a fire on Jimmy's chest.

"INSURRECTION NIPPED IN BUD!" shouted the first little man.

"PREZ DOES WHAT PREZ MUST DO!" shouted the second.

"What a sad thing, that Freeda should prove to be a traitor!" Phil said. "Well, let this be a lesson to all! A lesson that the disgusting traits that make those Inner Hornerites so disgusting, such as Disloyalty, such as undermining one's leaders via constant questioning, can even take root in us Outer Hornerites. I wouldn't be surprised if some of us didn't start getting smaller and doing mathematical proofs. We'll have to watch for that. We'll have to be vigilant. Jimmy, Vance, please help

Freeda remind us to be vigilant, by constructing an attractive yet sobering display of the components of Freeda, so people can witness Freeda's components, and thus learn from them! What a wonderful thing for Freeda, to be so very educational! In this way, her life will not have been a total waste!"

So the Special Friends made a display of Freeda's parts, by stringing some from trees and setting others on rocks, placing, near each, per Phil, a sign reading: "Loyalty—It's Super!"

Then, almost as an afterthought, Phil nodded to Jimmy, who plucked Old Gus out of the Peace-Encouraging Enclosure and disassembled him, which went very quickly, Old Gus being so frail, brittle, and greaseless.

"PROGRESS CONTINUES APACE!" shouted the second little man.

"TOTAL VICTORY IN SIGHT!" shouted the third.

A great high-pitched wailing now sounded from Inner Horner.

It may have been this that caused Phil's rack to spasm.

Oh shoot, wow, Phil thought, that really hurts.

He had only got this same spasming sensational once before in his life, and that had been the worse, due to, just after that, his speech would began suffering.

Darn, Phil thought. It are happening now, somewhat slight.

He'd better hurry, get this Phase III wropped up, so he could go homer and find that stupid brawn, and remont it.

"That one," Phil gasped, indicating Curtis, and Jimmy yanked Curtis out of the Peace-Encouraging Enclosure, and Jimmy unlatched Curtis's Lower Half, and Vance unbraided the nine tightly braided ropes that constituted Curtis's Upper Half, and Jimmy removed the three bolts joining Curtis's perfectly round head full of thick wavy hair to his Neck Platform, and soon Curtis had been reduced to a twitching pile of parts oozing hydraulic fluid.

At that moment, Dale, Citizen #9 from Greater Keller, burst out from behind the Outer Horner Cafe and sprinted off towards Greater Keller, his shock and disgust at all he had seen causing him to inscribe what was, for him, a remarkably linear path.

"What the heck was that?" said Melvin.

"It sure looked weird," said Leon.

"And it sure ran funny," said Larry.

The truth was, relative to the Inner and Outer Hornerites, the Greater Kellerites did look weird. They had no mechanical or botanical parts, and were tall and whippet-like and stood permanently leaning off to one side as if going around a bend, which, normally, they were.

They were also, it should be mentioned, huge: approximately three times the height of the Special Friends, with significantly less body fat. And longer legs. Their legs were long and lean from constant walking, and they never got tired, and their faces were slightly beveled and aerodynamic, and so, once you got them going, they were incredibly fast runners.

Dale, the fastest of all, reached Greater Keller just six minutes after he left the Border Area.

Nine minutes after Dale left the Border Area, the nation of Greater Keller, coffee cups clinking nervously against their saucers, listened as Dale concluded his report.

"Cliff, how are we doing?" President Rick tersely asked the National Enjoyment Assessor.

"Well, we've been better, sir," said Cliff. "Although our coffee cups are full and we have, on average, four cookies remaining on our plates, the National Life Enjoyment Index Score has dropped to an alarming Three out of Ten. I would attribute this to anxiety associated with Dale's report. In fact, Mr. President, knowing our people as I do, I foresee continued significant downturns in the NLEIS, if we do not in some way address Dale's findings."

"People will mope and feel guilty?" said President Rick.

"I'm afraid so," said Cliff.

"Our coffee will not taste as good?" said President Rick. "When regarding a beautiful vista or hearing a delightful bon mot, our hearts will not be as uplifted, due to we will be thinking of those people far away who need our help?"

"Basically, yes," said Cliff.

"Maybe we should send out an Expeditionary Force," said the First Daughter.

"Oh, gosh, I don't know," said President Rick. "I mean, if this new President is as bad as Dale says, isn't it possible that he might do something bad to our Expeditionary Force? And therefore, wouldn't it be better to keep everybody safe at home? That sounds much more Enjoyable to me."

"Sir, the nation is tense," said Cliff gravely. "It is asking itself how it can possibly stand idly by drinking gourmet coffee when an entire race is about to be disassembled. It wants to Enjoy, yes, but feels it will not be able to fully Enjoy until some sort of closure is reached."

"I'm just really torn about this," said President Rick. "If some of us get hurt, the NLEIS could easily drop below Three. It could even conceivably go into negative numbers."

"We could Suffer," said Lenore.

"We could Suffer, exactly," said President Rick.

"On the other hand," said the First Daughter, "if these people are as bad as Dale says, they could come here next."

"Talk about Suffering," said Kevin.

"They could destroy our coffee cart," said the First Lady.

"They could disassemble us," said Kelli.

"Sir," Cliff whispered urgently. "The NLEIS is dropping like a stone."

"Dang," said President Rick, who had been looking forward to that evening, when he planned on passing around some surprise éclairs and challenging his nation to write a collective national sonnet on the pleasurable sensation of eating an éclair while watching a sunset.

But President Rick knew his people, and knew that the only sonnets they would be able to write now would be sad guilt-racked sonnets, no matter how many éclairs he fed them.

So President Rick ordered Elroy, Citizen #6, the National Coffeemaker, to brew five thermoses of coffee, and had Dale lead a brief preliminary training hike into Outer Horner, during which Dale demonstrated various techniques he had found useful for running in a straight line.

Then the nation of Greater Keller sprinted into Outer Horner, commenting, as was their national habit, on the beauty of the landscape through which they were passing, but in uncharacteristically terse, joyless voices.

*   *   *

"All of them, sir?" Jimmy the Special Friend was saying at that very moment. "Even the ladies?"

"Even the kid?" said Vance.

"I do not see any lady or kids!" shouted Phil. "I only see some curvier Inner Hornerites with longer hair, and one smaller Inner Hornerite with two freakish brains! With Inner Hornerites there is no lady, there is no kid, there are only evil, which must be dealt with harsh, before it spread! Hurry, boys! Seize all remaining national asset, lift said national asses out from the Peace-Encouraging Enclosure plonto!"

So Jimmy plucked Carol and Elmer out of the Peace-Encouraging Enclosure, and Vance plucked Wanda and Little Andy out of the Peace-Encouraging Enclosure, and the entire remaining population of the once-great land of Inner Horner found itself suddenly suspended in the air, legs flailing, seconds from total extinction.

Which was when the Expeditionary Force of the Nation of Greater Keller arrived at the Border Area in five colossal, parallel, dust-raising arcs.

"What in the world?" said President Rick.

"Boys," Phil shouted frantically. "Arrest this invaderment!"

The Special Friends had never in their lives seen anyone bigger than themselves. Suddenly they nostalgically remembered their previous careers as Mud-Consistency Testing Associates. Those were the good old days, when the worst thing that ever happened to them was that occasionally Edna inadvertently left them out in the yard all night, covered in mud.

"SPECIAL FRIENDS FLEE BORDER AREA!" shouted the first little man.

"STRIPPING OFF BIG RED SHIRTS, THEY RUN LIKE WIND!" shouted the second.

"ALREADY THEY ARE OUT OF SIGHT!" shouted the third.

"PRESIDENT PHIL SPEECHLESS WITH HANGING-OPEN MOUTH AND LOOK OF TOTAL SHOCK ON FACE!" shouted the second.

"ANXIOUS NATION AWAITS PRESIDENTIAL STATEMENT!" shouted the third.

Actually, Phil felt, he wasn't feeling all that well. He was feeling totally devanced in terms of how good he could think. Where was that stupid brain? Where dud he left it? That thing had been offen a long time. No wonder no salvation thoughts were come winging out of him. He wanted to communerate to these idiotic tall circle-walking invaders they couldn't know how it was like, forced to live close to a national of inhuman puny coveting your wide open, claiming to be just as human, giving those hostility look just because you lived in a spacious total bounty of righteous plenty. Only suddenly he couldn't seem to speak so super.

Phil's legs gave out, and he sat on the ground near the Peace-Encouraging Enclosure.

"Sir?" said Larry. "Are you okay?"

It could not end this way, it could not end in any way but total triumph redemption of his dream of upward conquest, thereby him, Phil, in gold chair, and all the lessers, lying stretched out at his trenchant feet, citing his blessed nameplate.

"Cruel freight," he mumbled. "Working crosswise to my bold national, fate interdicted my glorious, and due to nefarious, all grand uplift purposes crash down, flags droop, crowds go home."

Then the weight of his brainless rack proved too much, and he slumped over, snagging his rack in the barbed wire of the Peace-Encouraging Enclosure.

A final spark flew out of his nosehole, and he was still.

A great silence fell across the Border Area.

"Mistakes were made," said Larry.

"Excesses were committed," said Leon.

"Let's get those poor people out of that cage, shall we?" said President Rick. "That doesn't look very Enjoyable."

Dale, Citizen #9, with the help of Kelli, Citizen #7, tore down the Peace-Encouraging Enclosure, and the nation of Inner Horner stumbled out.

"Our advice, to all of you people, is Enjoy!" said President Rick. "Life is full of beauty. Why fight? Why hate?

Learn to Enjoy, and you will have no need to fight, and no desire to! Love life, walk in a circle, learn to enjoy coffee! Will you do that? Will you promise to try that?"

The Inner Hornerites looked blankly at President Rick.

"Well, we have to be going!" said President Rick. "I'm sure you folks will figure everything out!"

And the Greater Kellerites started home in a loping victorious arc, their National Enjoyment Level an astonishing 9.8 out of Ten, due to their pride in their recent heroism and their anticipation of the many days of Enjoyable storytelling that lay ahead.

"I told Phil this would happen," said the mirror-faced Advisor.

"So did I," said the smiley Advisor.

"I said to him, Phil, honestly, who do you think you are, let's not get too big for our britches," said the mirror-faced Advisor.

"I think we all said that," said the mere mouth.

"HOW WAS NATION SO EASILY DUPED?" shouted the first little man.

"WHY DID NATION IGNORE REPEATED WARNINGS BY MEDIA?" shouted the second.

"NERVOUS-LOOKING ADVISORS LEAVE AREA AT FAST WALK!" shouted the third.

"MAJOR MEDIA FIGURES BRAVELY FOLLOW

STRANGE EXODUS FROM BORDER AREA, DETERMINED TO SEE WHAT IS UP WITH THAT!" shouted the first.

And the Advisors and media men left the Border Area, the Advisors discussing strategies for reminding the former President of how constantly loyal they had been to him, the media men feverishly whispering potential headlines out their rear-mouths.

The Inner Hornerites (Elmer, Carol, Little Andy, and Wanda), suddenly realizing they now outnumbered the Outer Hornerites (Leon, Larry, and Melvin), fell upon the Outer Hornerites with all the fury of a people who, naked and starving, had been imprisoned for days on end, in a cage, on the brink of extinction. Soon from out of the rising cloud of dust there flew a cotter pin (Melvin's) and a Temperature Gauge (Leon's), and Larry's Frontal Hairpiece, and several unidentified Teeth Plates, and suddenly it was the nation of Outer Horner, inside the cloud of dust, that found itself on the brink of extinction.

Which was when, in the sky above the Border Area, there appeared a hand so massive that its golden ring could easily have encircled the entire Border Area. Across its wrist ran a vast flower garden, one of its three fingers was mechanical, in its palm was what appeared to be a shimmering blue lake.

The Outer Hornerites and Inner Hornerites had all thought about the Creator, and talked about the Creator, and some of them had even prayed to the Creator, but none of them had ever dreamed the Creator was so big.

The fighting stopped, the dust cloud settled, the nations of Inner and Outer Horner stared up, wide-eyed and open-mouthed.

Then a second hand descended, with a vegetable garden running across the wrist, and two mechanical fingers, and a frozen lake in its palm, holding a spray can, and the Creator's left hand sprayed the Border Area, and the Outer and Inner Hornerites fell instantly asleep.

The two hands, working together, gently disassembled the Outer Hornerites.

Then they gently disassembled the Inner Hornerites.

Using the Inner and Outer Horner parts, they rapidly constructed fifteen entirely new little people.

The only parts they didn't use were Phil's parts. Phil's brain (retrieved from under his couch, covered in chip-crumbs and lint, giving off the hissing noise a Type C brain makes when off-gassing) they dropped into the stream, where several of the new fish, mistaking it for a misshapen fallen apple, began eating it. Phil's body, they mounted on a platform, after first spray-painting it black and mounting a plaque beneath it.

"PHIL," the plaque read. "MONSTER."

Then the massive hands lifted the new people up to a pair of giant indescribable lips and whispered, in a fundamentally untranslatable Creator-language, something that meant, approximately: THIS TIME, BE KIND TO ONE ANOTHER. REMEMBER: EACH OF YOU WANTS TO BE HAPPY. AND I WANT YOU TO. EACH OF YOU WANTS TO LIVE FREE FROM FEAR. AND I WANT YOU TO. EACH OF YOU ARE SECRETLY AFRAID YOU ARE NOT GOOD ENOUGH. BUT YOU ARE, TRUST ME, YOU ARE.

Then the left hand picked up the green string that constituted the boundary of the Short-Term Residency Zone, and the right hand picked up the red string that constituted the Inner Horner border, and the left hand took away the remnants of the Peace-Encouraging Enclosure, while the right hand planted a sign reading: "Welcome to New Horner."

Then the hands did that dusting-off thing hands do when they've just finished a difficult piece of work, and withdrew, majestically, through a large white cloud.

Soon the fifteen new people woke up, stretching and yawning. Where the heck were they? And who the heck were they? They felt sort of sore. Apparently, they concluded, by looking at the sign, they were New Hornerites, and lived in New Horner. Apparently, they concluded, reading the little name-tags around their necks, they each had a name.

They were, they all agreed, just amazingly hungry.

On the way to a nearby apple tree, they passed a hulking black mess on a platform.

"What is that thing?" said Gil.

"It's a Phil," said Clive.

"What is a Phil?" said Sally.

"A monster," said Leona.

"Apparently," said Fritz.

"Or maybe Monster was his last name?" said Gil. "You know: Phil Monster. Like: Hi, I'm Phil Monster? It's not entirely clear from the syntax."

"Whatever," said Sally. "Let's go eat."

Leona looked at Gil. *Syntax?* What the heck kind of word was that? What was Gil, some kind of big-shot? She hated big-shots, she suddenly realized. She'd have to watch Gil. She'd talk to Sally about it. Sally didn't seem like a big-shot. Sally seemed sensible and moral and down to earth. Sally, like Leona, was compressed and ball-shaped, unlike the freakishly elongated Gil.

As the months went by, the New Hornerites took to avoiding The Phil. Although nobody could exactly say why, The Phil gave them the creeps. Soon the path bowed out around it, weeds overtook it, and all that could be seen of The Phil was the tip of Phil's rack, which stuck out of the weeds like a bad flagpole. Animals burrowed in The Phil, birds nested there, balls accumulated there because the New Horner kids were too scared to retrieve them.

And that is where Phil is today: hidden in a thicket of weeds, not loved, not hated, just forgotten, rusting/rotting, with even the sign that proclaims his name fading away.

Except sometimes Leona comes to visit. She does not find The Phil monstrous, but strangely beautiful, and sometimes sits in the thicket for hours, dreaming, for reasons she can't quite explain, of a better world, run by humble, compressed, ball-shaped people, like her and Sally, who speak, when they speak at all, in short sentences, of their simple heroic dreams.

acknowledgments

The author wishes to thank the Lannan Foundation, the Syracuse University College of Arts and Sciences, and his colleagues and students in the Syracuse Creative Writing Program, for their generous support during the writing of this book.

IN PERSUASION NATION

For Paula, again, and always

CONTENTS

i.

I CAN SPEAK!™   101

my flamboyant grandson   111

jon   123

ii.

my amendment   171

the red bow   179

christmas   197

adams   211

iii.

93990   221

brad carrigan, american   233

in persuasion nation   275

iv.

bohemians   307

commcomm   323

i.

Our enemies will first assail the health of our
commerce, throwing up this objection and that to
innovative methods and approaches designed to
expand our prosperity, and thus our freedom.
Their old-fashioned clinging to obsolete ideas
only signals their extinction. In the end, we must
pity them: we are going forward with joy and
hope; they are being left behind, mired in fear.

—*Bernard "Ed" Alton,*
    Taskbook for the New Nation,
    Chapter 1. "New Man, New Growth-Community"

I CAN SPEAK!™

Mrs. Ruth Faniglia
210 Lester Way
Rochester, NY 14623

Dear Mrs. Faniglia,

We were very sorry to receive your letter of 23 Feb., which accompanied the I CAN SPEAK!™ you returned, much to our disappointment. We here at KidLuv believe that the I CAN SPEAK!™ is an innovative and essential educational tool that, used with proper parental guidance, offers a rare early-development opportunity for babies and toddlers alike. And so I thought I would take some of my personal time (I am on lunch) and try to address the questions you raised in your letter, which is here in front of me on my (cluttered!) desk.

First, may I be so bold as to suggest that some of your disappointment may stem from your own, perhaps unreasonable, expectations? Because in your letter, what you indicated, when I read it? Was that you think and/or thought that somehow the product can read your baby's mind? Our product cannot read your baby's mind, Mrs. Faniglia. No one can read a baby's mind. At least not yet. Although we are probably working on it! What the I CAN SPEAK!™ can do, however, is recognize *familiar aural patterns* and respond to these patterns in a way that makes *baby seem older*. Say baby sees a peach. If you or Mr. Faniglia (I hope I do not presume) were to loudly say something like: "What a delicious peach!" the I CAN SPEAK!™, hearing this, through that hole, that little slotted hole near the neck, might respond by saying something like: "I LIKE PEACH." Or: "I WANT PEACH." Or, if you had chosen the ICS2000 (which you did not, you chose the ICS1900, which is fine, perfectly good for most babies) the I CAN SPEAK!™ might even respond by saying something like: "FRUIT, ISN'T THAT ONE OF THE MAJOR FOOD GROUPS?"

Which would be pretty good for a six-month-old, don't you think, which my Warranty Response Card shows is the age of your son Derek, Derek Faniglia?

But here I must reiterate: That would not in reality be Derek speaking. Derek would not in reality know that a peach is fruit, or that fruit is a major food group. The I CAN SPEAK!™ knows it, however, and, from its position on Derek's face, gives the illusion that Derek knows it, by giving the illusion that Derek is speaking out of its twin moving SimuLips™. But that is it. That is all we claim.

Furthermore, in your letter, Mrs. Faniglia, you state that the I CAN SPEAK!™ "mask" (your terminology) takes on a "stressed-out look when talking that is not what a real baby's talking face appears like but is more like some nervous middle-aged woman." Well, maybe that is so, but with all due respect (and I say this with affection), you try it! You try making a latex face look and talk and move like the real face of an actual live baby! Inside are *over 5,000 separate circuits* and *390 moving parts*. And as far as looking like a middle-aged woman, we beg to differ. We do not feel that a middle-aged stressed-out woman has (1) no hair on head and (2) chubby cheeks and (3) fine downy facial hair. The ICS1900 unit is definitely the face of a baby, Mrs. Faniglia, we took over 2,500 photos of different babies and, using a computer, combined them to make this face on your unit, and on everybody else's unit, the face we call Male Composite 37 or, affectionately, "Little Roger." But what you possibly seem to be unhappy about is the fact that Little Roger's face is not Derek's face? To be frank, Mrs. Faniglia, many of you, our customers, have found it disconcerting that their baby looks different with the I CAN SPEAK!™ on, than with the I CAN SPEAK!™ off. Which we find so surprising. Did you not, we often wonder, look at the cover of the box? The ICS1900 is very plainly shown, situated on a sort of rack, looking facewise like Little Roger, albeit Little Roger is a bit crumpled and has a forehead furrow of sorts.

Which is why we came up with the ICS2100. With the ICS2100, your baby *looks just like your baby*. And because we do not want anyone to be unhappy with us, we would like to make you the gift of a complimentary ICS2100 upgrade! We would like to come to your house on Lester Way and make a personalized plaster cast of Derek's real, actual face! And soon, via FedEx, here will come Derek's face in a box, and when you slip that ICS2100 over Derek's head and Velcro the Velcro, he will look nearly exactly like himself, plus we have another free surprise, which is that, while at your house, we will tape his actual voice and use it to make our phrases, the phrases Derek will subsequently say. So not only will he look like himself, he will *sound like himself*, as he crawls around your home, appearing to speak!

Plus we will throw in several personalizing options.

Say you call Derek "Lovemeister." (I am using this example from my own personal home, as my wife Ann and I call our son Billy "Lovemeister," because he is so sweet.) With the ICS2100, you might choose to have Derek say—or appear to say—upon crawling into a room, "HERE COMES THE LOVEMEISTER!" or "STOP TALKING DIRTY, THE LOVEMEISTER HAS ARRIVED!" How we do this is, laser beams coming out of the earlobes, which sense the doorframe! From its position on the head of Derek, the I CAN SPEAK!™ knows it has just entered a room! And also you will have over one hundred Discretionary Phrases to more highly personalize Derek. You might choose to have Derek say, on his birthday, for example, "MOMMY AND DADDY, REMEMBER THAT TIME YOU CONCEIVED ME IN ARUBA?" (Although probably you did not in fact conceive Derek in Aruba. That we do not know. Our research is not that extensive.) Or say your dog comes up and gives Derek a lick? You might make Derek say (if your dog's name is Queenie, which our dog's name is Queenie): "QUEENIE, GIVE IT A REST!" Which, you know what? *Makes you love him more.* Because suddenly he is articulate. Suddenly he is not just sitting there going glub glub glub while examining a piece of his own feces on his own thumb, which is something we recently found our Billy doing. Sometimes we have felt that our childless friends think badly of us for having a kid who just goes glub glub glub in the corner while looking at his feces on his thumb. But now when childless friends are over, what we have found, Ann and I, is that there is something great about having your kid say something witty and self-possessed years before he or she would actually in reality be able to say something witty or self-possessed. The bottom line is, it's just *fun*, when you and your childless friends are playing cards, and your baby suddenly blurts out (in his *very own probable future voice*): "IT IS VERY POSSIBLE THAT WE STILL DON'T FULLY UNDER-STAND THE IMPORT OF ALL OF EINSTEIN'S FINDINGS!"

Here I must admit that we have several times seen a sort of softening in the eyes of our resolute childless friends, as if they too would suddenly like to have a baby.

And as far as what you said, about Derek sort of flinching whenever that voice issues forth from him? When that speaker near his mouth sort of buzzes his lips? May I say this is not unusual? What I suggest? Try putting the ICS on Derek for a short time at first, maybe ten minutes a day, then gradually building up his Wearing Time. That is what we did. And it worked super. Now Billy wears his even while sleeping. In fact, if we forget to put it back on after his bath, he pitches a fit. Sort of begs for it! He starts to say, you know, "Mak! Mak!" (Which we think is his word for mask.) And when we put the mask on and Velcro the Velcro, he says—or it says rather, the ICS2100 says—"GUTEN MORGEN, PAPA!" because we have installed the German Learning module. Or, for example, if his pants are not yet on, he'll say: "HOW ABOUT SLAPPING ON MY ROMPERS SO I CAN GET ON WITH MY DAY!" (I wrote that one, having done a little stand-up in my younger days.)

My point is, with the ICS2100, Billy is much, much cleverer than he ever was with the ICS1900. He has recently learned, for example, that if he dribbles a little milk out his mouth, down his chin, his SimuLips™ will issue a MOO sound. Which he really seems to get a kick out of! I'll be in the living room doing a little evening paperwork and from the kitchen I'll hear, you know, "MOO! MOO! MOO!" And I'll rush in, and there'll be this sort of lake of milk on the floor. And there'll be Billy, dribbling milk down his chin, until I yank the cup away, at which time he bellows: "DON'T FENCE ME IN!" (Ann's contribution—she was raised in Wyoming.)

Mrs. Faniglia, I, for one, do not believe that any baby wants to sit around all day going glub glub glub. My feeling is that a baby, sitting in its diaper, looking around at the world, thinks to itself, albeit in some crude nonverbal way: What the heck is wrong with me, why am I the only one saying glub glub glub while all these other folks are talking in whole complete sentences? And hence, possibly, lifelong psychological damage may result. Now, am I saying that your Derek runs the risk of feeling bad about himself as a grown-up because as a baby he felt he didn't know how to talk very good? It is not for me to say, Mrs. Faniglia, I am only in Sales. But I will say I am certainly not taking any chances with our Billy. My belief is that when Billy hears a competent, intelligent voice issuing from the area near his mouth, that makes him feel excellent about himself. And it makes me feel excellent about him. Not that I didn't feel excellent about him before. But now we can actually have a sort of conversation! And also—and most importantly— when that voice issues from his SimuLips™, he learns something invaluable, namely that, when he finally does begin speaking, he should *plan on speaking via using his mouth.*

Now, Mrs. Faniglia, you may be thinking: Hold on a sec, of course this guy loves his I CAN SPEAK!™, he probably got his for free. But no, Mrs. Faniglia, I got mine for two grand, just like you. We get no discounts, so much in demand is the I CAN SPEAK!™, and in addition, our management strongly encourages us—in fact you might say they even sort of *require* us—to purchase and use the I CAN SPEAK!™ at home, on our own kids. (Or even, in one case, the case of a Product Service Representative who has no kids, on his elderly senile mom! And although, yes, she looks sort of funny with that Little Roger face on her frail stooped frame, the family has really enjoyed hearing all the witty things she has to say, so much like her old self!) Not that I wouldn't use it otherwise. Believe me, I would. Since we upgraded to the ICS2100, things have been great, Billy says such wonderful things, while looking almost identical to himself, and is not nearly so, you know, boring as when we just had the ICS1900, which (frankly) says some rather predictable things, which I expect is partly why you were unhappy with it, Mrs. Faniglia, you seem like a very intelligent woman. When people come over now, sometimes we just gather around Billy and wait for his next howler, and just last weekend my supervisor, Mr. Ted Ames, stopped by (a super guy, he has really given me support, please let him know if you've found this letter at all helpful) and boy did we all crack up laughing, and did Mr. Ames ever start scribbling approving notes in his little green notebook, when Billy began rubbing his face very rapidly across the carpet, in order to make his ICS2100 shout: "FRICTION IS A COMMON AND USEFUL SOURCE OF HEAT!"

Mrs. Faniglia, it is nearing the end of my lunch, and I must wrap this up, but I hope I have been of service. On a personal note, I did not have the greatest of pasts when I came here, having been in a few scrapes and even rehab situations, but now, wow, the commissions roll in, and I have made a nice life for me and Ann and Billy. Not that the possible loss of my commission is the reason for my concern. Please do not think so. While it is true that, if you decline my upgrade offer and persist in your desire to return your ICS1900, my commission must be refunded, by me, to Mr. Ames, that is no big deal, I have certainly refunded commissions to Mr. Ames before, especially lately. I don't quite know what I'm doing wrong. But that is not your concern, Mrs. Faniglia. Your concern is Derek. My real reason for writing this letter, on my lunch break, is that, hard as we all work at KidLuv to provide innovative and essential development tools for families like yours, Mrs. Faniglia, it is always sort of a heartbreak when our products are misapprehended. Please do accept our offer of a free ICS2100 upgrade. We at KidLuv really love what kids are,

Mrs. Faniglia, which is why we want them to become something better as soon as possible. Baby's early years are so precious, and must not be wasted, as we are finding out, as our Billy grows and grows, learning new skills every day.

Sincerely yours,
Rick Sminks
Product Service Representative
KidLuv Inc.

my flamboyant grandson

I had brought my grandson to New York to see a show. Because what is he always doing, up here in Oneonta? Singing and dancing, sometimes to my old show-tune records, but more often than not to his favorite CD, *Babar Sings!*, sometimes even making up his own steps, which I do not mind, or rather I try not to mind it. Although I admit that once, coming into his room and finding him wearing a pink boa while singing, in the voice of the Old Lady, "I Have Never Met a Man Like That Elephant," I had to walk out and give it some deep thought and prayer, as was also the case when he lumbered into the parlor during a recent church Couples Dinner, singing "Big and Slow, Yet So Very Regal," wearing a tablecloth spray-painted gray, so as to more closely resemble Babar.

Being a man who knows something about grandfatherly disapproval, having had a grandfather who constantly taunted me for having enlarged calves—to the extent that even today, when bathing, I find myself thinking unkind thoughts about Grandfather—what I prayed on both occasions was: Dear Lord, he is what he is, let me love him no matter what. If he is a gay child, God bless him, if he is a non-gay child who simply very much enjoys wearing his grandmother's wig while singing "Edelweiss" to the dog, so be it, and in either case let me communicate my love and acceptance in everything I do.

Because where is a child to go for unconditional love, if not to his grandfather? He has had it tough, in my view, with his mother in Nevada and a father unknown, raised by his grandmother and me in an otherwise childless neighborhood, playing alone in a tiny yard that ends in a graveyard wall. The boys in his school are hard on him, as are the girls, as are his teachers, and recently we found his book bag in the Susquehanna, and recently also found, taped to the back of his jacket, a derogatory note, and the writing on it was not all that childish-looking, and there were rumors that his bus driver had written it.

Then one day I had a revelation. If the lad likes to sing and dance, I thought, why not expose him to the finest singing and dancing there is? So I called 1-800-CULTURE, got our Promissory Voucher in the mail, and on Teddy's birthday we took the train down to New York.

As we entered the magnificent lobby of the Eisner Theater, I was in good spirits, saying to Teddy, "The size of this stage will make that little stage I built you behind the garage look pathetic." When suddenly we were stopped by a stern young fellow (a Mr. Ernesti, I believe) who said, "We are sorry, sir, but you cannot be admitted on merely a Promissory Voucher, are you kidding us, you must take your Voucher and your Proof of Purchases from at least six of our Major Artistic Sponsors, such as AOL, such as Coke, and go at once to the Redemption Center on Forty-fourth and Broadway to get your real actual tickets, and please do not be late, as latecomers cannot be admitted, due to special effects which occur early, which require total darkness in order to simulate the African jungle at night."

Well, this was news to me. But I was not about to disappoint the boy.

We left the Eisner and started up Broadway, the Everly Readers in the sidewalk reading the Everly Strips in our shoes, the building-mounted miniscreens at eye level showing images reflective of the Personal Preferences we'd stated on our monthly Everly Preference Worksheets, the numerous Cybec Sudden Emergent Screens out-thrusting or down-thrusting inches from our faces, and in addition I could very clearly hear the sound-only messages being beamed to me and me alone via various Casio Aural Focusers, such as one that shouted out to me between Forty-second and Forty-third, "Mr. Petrillo, you chose Burger King eight times last fiscal year but only two times thus far this fiscal year, please do not forsake us now, there is a store one block north!" in the voice of Broadway star Elaine Weston, while at Forty-third a light-pole-mounted Focuser shouted, "Golly, Leonard, remember your childhood on the farm in Oneonta? Why not reclaim those roots with a Starbucks Country Roast?" in a celebrity-rural voice I could not identify, possibly Buck Owens. And then, best of all, in the doorway of PLC Electronics, a life-size Gene Kelly hologram suddenly appeared, tap-dancing, saying, "Leonard, my data indicates you're a bit of an old-timer like myself! Gosh, in our day, life was simpler, wasn't it, Leonard? Why not come in and let Frankie Z. explain the latest gizmos!" And he looked so real I called out to Teddy, "Teddy, look there, Gene Kelly, do you remember I mentioned him to you as one of the all-time greats?" But Teddy of course did not see Gene Kelly, Gene Kelly not being one of his Preferences, but instead saw his hero Babar, swinging a small monkey on his trunk while saying that his data indicated that Teddy did not yet own a Nintendo.

So that was fun, that was very New York, but what was not so fun was, by the time we got through the line at the Redemption Center, it was ten minutes until showtime, and my feet had swollen up the way they do shortly before they begin spontaneously bleeding, which they have done ever since a winter spent in the freezing muck of Cho-Bai, Korea. It is something I have learned to live with. If I can sit, that is helpful. If I can lean against something, also good. Best of all, if I can take my shoes off. Which I did, leaning against a wall.

All around and above us were those towering walls of light, curving across building fronts, embedded in the sidewalks, custom-fitted to light poles: a cartoon lion eating a man in a suit; a rain of gold coins falling into the canoe of a naked rain-forest family; a woman in lingerie running a bottle of Pepsi between her breasts; the Merrill Lynch talking fist asking, "Are you kicking ass or kissing it?"; a perfect human rear, dancing; a fake flock of geese turning into a field of Bebe logos; a dying grandmother's room filled with roses by a FedEx man who then holds up a card saying "No Charge."

And standing beneath all that bounty was our little Teddy, tiny and sad, whose grandfather could not even manage to get him into one crummy show.

So I said to myself, Get off the wall, old man, blood or no blood, just keep the legs moving and soon enough you'll be there. And off we went, me hobbling, Teddy holding my arm, making decent time, and I think we would have made the curtain. Except suddenly there appeared a Citizen Helper, who asked were we from out of town, and was that why, via removing my shoes, I had caused my Everly Strips to be rendered Inoperative?

I should say here that I am no stranger to innovative approaches to advertising, having pioneered the use of towable signboards in Oneonta back in the Nixon years, when I towed a fleet of thirty around town with a Dodge Dart, wearing a suit that today would be found comic. By which I mean I have no problem with the concept of the Everly Strip. That is not why I had my shoes off. I am as patriotic as the next guy. Rather, as I have said, it was due to my bleeding feet.

I told all this to the Citizen Helper, who asked if I was aware that, by rendering my Strips Inoperative, I was sacrificing a terrific opportunity to Celebrate My Preferences?

And I said yes, yes, I regretted this very much.

He said he was sorry about my feet, he himself having a trick elbow, and that he would be happy to forget this unfortunate incident if I would only put my shoes back on and complete the rest of my walk extremely slowly, looking energetically to both left and right, so that the higher density of Messages thus received would compensate for those I had missed.

And I admit, I was a little short with that Helper, and said, "Young man, these dark patches on my socks are blood, do you or do you not see them?"

Which was when his face changed and he said, "Please

do not snap at me, sir, I hope you are aware of the fact that I can write you up?"

And then I made a mistake.

Because as I looked at that Citizen Helper—his round face, his pale sideburns, the way his feet turned in—it seemed to me that I knew him. Or rather, it seemed that he could not be so very different from me when I was a young man, not so different from the friends of my youth—from Jeffie DeSoto, say, who once fought a Lithuanian gang that had stuck an M-80 up the ass of a cat, or from Ken Larmer, who had such a sweet tenor voice and died stifling a laugh in the hills above Koi-Jeng.

I brought out a twenty and, leaning over, said, "Look, please, the kid just really wants to see this show."

Which is when he pulled out his pad and began to write!

Now, even being from Oneonta, I knew that being written up does not take one or two minutes. We would be standing there at least half an hour, after which we would have to go to an Active Complaints Center, where they would check our Strips for Operability and make us watch that corrective video called *Robust Economy, Super Moral Climate!*, which I had already been made to watch three times last winter, when I was out of work and we could not afford cable.

And we would totally miss *Babar Sings!*

"Please," I said, "please, we have seen plenty of personalized messages, via both the building-mounted miniscreens at eye level and those suddenly out-thrusting Cybec Emergent Screens, we have learned plenty for one day, honest to God we have——"

And he said, "Sir, since when do you make the call as far as when you have received enough useful information from our Artistic Partners?"

And just kept writing me up.

Well, there I was, in my socks, there was Teddy, with a scared look in his eyes I hadn't seen since his toddler days, when he had such a fear of chickens that we could never buy Rosemont eggs due to the cartoon chicken on the carton, or, if we did, had to first cut the chicken off, with scissors we kept in the car for that purpose. So I made a quick decision, and seized that Citizen Helper's ticket pad and flung it into the street, shouting at Teddy, "Run! Run!"

And run he did. And run I did. And while that Citizen Helper floundered in the street, torn between chasing us and retrieving his pad, we raced down Broadway, and, glancing back over my shoulder, I saw a hulking young man stick out his foot, and down that Helper went, and soon I was handing our tickets to the same stern Mr. Ernesti, who was now less stern, and in we went, and took our seats, as stars appeared overhead and the Eisner was transformed into a nighttime jungle.

And suddenly there was Babar, looking with longing

toward Paris, where the Old Lady was saying that she had dreamed of someone named Babar, and did any of us know who this Babar was, and where he might be found? And Teddy knew the answer, from the Original Cast CD, which was *Babar is within us, in all of our hearts*, and he shouted it out with all of the other children, as the Old Lady began singing "The King Inside of You."

And let me tell you, from that moment, everything changed for Teddy. I am happy to report he has joined the play at school. He wears a scarf everywhere he goes, throwing it over his shoulder with what can only be described as bravado, and says, whenever asked, that he has decided to become an actor. This from a boy too timid to trick-or-treat! This from the boy we once found walking home from school in tears, padlocked to his own bike! There are no more late-night crying episodes, he no longer writes on his arms with permanent marker, he leaps out of bed in the morning, anxious to get to school, and dons his scarf, and is already sitting at the table eating breakfast when we come down.

The other day as he got off the bus I heard him say to his bus driver, cool as a cucumber, "See you at the Oscars."

When an Everly Reader is Reading, then suddenly stops, it is not hard to trace, and within a week I received a certified letter setting my fine at one thousand dollars, and stating that, in lieu of the fine, I could elect to return to the Originating Location of my Infraction (they included a map) and, under the supervision of that Citizen Helper, retrace my steps, shoes on, thus reclaiming a significant opportunity to Celebrate My Preferences.

This, to me, is not America.

What America is, to me, is a guy doesn't want to buy, you let him not buy, you respect his not buying. A guy has a crazy notion different from your crazy notion, you pat him on the back and say, Hey pal, nice crazy notion, let's go have a beer. America, to me, should be shouting all the time, a bunch of shouting voices, most of them wrong, some of them nuts, but please, not just one droning glamorous reasonable voice.

But do the math: a day's pay, plus train ticket, plus meals, plus taxis to avoid the bleeding feet, still that is less than one thousand.

So down I went.

That Citizen Helper, whose name was Rob, said he was glad about my change of heart. Every time a voice shot into my ear, telling me things about myself I already knew, every time a celebrity hologram walked up like an old friend, Rob checked a box on my Infraction Correction Form and said, "Isn't that amazing, Mr. Petrillo, that we can do that, that we can know you so well, that we can help you identify the things you want and need?"

And I would say, "Yes, Rob, that is amazing," sick in the gut but trying to keep my mind on the five hundred bucks I was saving, and all the dance classes that would buy.

As for Teddy, as I write this it is nearly midnight and he is tapping in the room above. He looks like a bird, our boy, he watches the same musical fifteen times in a row. Walking through the mall, he suddenly emits a random line of dialogue and lunges off to the side, doing a dance step that resembles a stumble, spilling his drink, plowing into a group of incredulous snickering Oneontans. He looks like no one else, acts like no one else, his clothes are increasingly like plumage, late at night he choreographs using plastic Army men, he fits no mold and has no friends, but I believe in my heart that someday something beautiful may come from him.

jon

Back in the time of which I am speaking, due to our Coor
dinators had mandated us, we had all seen that educational
video of *It's Yours to Do With What You Like!* in which teens
like ourselfs speak on the healthy benefits of getting off by
oneself and doing what one feels like in terms of self-
touching, which what we learned from that video was,
there is nothing wrong with self-touching, because love is a
mystery but the mechanics of love need not be, so go off
alone, see what is up, with you and your relation to your
own gonads, and the main thing is, just have fun, feeling no
shame!

And then nightfall would fall and our facility would fill
with the sounds of quiet fast breathing from inside our Privacy Tarps as we all experimented per the techniques taught

us in *It's Yours to Do With What You Like!* and what do you suspect, you had better make sure that that little gap between the main wall and the wall that slides out to make the Gender Areas is like really really small.

Which, guess what, it wasn't.

That is all what I am saying.

Also all what I am saying is, who could blame Josh for noting that little gap and squeezing through it snakelike in just his Old Navy boxers that Old Navy gave us to wear for gratis, plus who could blame Ruthie for leaving her Velcro knowingly un-Velcroed? Which soon all the rest of us heard them doing what the rest of us so badly wanted to be doing, only we, being more mindful of the rules than them, just laid there doing the self-stuff from the video, listening to Ruth and Josh really doing it for real, which believe me, even that was pretty fun.

And when Josh came back next morning so happy he was crying, that was a further blow to our morality, because why did our Coordinators not catch him on their supposedly nighttime monitors? In all of our hearts was the thought of, okay, we thought you said no boy-and-girl stuff, and yet here is Josh, with his Old Navy boxers in his hand and a hickey on his waist, and none of you guys is even saying boo?

Because I for one wanted to do right, I did not want to sneak through that gap, I wanted to wed someone when old enough (I will soon tell who) and relocate to the appropriate facility in terms of demographics, namely Young Marrieds, such as Scranton, PA, or Mobile, AL, and then along comes Josh doing Ruthie with imperity, and no one is punished, and soon the miracle of birth results and all our Coordinators, even Mr. Delacourt, are bringing Baby Amber stuffed animals? At which point every cell or chromosome or whatever it was in my gonads that had been holding their breaths was suddenly like, Dude, slide through that gap no matter how bad it hurts, squat outside Carolyn's Privacy Tarp whispering, Carolyn, it's me, please un Velcro your Privacy opening!

Then came the final straw that broke the back of me saying no to my gonads, which was I dreamed I was that black dude on MTV's *Hot and Spicy Christmas* (around like Location Indicator 34412, if you want to check it out) and Carolyn was the oiled-up white chick, and we were trying to earn the Island Vacation by miming through the ten Hot 'n' Nasty Positions before the end of "We Three Kings," only then, sadly, during Her On Top, Thumb In Mouth, her Elf Cap fell off, and as the Loser Buzzer sounded she bent low to me, saying, Oh, Jon, I wish we did not have to do this for fake in front of hundreds of kids on Spring Break doing the wave but instead could do it for real with just each other in private.

And then she kissed me with a kiss I can only describe as melting.

So imagine that is you, you are a healthy young dude who has been self-practicing all these months, and you wake from that dream of a hot chick giving you a melting kiss, and that same hot chick is laying or lying just on the other side of the sliding wall, and meanwhile in the very next Privacy Tarp is that sleeping dude Josh, who a few weeks before, a baby was born to the girl he had recently did it with, and nothing bad happened, except now Mr. Slippen sometimes let them sleep in.

What would you do?

Well, you would do what I did, you would, you would slip through, and when Carolyn un-Velcroed that Velcro wearing her blue Guess kimono, whispering, Oh my God, I thought you'd never ask, that would be the most romantic thing you had ever underwent.

And though I had many times seen LI 34321 for Honey Grahams, where the stream of milk and the stream of honey enjoin to make that river of sweet-tasting goodness, I did not know that, upon making love, one person may become like the milk and the other like the honey, and soon they cannot even remember who started out the milk and who the honey, they just become one fluid, this like honey/milk combo.

Well, that is what happened to us.

Which is why soon I had to go to Mr. Slippen hat in hand and say, Sir, Baby Amber will be having a little playmate if that is okay with you, to which he just rolled his eyes and crushed the plastic cup in his hand and threw it at my chest, saying, What are we running in here, Randy, a freaking playschool?

Then he said, Well, Christ, what am I supposed to do, lose two valuable team members because of this silliness? All right all right, how soon will Baby Amber be out of that crib or do I have to order your kid a whole new one?

Which I was so happy, because soon I would be a father and would not even lose my job.

A few days later, like how it was with Ruthie and Josh, Mr. Delacourt's brother the minister came in and married us, and afterward barbecue beef was catered, and we danced at our window while outside pink and purple balloons were released, and all the other kids were like, Rock on you guys, have a nice baby and all!

It was the best day of our lifes thus far for sure.

But I guess it is true what they say at LI 11006 about life throwing us not only curves and sliders but sometimes even worse, as Dodger pitcher Hector Jones throws from behind his back a grand piano for Allstate, because soon here came that incident with Baby Amber, which made everybody just loony.

Which that incident was, Baby Amber died.

Sometimes it was just nice and gave one a fresh spring-time feeling to sit in the much-coveted window seat, final-izing one's Summary while gazing out at our foliage strip, which sometimes slinking through it would be a cat from Rustic Village Apartments, looking so cute that one wished to pet or even smell it, with wishful petting being the feel-ing I was undergoing on the sad day of which I am telling, such as even giving the cat a tuna chunk and a sip of my Diet Coke! If cats even like soda. That I do not know.

And then Baby Amber toddled by, making this funny noise in her throat of not being very happy, and upon reaching the Snack Cart she like seized up and tumped over, giving off this sort of shriek.

At first we all just looked at her, like going, Baby Amber, if that is some sort of new game, we do not exactly get it, plus come on, we have a lot of Assessments to get through this morning, such as a First-Taste Session for Diet Ginger-Coke, plus a very critical First View of Dean Witter's Pre-liminary Clip Reel for their campaign of "Whose Ass Are You Kicking Today?"

But then she did not get up.

We dropped our Summaries and raced to the Observa-tion Window and began pounding, due to we loved her so much, her being the first baby we had ever witnessed living day after day, and soon the paramedics came and took her away, with one of them saying, Jesus, how stupid are you kids, anyway, this baby is burning up, she is like 107 with meningitis!

And maybe we were stupid, but also, I would like to see them paramedics do that many Assessments and still act smart, as we had a lot of stress on our plate at that time.

So next morning there was Carolyn all freaked out with her little baby belly, watching Amber's crib being dismantled by Physical Plant, who wiped all facility surfaces with Handi Wipes in case the meningitis was viral, and there was the rest of us, just like thrashing around the place kicking things down, going like, This sucks, this is totally fucked up!

Looking back, I commend Mr. Slippen for what he did next, which was he said, Christ, folks, all our hearts are broken, it is not just yours, do you or do you not think I have Observed this baby from the time she was born, do you or do you not think that I too feel like kicking things down while shouting, This sucks, this is totally fucked up? Only what would that accomplish, would that bring Baby Amber back? I am at a loss, in terms of how can we best support Ruth and Josh in this sad tragic time, is it via feeling blue and cranky, or via feeling refreshed and hopeful and thus better able to respond to their needs?

So that was a non-brainer, and we all voted to accept Mr. Slippen's Facility Morale Initiative, and soon were getting our Aurabon® twice a day instead of once, plus it seemed like better stuff, and I for one had never felt so glad or stress-free, and my Assessments became very nuanced, and I spent many hours doing and enjoying them and then re-doing and reenjoying them, and it was during this period that we won the McDorland Prize for Excellence in Assessing in the Midwest Region in our demographic category of White Teens.

The only one who failed to become gladder was Carolyn, who due to her condition of being pregnant could not join us at the place in the wall where we hooked in for our Aurabon®. And now whenever the rest of us hooked in she would come over and say such negative things as, Wake up and smell the coffee, you feel bad because a baby died, how about honoring that by continuing to feel bad, which is only natural, because a goddam baby died, you guys?

At night in our shared double Privacy Tarp in Conference Room 11, which our Coordinators had gave us so we would feel more married, I would be like, Honey look, your attitude only sucks because you can't hook in, once baby comes all will be fine, due to you'll be able to hook in again, right? But she always blew me off, like she would say she was thinking of never hooking in again and why was I always pushing her to hook in and she just didn't know who to trust anymore, and one night when the baby kicked she said to her abdomen, Don't worry angel, Mommy is going to get you Out.

Which my feeling was: Out? Hello? My feeling was, Hold on, I like what I have achieved, and when I thought of descending Out to somewhere with no hope of meeting luminaries such as actress Lily Farrell-Garesh or Mark Belay, chairperson of Thatscool.com, descending Out to, say, some lumberyard, like at LI 77656 for Midol, merely piling lumber as cars rushed past, cars with no luminaries inside, only plain regular people who did not know me from Adam, who, upon seeing me, saw just some mere guy stacking lumber having such humdrum thoughts as thinking, Hey, I wonder what's for lunch, duh—I got a cold flat feeling in my gut, because I did not want to undergo it.

Plus furthermore (and I said this to Carolyn) what will it be like for us when all has been taken from us? Of what will we speak of? I do not want to only speak of my love in grunts! If I wish to compare my love to a love I have previous knowledge of, I do not want to stand there in the wind casting about for my metaphor! If I want to say like, Carolyn, remember that RE/MAX one where as the redhead kid falls asleep holding that Teddy bear rescued from the trash, the bear comes alive and winks, and the announcer goes, Home is the place where you find yourself suddenly no longer longing for home (LI 34451)—if I want to say to Carolyn, Carolyn, LI 34451, check it out, that is how I feel about you—well, then, I want to say it! I want to possess all the articulate I can, because otherwise there we will be, in non-designer clothes, no longer even on TrendSetters & TasteMakers gum cards with our photos on them, and I will turn to her and say, Honey, uh, honey, there is a certain feeling but I cannot name it and cannot cite a precedent-type feeling, but trust me, dearest, wow, do I ever feel it for you right now. And what will that be like, that stupid standing there, just a man and a woman and the wind, and nobody knowing what nobody is meaning?

Just then the baby kicked my hand, which at that time was on Carolyn's stomach.

And Carolyn was like, You are either with me or agin me.

Which was so funny, because she was proving my point! Because you are either with me or agin me is what the Lysol bottle at LI 12009 says to the scrubbing sponge as they approach the grease stain together, which is making at them a threatening fist while wearing a sort of Mexican bandolera!

When I pointed this out, she removed my hand from her belly.

I love you, I said.

Prove it, she said.

* * *

So next day Carolyn and I came up to Mr. Slippen and said, Please, Mr. Slippen, we hereby Request that you supply us with the appropriate Exit Paperwork.

To which Mr. Slippen said, Guys, folks, tell me this is a joke by you on me.

And Carolyn said softly, because she had always liked Mr. Slippen, who had taught her to ride a bike when small in the Fitness Area, It's no joke.

And Slippen said, Holy smokes, you guys are possessed of the fruits of the labors of hundreds of thousands of talented passionate men and women, some of whom are now gone from us, they poured forth these visions in the prime of their lives, reacting spontaneously to the beauty and energy of the world around them, which is why these stories and images are such an unforgettable testimony to who we are as a nation! And you have it all within you! I can only imagine how thrilling that must be. And now, to give it all up? For what? Carolyn, for what?

And Carolyn said, Mr. Slippen, I did not see you raising your babies in such a confined environment.

And Slippen said, Carolyn, that is so, but also please note that neither I nor my kids have ever been on TrendSetters & TasteMakers gum cards and believe me, I have heard a few earfuls vis-à-vis that, as in: Dad, you could've got us In but no, and now, Dad, I am merely another ophthalmologist among millions of ophthalmologists. And please do not

think that is not something that a father sometimes strug-
gles with, in terms of coulda shoulda woulda.

And Carolyn said, Jon, you know what, he is not even
really listening to us.

And Slippen said, Randy, since when is your name Jon?

Because by the way my name is really Jon. Randy is just
what my mother put on the form the day I was Accepted,
although tell the truth I do not know why.

But in my dimmest mind I can very clear recall her
voice calling me Jon in my possibly baby days.

It is one thing to see all this stuff in your head, Carolyn
said. But altogether different to be Out in it, I would expect.

And I could see that she was softening into a like daughter role, as if wanting him to tell her what to do, and up
came LI 27493 (Prudential Life), where, with Dad en-
stroked in the hospital bed, Daughter asks should she
marry the guy who though poor has a good heart, and we
see the guy working with inner-city kids via spray-painting
a swingset, and Dad says, Sweetie the heart must lead you.
And then later here is Dad all better in a tux, and Daughter
hugging the poor but good dude while sneaking a wink at
Dad, who raises his glass and points at the groom's shoe,
where there is this little smudge of swingset paint.

I cannot comment as to that, Slippen said. Everyone is
different. Nobody can know someone else's experiences.

Larry, no offense but you are talking shit, Carolyn said.

We deserve better than that from you.

And Slippen looked to be softening, and I remembered when he would sneak all of us kids in doughnuts, doughnuts we did not even need to Assess but could simply eat with joy with jelly on our face before returning to our Focused Purposeful Play with toys we would Assess by coloring in on a sheet of paper either a smiling duck if the toy was fun or a scowling duck if the toy bit.

And Slippen said, Look, Carolyn, you are two very fortunate people, even chosen people. A huge investment was made in you, which I would argue you have a certain responsibility to repay, not to mention, with a baby on the way, there is the question of security, security for your future that I—

Uncle, please, Carolyn said, which was her trumpet cart, because when she was small he had let her call him that and now she sometimes still did when the moment was right, such as at Christmas Eve when all of our feelings was high.

Jesus, Slippen said. Look, you two can do what you want, clearly. I cannot stop you kids, but golly I wish I could. All that is required is the required pre-Exit visit to the Lerner Center, which as you know you must take before I can give you the necessary Exit Paperwork. When would you like to take or make that visit?

Now, Carolyn said.

Gosh, Carolyn, when did you become such a pistol? Mr. Slippen said, and called for the minivan.

The Lerner Center, even when reached via blackened-window minivan, is a trip that will really blow one's mind, due to all the new sights and sounds one experiences, such as carpet on floor is different from carpet on facility floor, such as smoke smell from the minivan ashtrays, whereas we are a No Smoking facility, not to mention, wow, when we were led in blindfolded for our own protection, so many new smells shot forth from these like sidewalkside blooms or whatever that Carolyn and I were literally bumping into each other like swooning.

Inside they took our blindfolds off, and, yes, it looked and smelled exactly like our facility, and like every facility across the land, via the PervaScent® system, except in other facilities across the land a lady in blue scrubs does not come up to you with crossed eyes, sloshing around a cup of lemonade, saying in this drunk voice like, *A barn is more than a barn it is a memory of a time when you were cared for by a national chain of caregivers who bring you the best of life with a self-less evening in Monterey when the stars are low you can be thankful to your Amorino Co broker!*

And then she burst into tears and held her lemonade so crooked it was like spilling on the Foosball table. I had no idea what Location Indicator or Indicators she was even at, and when I asked, she didn't seem to know what I meant by Location Indicator, and was like, *Oh I just don't know anymore what is going on with me or why I would expose that tenderest part of my baby to the roughest part of the forest where the going gets rough, which is not the accomplishment of any one man but an entire team of dreamers who dream the same dreams you dream in the best interests of that most important system of all, your family!*

Then this Lerner Center dude came over and led her away, and she slammed her hand down so hard on the Foosball table that the little goalie cracked and his head flew over by us, and someone said, Good one, Doreen, now there's no Foosball.

At which time luckily it was time for our Individual Consultation.

Who we got was this Mid-Ager from Akron, OH, who, when I asked my first question off my Question Card they gave us, which was, What is it like in terms of pain, he said, There is no pain except once I poked myself in my hole with a coffee stirrer and Jesus that smarted, but otherwise you can't really even feel it.

So I was glad to hear it, although not so glad when he showed us where he had poked his hole with the stirrer, because I am famous as a wimp among my peers in terms of gore, and he had opted not to use any DermaFill®, and you could see right in. And, wow, there is something about observing up close a raw bloody hole at the base of somebody's hair that really gets one thinking. And though he said, in Question No. 2, that his hole did not present him any special challenges in terms of daily maintenance, looking into that hole, I was like, Dude, how does that give you no challenges, it is like somebody blew off a firecracker inside your freaking neck!

And when Carolyn said Question No. 3, which was, How do you now find your thought processes, his brow dorkened and he said, Well, to be frank, though quite advanced, having been here three years, there are, if you will, places where things used to be when I went looking for them, brainwise, but now, when I go there, nothing is there, it is like I have the shelving but not the cans of corn, if you get my drift. For example, looking at you, young lady, I know enough to say you are pretty, but when I direct my brain to a certain place, to find there a more vivid way of saying you are pretty, watch this, some words will come out, which I, please excuse me, oh dammit—

Then his voice changed to this announcer voice and he was like, *These women know that for many generations entrenched deep in this ancient forest is a secret known by coffee growers since the dawn of time man has wanted one thing which is to watch golf in peace will surely follow once knowledge is dispersed via the World Book is a super bridge across the many miles the phone card can close the gap!*

And his eyes were crossing and he was sputtering, which would have been sort of funny if we did not know that soon our eyes would be the crossing eyes and out of our mouths would the sputter be flying.

Then he got up and fled from the room, hitting himself hard in the face.

And I said to Carolyn, Well, that about does it for me.

And I waited for her to say that about did it for her, but she only sat there looking conflicted with her hand on her belly.

Out in the Common Room, I took her in my arms and said, Honey, I do not really think we have it all that bad, why not just go home and love each other and our baby when he or she comes, and make the best of all the blessings what we have been given?

And her head was tilted down in this way that seemed to be saying, Yes, sweetie, my God, you were right all along.

But then a bad decisive thing happened, which was this old lady came hobbling over and said, Dear, you must wait until Year Two to truly know, some do not thrive but others do, I am Year Two, and do you know what? When I see a bug now, I truly see a bug, when I see a paint chip I am truly seeing that paint chip, there is no distraction and it is so sweet, nothing in one's field of vision but what one opts to put there via moving one's eyes, and also do you hear how well I am speaking?

Out in the minivan I said, Well, I am decided, and Carolyn said, Well, I am, too. And then there was this long dead silence, because I knew and she knew that what we had both decided was not the same decision, not at all, that old crony had somehow rung her bell!

And I said, How do you know what she said is even true?

And she said, I just know.

That night in our double Privacy Tarp, Carolyn nudged me awake and said, Jon, doesn't it make sense to make our mistakes in the direction of giving our kid the best possible chance at a beautiful life?

And I was like, Chick, please take a look in the Fridge, where there is every type of food that must be kept cold, take a look on top of the Fridge, where there is every type of snack, take a look in our Group Closet, which is packed with gratis designerwear such as Baby Gap and even Baby Ann Taylor, whereas what kind of beautiful life are you proposing, with a Fridge that is empty both inside and on top, and the three of us going around all sloppenly, because I don't know about you but my skill set is pretty limited in terms of what do I know how to do, and if you go into the Fashion Module for Baby Ann Taylor and click with your blinking eyes on Pricing Info you will find that they are not just giving that shit away.

And she said, Oh, Jon, you break my heart, that night when you came to my Tarp you were like a lion taking what he wanted but now you are like some bunny wiffling his nose in fright.

Well, that wasn't nice, and I told her that wasn't nice, and she said, Jesus, don't whine, you are whining like a bunny, and I said I would rather be a bunny than a rag, and she said maybe I better go sleep somewhere else.

So I went out to Boys and slept on the floor, it being too late to check out a Privacy Tarp.

And I was pissed/sad, because no dude likes to think of himself as a rabbit, because once your girl thinks of you as a rabbit, how will she ever again think of you as a lion? And all of the sudden I felt very much like starting over with someone who would always think of me as a lion and never as a rabbit, and who really got it about how lucky we were.

Laying there in Boys, I did what I always did when confused, which was call up my Memory Loop of my mom, where she is baking a pie with her red hair up in a bun, and as always she paused in her rolling and said, Oh, my little man, I love you so much, which is why I did the most difficult thing of all, which was part with you my darling, so that you could use your exceptional intelligence to do that most holy of things, help other people. Stay where you are, do not get distracted, have a content and productive life, and I will be happy too.

Blinking on End, I was like, Thanks, Mom, you have always been there for me, I really wish I could have met you in person before you died.

In the morning Slippen woke me by giving me the light shock on the foot bottom which was sometimes useful to help us arise if we had to arise early and were in need of assistance, and said to please accompany him, as we had a bit of a sticky wicket in our purview.

Waiting in Conference Room 6 were Mr. Dove and Mr. Andrews and Mr. Delacourt himself, and at the end of the table Carolyn, looking small, with both hands on her pile of Exit Paperwork and her hair in braids, which I had always found cute, her being like that milkmaid for Swiss Rain Chocolate (LI 10003), who suddenly throws away her pail and grows sexy via taking out her braids, and as some fat farm ladies line up by a silo and also take out their braids to look sexy their thin husbands look dubious and run for the forest.

Randy, Mr. Dove said, Carolyn here has evinced a desire to Exit. What we would like to know is, being married, do you have that same desire?

And I looked at Carolyn like, You are jumping to some

conclusion because of one little fight, when it was you who called me the rabbit first, which is the only reason I called you rag?

It's not because of last night, Jon, Carolyn said.

Randy, I sense some doubt? Mr. Dove said.

And I had to admit some doubt was being felt by me, because it seemed more than ever like she was some sort of malcontentish girl who would never be happy no matter how good things were.

Maybe you kids would like some additional time, Mr. Andrews said. Some time to talk it over and be really sure.

I don't need any additional time, Carolyn said.

And I said, You're going no matter what? No matter what I do?

And she said, Jon, I want you to come with me so bad, but, yes, I'm going.

And Mr. Dove said, Wait a minute, who is Jon?

And Mr. Andrews said, Randy is Jon, it is apparently some sort of pet name between them.

And Mr. Slippen said to us, Look, guys, I have been married for nearly thirty years and it has been my experience that, when in doubt, take a breath. Err on the side of being together. Maybe, Carolyn, the thing to do is, I mean, your Paperwork is complete, we will hold on to it, and maybe Randy, as a concession to Carolyn, you could complete your Paperwork, and we'll hold on to it for you, and when you both decide the time is right, all you have to do is say the word and we will—

I'm going today, Carolyn said. As soon as possible.

And Mr. Dove looked at me and said, Jon, Randy, whoever, are you prepared to go today?

And I said no. Because what is her rush, I was feeling, why is she looking so frantic with furrowed anxious brow like that Claymation chicken at LI 98473 who says the sky is falling the sky is falling and turns out it is only a Dodge Ramcharger, which crushes her from on high and one arm of hers or wing sticks out with a sign that says March Madness Daze?

And Slippen said, Guys, guys, I find this a great pity. You are terrific together. A real love match.

Carolyn was crying now and said, I am so sorry, but if I wait I might change my mind, which I know in my heart would be wrong.

And she thrust her Exit Paperwork across at Slippen.

Then Dove and Andrews and Delacourt began moving with great speed, as if working directly from some sort of corporate manual, which actually they were, Mr. Dove had some photocopied sheets, and reading from the sheets, he asked was there anyone with whom she wished to have a fond last private conversation, and she said, Well duh, and we were both left briefly alone.

She took a deep breath while looking at me all tender

and said, Oh Gadzooks. Which that broke my heart, Gadzooks being what we sometimes said at nice privacy moments in our Privacy Tarp when overwhelmed by our good luck in terms of our respective bodies looking so hot and appropriate, Gadzooks being from LI 38492 for Zookers Gum, where the guy blows a bubble so Zookified it ingests a whole city and the city goes floating up to Mars.

At this point her tears were streaming down and mine also, because up until then I thought we had been so happy.

Jon, please, she said.

I just can't, I said.

And that was true.

So we sat there quiet with her hands against my hands like Colonel Sanders and his wife at LI 87345, where he is in jail for refusing to give up the recipe for KFC Haitian MiniBreasts, and then Carolyn said, I didn't mean that thing about the rabbit, and I scrinkled up my nose rabbit-like to make her laugh.

But apparently in the corporate manual there is a time limit on fond last private conversations, because in came Kyle and Blake from Security, and Carolyn kissed me hard, like trying to memorize my mouth, and whispered, Someday come find us.

Then they took her away, or she took them away rather, because she was so far in front that they had to like run to keep up as she clomped loudly away in her Kenneth Cole boots, which by the way they did not let her keep those, because that night, selecting my pajamas, I found them back in the Group Closet.

Night after night after that I would lay or lie alone in our Privacy Tarp, which now held only her nail clippers and her former stuffed dog Lefty, and during the days Slippen let me spend many unbillable hours in the much-coveted window seat, just scanning some images or multiscanning some images, and around me would be the other facility Boys and Girls, all Assessing, all smiling, because we were still on the twice-a-day Aurabon®, and thinking of Carolyn in those blue scrubs, alone in the Lerner Center, I would apply for additional Aurabon® via filling out a Work-Affecting Mood-Problem Notification, which Slippen would always approve, being as he felt so bad for me.

And the Aurabon® would make things better, as Aurabon® always makes things better, although soon what I found was, when you are hooking in like eight or nine times a day, you are always so happy, and yet it is a kind of happy like chewing on tinfoil, and once you are living for that sort of happy, you soon cannot be happy enough, even when you are very very happy and are even near tears due to the beauty of the round metal hooks used to hang your facility curtains, you feel this intense wish to be even happier, so

you tear yourself away from the beautiful curtain hooks
and with shaking happy hands fill out another Work-Affecting Mood-Problem Notification, and then, because nothing
in your facility is beautiful enough to look at with your new
level of happiness, you sit in the much-coveted window seat
and start lendelling in this crazy uncontrolled way, calling
up, say, the Nike one with the Hanging Gardens of Babylon
(LI 89736), and though it is beautiful, it is not beautiful
enough, so you scatter around some Delicate Secrets lingerie models from LI 22314, and hang fat Dole oranges and
bananas in the trees (LI 76765), and add like a sky full of
bright stars from LI 74638 for Crest, and from the Smell
Palate supplied by the antiallergen Capaviv® you fill the air
with jasmine and myrrh, but still that is not beautiful
enough, so you blink on End and fill out another Work-Affecting Mood-Problem Notification, until finally one day
Mr. Dove comes over and says, Randy, Jon, whatever you are
calling yourself these days—a couple of items. First, it
seems to us that you are in some private space not helpful to
you, and so we are cutting back your Aurabon® to twice a day
like the other folks, and please do not sit in that window seat
anymore, it is hereby forbidden to you, and plus we are going
to put you on some additional Project Teams, since it is our
view that idle hands are the devil's work area. Also, since you
are only one person, it is not fair, we feel, for you to have a
whole double Privacy Tarp to yourself, you must, it seems to

us, rejoin your fellow Boys in Boys.

So that night I went back with Rudy and Lance and Jason and the others, and they were nice, as they are always nice, and via No. 10 cable Jason shared with me some Still Photos from last year's Christmas party, of Carolyn hugging me from behind with her cute face appearing beneath my armpit, which made me remember how after the party in our Privacy Tarp we played a certain game, which it is none of your beeswax who I was in that game and who she was, only believe me, that was a memorable night, with us watching the snow fall from the much-coveted window seat, in which we sat snuggling around midnight, when we had left our Tarp to take a break for air, and also we were both sort of sore.

Which made it all that much more messed-up and sad to be sleeping once again alone in Boys.

When the sliding wall came out to make our Gender Areas, I noticed they had fixed it so nobody could slide through anymore, via five metal rods. All we could do was, by putting our mouths to the former gap, say good night to the Girls, who all said good night back from their respective Privacy Tarps in this sort of muffled way.

But I did not do that, as I had nobody over there I wished to say good night to, they all being like merely sisters to me, and that was all.

*   *   *

So that was the saddest time of my life thus far for sure.

Then one day we were all laying or lying on our stomachs playing Hungarian Headchopper for GameBoy, a new proposed one where you are this dude with a scythe in your mother's garden, only what your mother grows is heads, when suddenly a shadow was cast over my game by Mr. Slippen, which freaked up my display, and I harvested three unripe heads, but the reason Slippen was casting his shadow was, he had got a letter for me, from Carolyn!

And I was so nervous opening it, and even more nervous after opening it, because inside were these weird like marks I could not read, like someone had hooked a pen to the back leg of a bird and said, Run little bird, run around this page and I will mail it for you. And the parts I could read were bumming me out even worse, such as she had wrote all sloppenly, *Jon a abbot is a cove, a glen, it is something with prayerful guys all the livelong day in silence as they move around they are sure of one thing which is the long-term stability of a product we not only stand behind we run behind since what is wrong with taking a chance even if that chance has horns and hoofs and it is just you and your worst fear in front of ten thousand screaming supporters of your last chance to be the very best you can be?*

And then thank God it started again looking like the pen on the foot of the running bird.

I thought of how hot and smart she had looked when

doing a crossword with sunglasses on her head in Hilfiger cutoffs, I thought of her that first night in her Privacy Tarp, naked except for her La Perla panties in the light that came from the Exit sign through the thin blue Privacy Tarp, so her flat tummy and not-flat breasts and flirty smile were all blue, and then all of the sudden I felt like the biggest jerk in the world, because why had I let her go? It was like I was all of the sudden waking up! She was mine and I was hers, she was so thin and cute, and now she was at the Lerner Center all alone? Shaking and scared with a bloody hole in her neck and our baby in her belly, hanging out with all those other scared shaking people with bloody holes in their necks, only none of them knew her and loved her like I did? I had done such a dumb-shit thing to her, all the time thinking it was sound reasoning, because isn't that how it is with our heads, when we are in them it always makes sense, but then later, when you look back, we sometimes are like, I am acting like a total dumbass!

Then Brad came up and was like, Dude, time to hook in.

And I was like, Please Brad, do not bother me with that shit at this time.

And I went to get Slippen, only he was at lunch, so I went to get Dove and said, Sir, I hereby Request my appropriate Exit Paperwork.

And he said, Randy, please, you're scaring me, don't act rash, have a look out the window.

I had a look, and tell the truth it did not look that good, such as the Rustic Village Apartments, out of which every morning these bummed-out-looking guys in the plainest non-designer clothes ever would trudge out and get in their junky cars. And was someone joyfully kissing them goodbye, like saying when you come home tonight you will get a big treat, which is me? No, the person who should have been kissing them with joy was yelling, or smoking, or yelling while smoking, and when the dudes came home they would sit on their stoops with heads in hand, as if all day long at work someone had been pounding them with clubs on their heads, saying they were jerks.

Then Mr. Dove said, Randy, Randy, why would a talented young person like yourself wish to surrender his influence in the world and become just another lowing cattle in the crowd, don't you know how much people out there look up to you and depend on you?

And that was true. Because sometimes kids from Rustic Village would come over and stand in our lava rocks with our TrendSetters & TasteMakers gum cards upheld, pressing them to our window, and when we would wave to them or strike the pose we were posing on our gum cards, they would race back all happy to their crappy apartments, probably to tell their moms they had seen the real actual us, which was probably like the high point of their weeks.

But still, when I thought of those birdlike markings of

Carolyn's letter, I don't know, something just popped, I felt I was at a distinct tilt, and I blurted out, No, no, just please bring me the freaking Paperwork, I am Requesting, and I thought when I Requested you had to do it!

And Dove said sadly, We do, Randy, when you Request, we have to do it.

Dove called the other Coordinators over and said, Larry, your little pal here has just Requested his Paperwork.

And Slippen said, I'll be damned.

What a waste, Delacourt said. This is one super kid.

One of our best, Andrews said.

Which was true, with me five times winning the Cooperative Spirit Award and once even the Denny O'Malley Prize, Denny O'Malley being this Assessor in Chicago, IL, struck down at age ten, who died with a smile on his face of leukemia.

Say what you will, it takes courage, Slippen said. Going after one's wife and all.

Yes and no, Delacourt said. If you, Larry, fall off a roof, does it help me to go tumbling after you?

But I am not your wife, Slippen said. Pregnant wife.

Wife or no, pregnant or no, Delacourt said. What we then have are two folks not feeling so good in terms of that pavement rushing up. No one is helped. Two are crushed. In effect three are crushed.

Baby makes three, Andrews said.

Baby does make three, said Delacourt.

Although anything is possible, Slippen said. You know, the two of them together, the three of them, maybe they could make a go of it—

Larry, whose side are you on? Dove said.

I am on all sides, Slippen said.

You see this thing from various perspectives, Andrews said.

Anyway, this is academic, Delacourt said. He has Requested his Paperwork and we must provide it.

His poor mother, Dove said. The sacrifices she made, and now this.

Oh, please, Slippen said. His mother.

Larry, sorry, did you say something? Dove said.

Which mother did he get? Slippen said.

Larry, please go to that Taste-and-Rate in Conference Room 6, Delacourt said. See how they are doing with those CheezWands.

Which mother did we give him? Slippen said. The redhead baking the pie? The blonde in the garden?

Larry, honestly, Dove said. Are you freaking out?

The brunette at prayer? Slippen said. Who, putting down her prayer book, says, as they all say: Stay where you are, do not get distracted, have a content and productive life, and I will be happy too?

Larry has been working too hard, Andrews said.

Plus taking prescription pills not prescribed to him, Delacourt said.

I have just had it with all of this, Slippen said and stomped off to the Observation Room.

Ha, that Larry! Dove said. He did not even know your mom, Randy.

Only we did, Andrews said.

Very nice lady, Delacourt said.

Made terrific pies, Dove said.

And I was like, Do you guys think I am that stupid, I know something is up, because how did Slippen know my mom's exact words said to me on my private Memory Loop?

Then there was this long silence.

Then Delacourt said, Randy, when you were a child, you thought as a child. Do you know that one?

And I did know that one, it being LI 88643 for Trojan Ribbed.

Well, you are not a child anymore, he said. You are a man. A man in the middle of making a huge mistake.

We had hoped it would not come to this, Dove said.

Please accompany us to the Facility Cinema, Delacourt said.

Which that was a room off of Dining, with a big-screen

plasma TV and Pottery Barn leather couch and a deluxe Orville Redenbacher Corn Magician.

Up on the big-screen came this old-fashioned-looking film of a plain young girl with stringy hair, smoking a cigarette in a house that looked pretty bad.

And this guy unseen on the video said, Okay, tell us precisely why, in your own words.

And the girl said, Oh, I dunno, due to my relation with the dad, I got less than great baby interest?

Okay, said the unseen voice. And the money is not part?

Well, sure, yeah, I can always use money, she said.

But it is not the prime reason? the voice said. It being required that it not be the prime reason, but rather the prime reason might be, for example, your desire for a better life for your child?

Okay, she said.

Then they pulled back and you could see bashed-out windows with cardboard in them and the counters covered with dirty dishes and in the yard a car up on blocks.

And you have no objections to the terms and conditions? the voice said. Which you have read in their entirety?

It's all fine, the girl said.

Have you read it? the voice said.

I read in it, she said. Okay, okay, I read it cover to freaking cover.

And the name change you have no objection to? the voice said.

Okay, she said. Although why Randy?

And the No-Visit Clause you also have no objection to? the voice said.

Fine, she said, and took a big drag.

Then Dove tapped on the wall twice and the movie Paused.

Do you know who that lady is, Randy? he said.

No, I said.

Do you know that lady is your mom? he said.

No, I said.

Well, that lady is your mom, Randy, he said. We are sorry you had to learn it in this manner.

And I was like, Very funny, that is not my mom, my mom is pretty, with red hair in a bun.

Randy, we admit it, Delacourt said. We gave some of you stylized mothers, in your Memory Loops, for your own good, not wanting you to feel bad about who your real mothers were. But in this time of crisis we must give you the straight skinny. That is your real mother, Randy, that is your real former house, that is where you would have been raised, had your mother not answered our ad all those years ago, that is who you are. So much in us is hardwired! You cannot fight fate without some significant help from an intervening entity, such as us, such as our resources, which we have poured into you in good faith all these years. You are a prince, we have made you a prince. Please do not descend back into the muck.

Please reconsider, Randy, Dove said. Sleep on it.

Will you? Delacourt said. Will you at least think about it?

Tell the truth, that thing with my mom had freaked me out, it was like my foundation had fallen away, like at LI 83743 for Advil, where the guy's foundation of his house falls away and he thunks his head on the floor of Hell and thus needs a Advil, which the devil has some but won't give him any.

So I said I would think about it.

As he left, Dove unhit Pause, and I had time to note many things on that video, such as that lady's teeth were not good, such as my chin and hers were similar, such as she referred to our dog as Shit Machine, which what kind of name is that for a dog, such as at one point they zoomed in on this little baby sitting on the floor in just a diaper, all dirty and looking sort of dumb, and I could see very plain it was me.

Just before Dinner, Dove came back in.

Randy, your Paperwork, per your Request, he said. Do you still want it?

I don't know, I said. I'm not sure.

You are making me very happy, Dove said.

And he sent in Tony from Catering with this intense Dinner of steak au poivre and our usual cheese tray with Alsatian olives, and a milkshake in my monogrammed cup, and while I watched *Sunset Terror Home* on the big-screen, always a favorite, Bedtime passed and nobody came and got me, them letting me stay up as late as I wanted.

Later that night in my Privacy Tarp I was wakened by someone crawling in, which, hitting my Abercrombie & Fitch nightlight, I saw it was Slippen.

Randy, I am so sorry for my part in all of this, he whispered. I just want to say you are a great kid and always have been since Day One and in truth I at times have felt you were more of a son than my own personal sons, and likewise with Carolyn, who was the daughter I never had.

Well I did not know what to say to that, it being so personal and all, plus he was like laying or lying practically right on top of me and I could smell wine on his breath. We had always learned in Religion that if something is making you uncomfortable you should just say it, so I just said it, I said, Sir, this is making me uncomfortable.

You know what is making me uncomfortable? he said. You farting around in here while poor Carolyn sits in the Lerner

Center all alone, big as a house, scared to death. Randy, one only has one heart, and when that heart is breaking via thinking of what is in store for poor Carolyn, one can hardly be blamed for stepping in, can one? Can one? Randy, do you trust me?

He had always been good to me, having taught me so much, like how to hit a Wiffle and how to do a push-up, and once he even brought in this trough and taught me and Ed and Josh to fish, and how fun was that, all of us laughing and feeling around on the floor for the fish we kept dropping during those moments of involuntary blindness that would occur as various fish-related LIs flashed in our heads, like the talking whale for Stouffer's FishMeals (LI 38322), like the fish and loafs Jesus makes at LI 83722 and then that one dude goes, Lord, this bread is dry, can you not summon up some ButterSub?

I do trust you, I said.

Then come on, he said, and crawled out of my Privacy Tarp.

We crossed the Common Area and went past Catering, which I had never been that far before, and soon were standing in front of this door labeled Caution Do Not Open Without Facility Personnel Accompaniment.

Randy, do you know what is behind this door? Slippen said.

No, I said.

Take a look, he said.

And smiling a smile like that mother on Christmas morning at LI 98732 for Madpets.com, who throws off that tablecloth to reveal a real horse in their living room chewing on the rug, Slippen threw open that door.

Looking out, I saw no walls and no rug and no ceiling, only lawn and flowers, and above that a wide black sky with stars, which all of that made me a little dizzy, there being no glass between me and it.

Then Slippen very gently pushed me Out.

And I don't know, it is one thing to look out a window, but when you are Out, actually Out, that is something very powerful, and how embarrassing was that, because I could not help it, I went down flat on my gut, checking out those flowers, and the feeling of the one I chose was like the silk on that Hermès jacket I could never seem to get Reserved because Vance was always hogging it, except the flower was even better, it being very smooth and built in like layers? With the outside layer being yellow, and inside that a white thing like a bell, and inside the white bell-like thing were fifteen (I counted) smaller bell-like red things, and inside each red thing was an even smaller orange two-dingly-thing combo.

Which I was like, Dude, who thought this shit up? And though I knew very well from Religion it was God, still I

had never thought so high of God as I did just then, seeing
the kind of stuff He could do when He put His or Her mind
to it.

Also amazing was, laying there on my gut, I was able to
observe very slowly some grass, on a blade basis! And what
I found was, each blade is its total own blade, they are not
all exact copies as I had always thought when looking at the
Rustic Village Apartments lawn from the much-coveted
window seat. No, each blade had a special design of up-and-
down lines on it, plus some blades were wider than others,
and some were yellow, with some even having little holes
that I guessed had been put there via bugs chewing them?

By now as you know I am sometimes a kidder, with Humor always ranked by my peers as one of my Principal Pos-
itives on my Yearly Evaluation, but being totally serious? If
I live one million years I will never forget all the beautiful
things I saw and experienced in that kickass outside yard.

Isn't it something? Slippen said. But look, stand up, here
is something even better.

And I stood up, and here came this bland person in blue
scrubs, and my first thought was, Ouch, why not accentuate
that killer bone structure with some makeup, and also what
is up with that dull flat hair, did you never hear of Bumble
& Bumble Plasma Volumizer?

And then she said my name.

Not my name of Randy but my real name of Jon.

Which is how I first got the shock of going, Oh my God, this poor washed-out gal is my Carolyn.

And wow was her belly ever bigger.

Then she touched my face very tender and said, *The suspense of waiting is over and this year's Taurus far exceeds expectations already high in this humble farming community.*

And I was like, Carolyn?

And she was like, *The beauty of a reunion by the sea of this mother and son will not soon again be parted and all one can say is amen and open another bag of chips, which by spreading on a thin cream on the face strips away the harsh effect of the destructive years.*

Then she hugged me, which is when I saw the gaping hole in her neck where her gargadisk had formerly been.

But tell you the truth, even with a DermaFilled® neck-hole and nada makeup and huge baby belly, still she looked so pretty, like someone had put a light inside her and switched it on.

But I guess it is true what they say at LI 23005, life is full of ironic surprises, where that lady in a bikini puts on sun-screen and then there is this nuclear war and she takes a sip of her drink only she has been like burned to a crisp, because all that time Out not one LI had come up, as if my mind was stymied or holding its breath, but now all of the sudden here came all these LIs of Flowers, due to I had seen those real-life flowers, such as big talking daisies for

Polaroid (LI 10119), such as that kid who drops a jar of applesauce but his anal mom totally melts when he hands her a sunflower (LI 22365), such as the big word PFIZER that as you pan closer is made of roses (LI 88753), such as LI 73486, where as you fly over wildflowers to a Acura Legend on a cliff the announcer goes, Everyone is entitled to their own individual promised land.

And I blinked on Pause but it did not Pause, and blinked on End but it did not End.

Then up came LIs of Grass, due to I had seen that lawn, such as an old guy sprinkling grass seed while repetitively checking out his neighbor-girl who is sunbathing, and then in spring he only has grass in that one spot (LI 11121), such as LI 76567, with a sweeping lawn leading up to a mansion for Grey Poupon, such as (LI 00391) these grass blades screaming in terror as this lawnmower approaches but then when they see it is a Toro they put on little party hats.

Randy, can you hear me? Slippen said. Do you see Carolyn? She has been waiting out here an hour. During that hour she has been going where she wants, looking at whatever she likes. See what she is doing now? Simply enjoying the night.

And that was true. Between flinches and blinks on End I could dimly persee her sitting cross-legged near me, not flinching, not blinking, just looking pretty in the moonlight with a look on her face of deep concern for me.

george saunders

Randy, this could all be yours, Slippen was saying. This world, this girl!

And then I must have passed out.

Because when I came to I was sitting inside that door marked Caution Do Not Open Without Facility Personnel Accompaniment, with my Paperwork in my lap and all my Coordinators standing around me.

Randy, Dove said. Larry Slippen here claims that you wish to Exit. Is this the case? Did you in fact Request your Paperwork, then thrust it at him?

Okay, I said. Yes.

So they rushed me to Removals, where this nurse named Vivian was like, Welcome, please step behind that screen and strip off, then put these on.

Which I did, I dropped my Calvin Klein khakis and socks and removed my Country Road shirt as well as my Old Navy boxers, and put on the dreaded blue scrubs.

Best of luck, Randy, Slippen said, leaning in the door. You'll be in my prayers.

Out out out, Vivian said.

Then she gave me this Patient Permission Form, which the first question was, Is patient aware of risk of significantly reduced postoperative brain function?

And I wrote, Yes.

164

And then it said, Does patient authorize Dr. Edward Kenton to perform all procedures associated with a complete gargadisk removal, including but not limited to e-wire severance, scar-tissue removal, forceful Kinney Maneuver (if necessary to fully disengage gargadisk), suturing, and postoperative cleansing using the Foreman Vacuum Device, should adequate cleaning not be achievable via traditional methods?

And I wrote, Yes.

I have been here since Wednesday, due to Dr. Kenton is at a wedding.

I want to thank Vivian for all this paper, and Mr. Slippen for being the father I never had, and Carolyn for not giving up on me, and Dr. Kenton, assuming he does not screw it up.

(Ha ha, you know what, Dr. Kenton, I am just messing with you, even if you do screw it up, I know you tried your best. Only please do not screw it up, ha ha ha!)

Last night they let Carolyn send me a fax from the Lerner Center, and it said, I may not look my best or be the smartest apple on the applecart, but believe me, in time I will again bake those ninety-two pies.

And I faxed back, However you are is fine with me, I will see you soon, look for me, I will be the one with the ripped-up neck, smacking himself in the head!

No matter what, she faxed, at least we will now have a

life, that life dreamed of by so many, living in freedom with all joys and all fears, let it begin, I say, the balloon of our excitement will go up up up, to that land which is the land of true living, we will not be denied!

I love you, I wrote.

Love you too, she wrote.

Which I thought that was pretty good, it being so simple and all, and it gave me hope.

Because maybe we can do it.

Maybe we can come to be normal, and sit on our porch at night, the porch of our own house, like at LI 87326, where the mom knits and the dad plays guitar and the little kid works very industrious with his Speak & Spell, and when we talk, it will make total sense, and when we look at the stars and moon, if choosing to do that, we will not think of LI 44387, where the moon frowns down at this dude due to he is hiding in his barn eating Rebel CornBells instead of proclaiming his SnackLove aloud, we will not think of LI 09383, where this stork flies through some crying stars who are crying due to the baby who is getting born is the future Mountain Dew Guy, we will not think of that alien at LI 33081 descending from the sky going, Just what is this thing called a Cinnabon?

In terms of what we will think of, I do not know. When I think of what we will think of, I draw this like total blank and get scared, so scared my Peripheral Area flares up green, like when I have drank too much soda, but tell the truth I am curious, I think I am ready to try.

ii.

They will attempt to insinuate themselves into
the very fabric of our emotional lives, demanding
the dissolution of the distinction between beloved
and enemy, friend and foe, neighbor and stranger.
They will, citing equality, deny our right to make
critical moral distinctions. Crying peace, they will
deny our right to defend, in whatever manner is
most expedient, the beloved. Under the guise of
impartiality, they will demand we disavow all
notions of tradition, family, friends, tribe, and even
nation. But are we animals, forced to look blankly
upon the rich variety of life, disallowed the privilege of making moral distinctions, dead to love,
forbidden from preferring this to that?

—*Bernard "Ed" Alton,*
Taskbook for the New Nation,
Chapter 3. "Are We Not We? Are They Not Them?"

my amendment

Mr. Terence Rackman

Leadville Courier-Examiner

Leadville, PA 13245

Re: "Not in This Town, Friend," June 15 issue, "My Turn"

Lifestyle Section

Dear Mr. Rackman,

Very much enjoyed your recent article and wish to weigh in with some of my thoughts on this troubling matter. I agree with all you had to say. Like any sane person, I am against Same-Sex Marriage, and in favor of a constitutional amendment to ban it.

To tell the truth, I feel that, in the interest of moral rigor, it is necessary for us to go a step further, which is why I would like to propose a supplementary constitutional amendment.

In the town where I live, I have frequently observed a

phenomenon I have come to think of as Samish-Sex Marriage. Take, for example, "K," a male friend of mine, of slight build, with a ponytail. "K" is married to "S," a tall, stocky female with extremely short hair, almost a crew cut. Often, while watching "K" play with his own ponytail as "S" towers over him, I have wondered, Isn't it odd that this somewhat effeminate man should be married to this somewhat masculine woman? Is "K" not, at some level, imperfectly expressing a slight latent desire to be married to a man? And is not "S," at some level, imperfectly expressing a slight latent desire to be married to a woman?

Then I ask myself, Is this truly what God had in mind?

Take the case of "L," a female friend with a deep, booming voice. I have often found myself looking askance at her husband, "H." Though "H" is basically pretty masculine, having neither a ponytail nor a tight feminine derriere like "K," still I wonder: "H," when you are having marital relations with "L," and she calls out your name in that deep, booming, nearly male voice, and you continue having marital relations with her (i.e., you are not "turned off"), does this not imply that you, "H," are, in fact, still "turned on"? And doesn't this indicate that, on some level, you, "H," have a slight latent desire to make love to a man?

Or consider the case of "T," a male friend with an extremely small penis. (We attend the same gym.) He is married to "O," an average-looking woman who knows how to fix cars. I wonder about "O." How does she know so much about cars? Is she not, by tolerating this non-car-fixing, short-penised friend of mine, indicating that, at some level, she wouldn't mind being married to a woman, and is therefore, perhaps, a tiny bit functionally gay?

And what about "T?" Doesn't the fact that "T" can stand there in the shower room at our gym, confidently toweling off his tiny unit, while "O" is at home changing their spark plugs with alacrity, indicate that it is only a short stroll down a slippery slope before he is completely happy being the "girl" in their relationship, from which it is only a slight fey hop down the same slope before "T" is happily married to another man, perhaps my car mechanic, a handsome Portuguese fellow I shall refer to as "J"?

Because my feeling is, when God made man and woman He had something very specific in mind. It goes without saying that He did not want men marrying men, or women marrying women, but also what He did not want, in my view, was feminine men marrying masculine women.

Which is why I developed my Manly Scale of Absolute Gender.

Using my Scale, which assigns numerical values according to a set of masculine and feminine characteristics, it is now easy to determine how Manly a man is and how Fem a woman is, and, therefore how close to a Samish-Sex Marriage a given marriage is.

Here's how it works: Say we determine that a man is an 8 on the Manly Scale, with 10 being the most Manly of all and 0 basically a Neuter. And say we determine that his fiancée is a -6 on the Manly Scale, with a -10 being the most Fem of all. Calculating the difference between the man's rating and the woman's rating—the Gender Differential— we see that this proposed union is not, in fact, a Samish-Sex Marriage, which I have defined as "any marriage for which the Gender Differential is less than or equal to 10 points."

Friends whom I have identified as being in Samish-Sex Marriages often ask me, Ken, given that we have scored poorly, what exactly would you have us do about it?

Well, one solution I have proposed is divorce—divorce followed by remarriage to a more suitable partner. "K," for example, could marry a voluptuous high-voiced NFL cheerleader, who would more than offset his tight feminine derriere, while his ex-wife, "S," might choose to become involved with a lumberjack with very large arms, thereby neutralizing her thick calves and faint mustache.

Another, and of course preferable, solution would be to *repair* the existing marriage, converting it from a Samish-Sex Marriage to a healthy Normal Marriage, by having the feminine man become more masculine, and/or the masculine woman become more feminine.

Often, when I propose this, my friends become surly. How dare I, they ask. What business is it of mine? Do I think it is easy to change in such a profound way?

To which I say, It is not easy to change, but it is possible.

I know, because I have done it.

When young, I had a tendency to speak too quickly, while gesturing too much with my hands. Also, my opinions were unfirm. I was constantly contradicting myself in that fast voice, while gesturing like a girl. Also, I cried often. Things seemed so sad. I had long blond hair, and liked it. My hair was layered and fell down across my shoulders, and, I admit it, I would sometimes slow down when passing a shopwindow, to look at it, to look at my hair! I had a strange constant feeling of being happy to be alive. This feeling of infinite future possibility sometimes caused me to laugh when alone, or even, on occasion, to literally skip down the street, before pausing in front of a shopwindow and giving my beautiful hair a cavalier toss.

To tell the truth, I do not think I would have scored very high on my Manly Scale, if the Scale had been invented at that time, by me. I suspect I would have scored so Fem on the Test that I would have been prohibited from marrying my wife, "P," the love of my life.

And I think, somewhere in my heart, I knew that.

I knew I was too Fem.

So what did I do about it? Did I complain? Did I whine? Did I expect activist judges to step in on my behalf, manipulating the system to accommodate my peculiarity?

No, I did not.

What I did was, I changed. I undertook what I like to think of as a classic American project of self-improvement. I made videos of myself talking, and studied these, and in time succeeded in training myself to speak more slowly, while almost never moving my hands. Now, if you ever meet me, you will observe that I always speak in an extremely slow and manly and almost painfully deliberate way, with my hands either driven deep into my pockets or held stock-still at the end of my arms, which are bent slightly at the elbows, as if I were ready to respond to the slightest provocation by punching you in the face. As for my opinions, they are very firm. I rarely change them. When feeling like skipping, I absolutely do not skip. As for my long beautiful hair—well, I am lucky, in that I am rapidly going bald. Every month, when I recalculate my ranking on the Manly Scale, I find myself becoming more and more Manly, as my hair gets thinner and my girth increases, thickening my once lithe, almost girlish, physique, thus insuring the continuing morality and legality of my marriage to "P."

My point is simply this: If I was able to effect these tremendous positive changes in my life, to avoid finding myself in the moral/legal quagmire of a Samish-Sex Marriage, why can't "K," "S," "L," "H," "T," and "O" do the same?

I implore anyone who finds themselves in a Samish-Sex Marriage: Change. If you are a feminine man, become more manly. If you are a masculine woman, become more feminine. If you are a woman and are thick-necked or lumbering, or have ever had the slightest feeling of attraction to a man who is somewhat pale and fey, deny these feelings and, in a spirit of self-correction, try to become more thin-necked and light-footed, while, if you find it helpful, watching videos of naked masculine men, to sort of retrain yourself in the proper mode of attraction. If you are a man, and, upon seeing a thick-waisted, athletic young woman walking with a quasi-mannish gait through your local grocery, you imagine yourself in a passionate embrace with her, in your car, a car that is parked just outside, and which is suddenly, in your imagination, full of the smell of her fresh young breath—well, stop thinking that! Are you a man or not?

I, for one, am sick and tired of this creeping national tendency to let certain types of people take advantage of our national good nature by marrying individuals who are essentially of their own gender. If this trend continues, before long our towns and cities will be full of people like "K," "S," "L," "H," "T," and "O" "asserting their rights" by dating, falling in love with, marrying, and spending the rest of their lives with whomever they please.

I, for one, am not about to stand by and let that happen.

Because then what will we have? A nation ruled by the anarchy of unconstrained desire. A nation of willful human hearts, each lurching this way and that, reaching out for whatever it spontaneously desires, totally unconcerned about the external form in which that desired thing is embodied.

That is not the kind of world in which I wish to live.

I, for one, intend to become ever more firmly male, enjoying my golden years, while watching "P" become ever more female, each of us vigilant for any hint of ambiguity in the other.

And as our children, "G" and "M," grow, should they begin to show the slightest hint of some lingering residue of the opposite gender, "P" and I will lovingly pull them aside and list all the particulars by which we were able to identify their unintentional deficiency.

Then, together, we will devise a suitable correction.

And in this way, the race will go on.

Sincerely,
Ken Byron
115 Delton Way
Leadville, PA 13246

the red bow

Next night, walking out where it happened, I found her little red bow.

I brought it in, threw it down on the table, said: My God my God.

Take a good look at it and also I'm looking at it, said Uncle Matt. And we won't ever forget it, am I right?

First thing of course was to find the dogs. Which turns out, they were holed up back of the—the place where the little kids go, with the plastic balls in cages, they have birthday parties and so forth—holed up in this sort of nest of tree debris dragged there by the Village.

Well we lit up the debris and then shot the three of them as they ran out.

But that Mrs. Pearson, who'd seen the whole—well she

said there'd been four, four dogs, and next night we found that the fourth had gotten into Mullins Run and bit the Elliotts' Sadie and that white Muskerdoo that belonged to Evan and Millie Bates next door.

Jim Elliott said he would put Sadie down himself and borrowed my gun to do it, and did it, then looked me in the eye and said he was sorry for our loss, and Evan Bates said he couldn't do it, and would I? But then finally he at least led Muskerdoo out into that sort of field they call The Concourse, where they do the barbecues and whatnot, giving it a sorrowful little kick (a gentle kick, there was nothing mean in Evan) whenever it snapped at him, saying Musker Jesus!—and then he said, *Okay, now*, when he was ready for me to do it, and I did it, and afterwards he said he was sorry for our loss.

Around midnight we found the fourth one gnawing at itself back of Bourne's place, and Bourne came out and held the flashlight as we put it down, and helped us load it into the wheelbarrow alongside Sadie and Muskerdoo, our plan being—Dr. Vincent had said this was best—to burn those we found, so no other animal would—you know, via feeding on the corpses—in any event, Dr. Vincent said it was best to burn them.

When we had the fourth in the wheelbarrow my Jason said: Mr. Bourne, what about Cookie?

Well no I don't believe so, said Bourne.

He was an old guy and had that old-guy tenderness for the dog, it being pretty much all he had left in the world, such as for example he always called it *friend-of-mine*, as in: How about a walk, friend-of-mine?

But she is mostly an outside dog? I said.

She is almost completely an outside dog, he said. But still, I don't believe so.

And Uncle Matt said: Well, Lawrence, I for one am out here tonight trying to be certain. I think you can understand that.

I can, Bourne said, I most certainly can.

And Bourne brought out Cookie and we had a look.

At first she seemed fine, but then we noticed she was doing this funny thing where a shudder would run through her and her eyes would all of a sudden go wet, and Uncle Matt said: Lawrence, is that something Cookie would normally do?

Well, ah . . ., said Mr. Bourne.

And another shudder ran through Cookie.

Oh Jesus Christ, said Mr. Bourne, and went inside.

Uncle Matt told Seth and Jason to trot out whistling into the field and Cookie would follow, which she did, and Uncle Matt ran after, with his gun, and though he was, you know, not exactly a runner, still he kept up pretty good just via sheer effort, like he wanted to make sure this thing got done right.

Which I was grateful to have him there, because I was too tired in my mind and my body to know what was right anymore, and sat down on the porch, and pretty soon heard this little pop.

Then Uncle Matt trotted back from the field and stuck his head inside and said: Lawrence do you know, did Cookie have contact with other dogs, was there another dog or dogs she might have played with, nipped, that sort of thing?

Oh get out, get away, said Bourne.

Lawrence my God, said Uncle Matt. Do you think I like this? Think of what we've been through. Do you think this is fun for me, for us?

There was a long silence and then Bourne said well all he could think of was that terrier at the Rectory, him and Cookie sometimes played when Cookie got off her lead.

When we got to the Rectory, Father Terry said he was sorry for our loss, and brought Merton out, and we watched a long time and Merton never shuddered and his eyes remained dry, you know, normal.

Looks fine, I said.

Is fine, said Father Terry. Watch this: Merton, genuflect.

And Merton did this dog stretchy thing where he sort of like bowed.

Could be fine, said Uncle Matt. But also could be he's

sick but just at an early stage.

We'll have to be watchful, said Father Terry.

Yes, although, said Uncle Matt. Not knowing how it spreads and all, could it be we are in a better-safe-than-sorry type of situation? I don't know, I truly don't know. Ed, what do you think?

And I didn't know what I thought. In my mind I was all the time just going over it and over it, the before, the after, like her stepping up on that footstool to put that red bow in, saying these like lady phrases to herself, such as, Well Who Will Be There, Will There Be Cakes?

I hope you are not suggesting putting down a perfectly healthy dog, said Father Terry.

And Uncle Matt produced from his shirt pocket a red bow and said: Father, do you have any idea what this is and where we found it?

But it was not the real bow, not Emily's bow, which I kept all the time in my pocket, it was a pinker shade of red and was a little bigger than the real bow, and I recognized it as having come from our Karen's little box on her dresser.

No I do not know what that is, said Father Terry. A hair bow?

I for one am never going to forget that night, said Uncle Matt. What we all felt. I for one am going to work to make sure that no one ever again has to endure what we had to endure that night.

I have no disagreement with that at all, said Father Terry.

It is true you don't know what this is, Uncle Matt said, and put the bow back in his pocket. You really really have no experience whatsoever of what this is.

Ed, Father Terry said to me. Killing a perfectly healthy dog has nothing to do with—

Possibly healthy but possibly not, said Uncle Matt. Was Cookie bitten? Cookie was not. Was Cookie infected? Yes she was. How was Cookie infected? We do not know. And there is your dog, who interacted with Cookie in exactly the same way that Cookie interacted with the known infected animal, namely through being in close physical proximity.

It was funny about Uncle Matt, I mean funny as in great, admirable, this sudden stepping up to the plate, because previously—I mean, yes, he of course loved the kids, but had never been particularly—I mean he rarely even spoke to them, least of all to Emily, her being the youngest. Mostly he just went very quietly around the house, especially since January when he'd lost his job, avoiding the kids really, a little ashamed almost, as if knowing that, when they grew up, they would never be the out-of-work slinking-around uncle, but instead would be the owners of the house where the out-of-work slinking uncle etc., etc.

But losing her had, I suppose, made him realize for the

first time how much he loved her, and this sudden strength—focus, certainty, whatever—was a comfort, because tell the truth I was not doing well at all—I had always loved autumn and now it was full autumn and you could smell woodsmoke and fallen apples but all of the world, to me, was just, you know, flat.

It is like your kid is this vessel that contains everything good. They look up at you so loving, trusting you to take care of them, and then one night—what gets me, what I can't get over, is that while she was being—while what happened was happening, I was—I had sort of snuck away downstairs to check my e-mail, see, so that while—while what happened was happening, out there in the schoolyard, a few hundred yards away, I was sitting there typing—typing!—which, okay, there is no sin in that, there was no way I could have known, and yet—do you see what I mean? Had I simply risen from my computer and walked upstairs and gone outside and for some reason, any reason, crossed the schoolyard, then believe me, there is not a dog in the world, no matter how crazy—

And my wife felt the same way and had not come out of our bedroom since the tragedy.

So Father you are saying no? said Uncle Matt. You are refusing?

I pray for you people every day, Father said. What you are going through, no one ever should have to go through.

Don't like that man, Uncle Matt said as we left the Rectory. Never have and never will.

And I knew that. They had gone to high school together and there had been something about a girl, some last-minute prom-date type of situation that had not gone in Uncle Matt's favor, and I think some shoving on a ballfield, some name-calling, but all of this was years ago, during like say the Kennedy administration.

He will not observe that dog properly, said Uncle Matt. Believe me. And if he does notice something, he won't do what is necessary. Why? Because it's his dog. *His* dog. Everything that's his? It's special, above the law.

I don't know, I said. Truly I don't.

He doesn't get it, said Uncle Matt. He wasn't there that night, he didn't see you carrying her inside.

Which, tell the truth, Uncle Matt hadn't seen me carrying her inside either, having gone out to rent a video—but still, yes, I got his drift about Father Terry, who had always had a streak of ego, with that silver hair with the ripples in it, and also he had a weight set in the Rectory basement and worked out twice a day and had, actually, a very impressive physique, which he showed off, I felt—we all felt—by ordering his priest shirts perhaps a little too tight.

Next morning during breakfast Uncle Matt was very quiet and finally said, well, he might be just a fat little unemployed guy who hadn't had the education some had, but love was love, honoring somebody's memory was honoring somebody's memory, and since he had no big expectations for his day, would I let him borrow the truck, so he could park it in the Burger King lot and keep an eye on what was going on over at the Rectory, sort of in memory of Emily?

And the thing was, we didn't really use that truck anymore and so—it was a very uncertain time, you know, and I thought, Well, what if it turns out Merton really is sick, and somehow gets away and attacks someone else's—so I said yes, he could use the truck.

He sat all Tuesday morning and Tuesday afternoon, I mean not leaving the truck once, which for him—he was not normally a real dedicated guy, if you know what I mean. And then Tuesday night he came charging in and threw a tape in the VCR and said watch, watch this.

And there on the TV was Merton, leaning against the Rectory fence, shuddering, arching his back, shuddering again.

So we took our guns and went over.

Look I know I know, said Father Terry. But I'm handling it here, in my own way. He's had enough trouble in his life, poor thing.

Say what? said Uncle Matt. Trouble in his life? You are saying to this man, this father, who has recently lost—the dog has had *trouble in his life*?

Well, however, I should say—I mean, that was true. We all knew about Merton, who had been brought to Father Terry from this bad area, one of his ears sliced nearly off, plus it had, as I understood it, this anxiety condition, where it would sometimes faint because dinner was being served, I mean, it would literally pass out due to its own anticipation, which, you know, that couldn't have been easy.

Ed, said Father Terry. I am not saying Merton's trouble is, I am not comparing Merton's trouble to your—

Christ let's hope not, said Uncle Matt.

All's I'm saying is I'm losing something too, said Father Terry.

Ho boy, said Uncle Matt. Ho boy ho boy.

Ed, my fence is high, said Father Terry. He's not going anywhere, I've also got him on a chain in there. I want him to—I want it to happen here, just him and me. Otherwise it's too sad.

You don't know from sad, said Uncle Matt.

Sadness is sadness, said Father Terry.

Blah blah blah, said Uncle Matt. I'll be watching.

Well later that week this dog Tweeter Deux brought down a deer in the woods between the TwelvePlex and the Episcopal church, and that Tweeter Deux was not a big dog, just, you know, crazed, and how the DeFrancinis knew she had brought down a deer was, she showed up in the living room with a chewed-off foreleg.

And that night—well the DeFrancini cat began racing around the house, and its eyes took on this yellow color, and at one point while running it sort of locked up and skidded into the baseboard and gave itself a concussion.

Which is when we realized the problem was bigger than we had initially thought.

The thing was, we did not know and could not know how many animals had already been infected—the original four dogs had been at large for several days before we found them, and any animal they might have infected had been at large for nearly two weeks now, and we did not even know the precise method of infection—was it bites, spit, blood, was something leaping from coat to coat? We knew it could happen to dogs, it appeared it could happen to cats— what I'm saying is, it was just a very confusing and frightening time.

So Uncle Matt got on the iMac and made up these fliers, calling a Village Meeting, and at the top was a photo he'd taken of the red bow (not the real bow but Karen's pinkish red bow, which he'd color-enhanced on the iMac to make it redder and also he had superimposed Emily's communion photo) and along the bottom it said FIGHT THE OUTRAGE, and underneath in smaller letters it said something along the lines of, you know, Why do we live in this world but to love what is ours, and when one of us has cruelly lost what we loved, it is the time to band together to stand up to that which threatens that which we love, so that no one else ever has to experience this outrage again. Now that we have known and witnessed this terrific pain, let us resolve together to fight against any and all circumstances which might cause or contribute to this or a similar outrage now or at any time in the future—and we had Seth and Jason run these around town, and on Friday night ended up with nearly four hundred people in the high school gym.

Coming in, each person got a rolled-up FIGHT THE OUTRAGE poster of the color-enhanced bow, and also on these Uncle Matt had put in—I objected to this at first, until I saw how people responded—well he had put in these tiny teethmarks, they were not meant to look real, they were just, you know, as he said, symbolic reminders, and down in one corner was Emily's communion photo and in the opposite corner a photo of her as a baby, and Uncle Matt had hung a larger version of that poster (large as a closet) up over the speaker's podium.

And I was sort of astonished by Uncle Matt, I mean, he was showing so much—I'd never seen him so motivated. This was a guy whose idea of a big day was checking the mail and getting up a few times to waggle the TV antenna—and here he was, in a suit, his face all red and sort of proud and shiny—

Well Uncle Matt got up and thanked everyone for coming, and Mrs. DeFrancini, owner of Tweeter Deux, held up that chewed-up foreleg, and Dr. Vincent showed slides of cross-sections of the brain of one of the original four dogs, and then at the end I talked, only I got choked up and couldn't say much except thanks to everybody, their support had meant the world to us, and I tried to say about how much we had all loved her, but couldn't go on.

Uncle Matt and Dr. Vincent had, on the iMac, on their own (not wanting to bother me) drawn up what they called a Three-Point Emergency Plan, which the three points were: (1) All Village animals must immediately undergo an Evaluation, to determine was the animal Infected, (2) All Infected or Suspected Infected animals must be destroyed at once, and (3) All Infected or Suspected Infected animals, once destroyed, must be burned at once to minimize the possibility of Second-Hand Infection.

Then someone asked could they please clarify the meaning of "suspected"?

Suspected, you know, said Uncle Matt. That means we suspect and have good reason to suspect that an animal is, or may be, Infected.

The exact methodology is currently under development, said Dr. Vincent.

How can we, how can you, ensure that this assessment will be fair and reasonable though? the guy asked.

Well that is a good question, said Uncle Matt. The key to that is, we will have the assessment done by fair-minded persons who will do the Evaluation in an objective way that seems reasonable to all.

Trust us, said Dr. Vincent. We know it is so very important.

Then Uncle Matt held up the bow—actually a new bow, very big, about the size of a ladies' hat, really, I don't know where he found that—and said: All of this may seem confusing but it is not confusing if we remember that it is all about *This*, simply *This*, about honoring *This*, preventing *This*.

Then it was time for the vote, and it was something like 393 for and none against, with a handful of people abstaining (which I found sort of hurtful), but then following the vote everyone rose to their feet and, regarding me and Uncle Matt with—well they were smiling these warm smiles, some even fighting back tears—it was just a very nice, very kind moment, and I will never forget it, and will be grateful for it until the day I die.

After the meeting Uncle Matt and Trooper Kelly and a few others went and did what had to be done in terms of Merton, over poor Father Terry's objections—I mean, he was upset about it, of course, so upset it took five men to hold him back, him being so fit and all—and then they brought

Merton, Merton's body, back to our place and burned it, out at the tree line where we had burned the others, and someone asked should we give Father Terry the ashes, and Uncle Matt said why take the chance, we have not ruled out the possibility of airborne transmission, and putting on the little white masks supplied by Dr. Vincent, we raked Merton's ashes into the swamp.

That night my wife came out of our bedroom for the first time since the tragedy, and we told her everything that had been happening.

And I watched her closely, to see what she thought, to see what I should think, her having always been my rock.

Kill every dog, every cat, she said very slowly. Kill every mouse, every bird. Kill every fish. Anyone objects, kill them too.

Then she went back to bed.

Well that was—I felt so bad for her, she was simply not herself—I mean, this was a woman who, finding a spider, used to make me take it outside in a cup. Although, as far as killing all dogs and cats—I mean, there was a certain—I mean, if you did that, say, killed every dog and cat, regardless of were they Infected or not, you could thereby guarantee, to 100 percent, that no other father in town would ever again have to carry in his—God there is so much I don't remember about that night but one thing I do remember is, as I brought her in, one of her little clogs thunked off onto the linoleum, and still holding her I bent down to—and she wasn't there anymore, she wasn't, you know, there, inside her body. I had passed her thousands of times on the steps, in the kitchen, had heard her little voice from everywhere in the house and why, why had I not, every single time, rushed up to her and told her everything that I—but of course you can't do that, it would malform a child, and yet—

What I'm saying is, with no dogs and no cats, the chance that another father would have to carry his animal-murdered child into their home, where the child's mother sat, doing the bills, happy or something like happy for the last time in her life, happy until the instant she looked up and saw—what I guess I'm saying is, with no dogs and no cats, the chance of that happening to someone else (or to us again) goes down to that very beautiful number of Zero.

Which is why we eventually did have to enact our policy of sacrificing all dogs and cats who had been in the vicinity of the Village at the time of the incident.

But as far as killing the mice, the birds, the fish, no, we had no evidence to support that, not at that time anyway, and had not yet added the Reasonable Suspicion Clause to the Plan, and as far as the people, well my wife wasn't herself, that's all there was to it, although soon what we found was—I mean, there was something prescient about what she'd said, because in time we did in fact have to enact some very specific rules regarding the physical process of extracting the dogs and/or cats from a home where the owner was being unreasonable—or the fish, birds, whatever—and also had to assign specific penalties should these people, for example, assault one of the Animal Removal Officers, as a few of them did, and finally also had to issue some guidelines on how to handle individuals who, for whatever reason, felt it useful to undercut our efforts by, you know, obsessively and publicly criticizing the Five- and Six-Point Plans, just very unhappy people.

But all of that was still months away.

I often think back to the end of that first Village Meeting, to that standing-ovation moment. Uncle Matt had also printed up T-shirts, and after the vote everyone pulled the T-shirt with Emily's smiling face on it over his or her own shirt, and Uncle Matt said that he wanted to say thank you from the bottom of his heart, and not just on behalf of his family, this family of his that had been sadly and irreversibly malformed by this unimaginable and profound tragedy, but also, and perhaps more so, on behalf of all the families we had just saved, via our vote, from similar future profound unimaginable tragedies.

And as I looked out over the crowd, at all those T-shirts—I don't know, I found it deeply moving, that all of those good people would feel so fondly toward her, many of whom had not even known her, and it seemed to me that somehow they had come to understand how good she had been, how precious, and were trying, with their applause, to honor her.

christmas

I was twenty-six, beyond broke, back in my hometown, living in my aunt's basement. Having courted and won a girl I had courted but never come close to winning in high school, I was now losing her via my pathetically dwindling prospects. One night she said: "I'm not saying I'm great or anything, but still I think I deserve better than this."

My uncle called in a favor and soon I was on a roofing crew, one of three grunts riding from job to job in the freezing open back of a truck. My fellow grunts, Tyrell and John, were the only black guys on the crew, and hence I was known as The Great White Hope. Once everyone had seen me work, I became The Great White Dope. Our job was to move the hot tar from a vat on the ground to the place on the roof where the real roofing was done. Tyrell had a thick

Mississippi accent and no top teeth. Not once so far had I understood a word he said. He stayed on the ground, working the pulley, muttering obscenities at passing grannies and schoolgirls. John was forty-two, gentle-voiced, dignified, with a salt-and-pepper beard and his own roofing tools, which he brought to work every day, though he was never allowed to do anything but lug tar. John had roofed, he claimed, all his adult life, and in fact had virtuosoed his way into this job, by appearing on the job site one day and out-shingling the best white shingler.

"I guess I don't remember that," said Rick, our supervisor.

"I don't think you were there that day maybe," said John. "It was Lawrence hired me."

Lawrence was dead now, a famous Fezziwiggian presence, mourned by all.

"You are so full of shit," said Rick. "If you were so fast then, why are you so shitty now?"

"You roof like my mother," said Terry, the owner's brother.

"Maybe your mother roofs good," John mumbled.

"She don't," said Terry. "But still she's faster than you."

All that fall, John grieved the fact that he was not allowed to do the real and dignified work of a master roofer.

"It ain't right," he'd say to me. "I can do it. They need to give me a chance. I'm an older man. Got responsibilities. Can't just keep carrying tar my whole life."

In late November, talk turned to the yearly Christmas party. Drinks and food were to be on Walter, the owner. People got shitfaced. Also there was gambling.

"Then we're gonna see," Rick said one day. "We're gonna see if John here is a better gambler than he is a roofer."

"You gotta hope," said Terry.

"As a roofer, John, face it, you suck," Rick said. "Nice guy, shit roofer."

"Too fucking slow, John," Terry said. "We keep giving you chances and you keep screwing it up."

"But maybe why he's a shit roofer is, he's a gambling man," said Rick.

"What y'all are gonna find out is, I'm a roofer and a gambler both," said John.

"Excuse me saying it," Rick said when John had gone down to help Tyrell load the cauldron. "But that is a prime example of nigger-think. He *thinks* he's a roofer because he *says* he is. *Thinks* he can gamble because he *says* he can."

"Has fourteen kids and lets the welfare pay," said Terry.

One payday John asked could I give him a ride home. I gave him a ride, but turned out, not to his home. We drove deep into Southshore, past houses we'd roofed, then into an area too poor to roof, down a block of slumping two-flats.

"My friend's place," John said. "I'm gonna get you and your lady some Sherman Juice, so you can have a little party."

What was Sherman Juice? We'd started drinking at the shop and I was now too drunk to ask. In the kitchen, under dueling photos of MLK and JFK, sat an ancient black woman in a rocking chair. A mad kid dashed around, humming at me: *You devil, you white*. John's friend did not have any Sherman Juice, but did have a Polaroid of his girlfriend going down on him. In the photo, taken from his POV, we could see, in addition to his penis, his feet, in black socks. She was looking at the camera, smiling, sort of.

"Wow, is she pretty," I said politely.

The friend and I sat there together, admiring her. Then John and I went somewhere else. Where we went was John's wife's apartment. They lived apart. Living apart, they got more money and, with more money, they could buy a house sooner. In the apartment was a TV and four-teen kids around it. John named them, rapid-fire, with only a few stumbles.

"You really have fourteen kids," I said.

"Yes I do," he said. "Every one mine. Right, baby?"

"I should hope so," said his wife.

No chairs, no couch, newspapers on the windows. John and his wife cuddled on a blanket.

"When we get our real house, you come over," John's

wife said. "Bring your lady."

"Bring your lady, we'll all of us have dinner," John said.

"I hope that day come soon," said John's wife.

"I hope it come damn soon," John said. "I don't like all this living separate from my babies."

The kids giggled that he'd said *damn*. He went around kissing them all as I paced and lectured myself in the hall, trying to sober up for the long drive home.

As long as it didn't snow, we could roof. Every morning I woke at four, checked for snow. If no snow, I called in. If someone skill-less and slow might be useful that day, Walter told me come down. I rose, put on all five of my shirts (I had no coat), and drove down in my Nova, deicing the windshield as I went, via reaching out the window and hacking with a putty knife I kept for that purpose.

From the roofs, the city looked medieval, beautiful. I wrote poems in my head, poems that fizzled out under the weight of their own bloat: *O Chicago, giver and taker of life, city of bald men in pool halls, also men of hair, men who have hair, hairy men, etc., etc.* On the roofs we found weird things: a dead rat, a bike tire, somebody's dragon-headed pool floatie, all frozen stiff.

Mid-December then and still no snow. Strange Chicago crèches appeared in front yards: Baby Jesus, freed from the manger, leaned against a Santa sled half his height. He was crouching, as if about to jump; he wore just a diaper. Single strings of colored lights lay across bushes, as if someone had hatefully thrown them there. We patched the roof of a Jamaican immigrant whose apartment had nothing in it but hundreds of rags, spread across the floor and hanging from interior clotheslines. Nobody asked why. As we left, she offered us three DietRite Colas.

Then it was the Christmas party. The way we knew it was festive was, the metal shop had been cleared of dog shit. It had also been cleared of the dog, a constantly barking mutt who even bit Walter. He bit Walter, he bit the shovel-head Walter thrust at him, sometimes we came in and found him resolutely gnawing the leg of the worktable with a fine sustained hatred. Tonight, festively, the dog was locked in the cab of a truck. Now and then he would hurl himself against the windshield and somebody, festively, would fling at the windshield a plastic fork or hamburger bun. The other components of the festivity were a plate of cold cuts on the table where normally the gutters were pre-bent, a garbage can full of iced beer, and a ripped-off cardboard box holding some dice.

We ate, we drank, the checks were distributed, we waddled drunkenly across Prairie Island to the Currency Exchange, to cash the checks, after which the gambling began. I didn't know a thing about gambling and didn't want to. I rolled my four fresh hundreds and put them in the front pocket of my tar-stiff jeans, now and then patting the pocket to make sure the hundreds were still real.

Finally, in terms of money, I got it: money forestalled disgrace. I thought of my aunt, who worked three jobs and whom I had not yet paid a dime for food, thought of my girlfriend, who now paid whenever we went out, which was never, because my five shirts were too stained with tar.

"You ain't gambling, Tyrell?" said Rick.

Tyrell said something nobody got, and disappeared out the door.

"I suspect Tyrell is pussy-bound," said Terry.

"Smart man," said Rick.

John did gambler-things with his shirtsleeves, spat on his hands, hopped around on one foot, blew on the dice. Then he laid his four hundreds out near the craps box and gave them a lecture. They were to go forth and multiply. They were to find others of their kind and come scampering back.

Rick had gone to the bank that morning. He showed us his roll. It held maybe three thousand. His wife didn't dare say shit about it. Who earned it, him or her? "I do," he answered himself.

The gambling began. One by one the guys lost what they felt they could lose and drifted back to stand against the worktable and diddle with the soldering irons. Soon only John was left. Why was John left? Rick kept taunting.

A whole autumn of such taunts now did their work. All belittled men dream of huge redemption. Here was John, dreaming. In response to John's dreaming, Rick and Terry began to speak in mock-professorial diction.

"Look at this, kindly look at this," Rick shouted. "John is not, after all, any more a gambler than he is a ergo roofer. That is, he is a equally sucky gambler as he is a suckass roofer."

"Are you saying," said Terry, "that his gambling, in terms of how much does it suck, sucks exactly as much as does suck his roofing?"

"Perzackly, yup, that is just what I am saying, doctor," Rick burped.

John burned. They were going to see. They were going to see that the long years of wrongs done him had created a tremendous backlog of owed good luck, which was going to surge forward now, holy and personal.

And see they did. Soon John was down to his last hundred, and then he broke it, and then he was down to his last twenty. Then Rick cackled, and John threw his sole remaining five at Rick's chest. Rick caught it, kissed it, added it to his tremendous wad.

A light went on in my head, and has stayed on ever since: It was all about capital. Rick could lose and lose and never really lose. Once John dipped below four hundred, he was dead. He was dead now.

Which was when Walter came in and passed out the bonus checks.

Walter was the owner, the big man. Tonight he was wearing a tie. Afternoons he drove from site to site in his Lincoln, cranking out estimates, listening to opera, because, he said, though it was fag music, it floated his boat.

John took his check, made for the door. I followed him out.

"You're doing right," I said. "Go on home."

"Ain't going home," John said, and numb-footed across Prairie Island again.

"No no no," I mumbled, vividly drunk, suddenly alive. What had happened to me? Christ, where was I? Whither my promise, my easy season of victories, my field of dominant, my dominant field of my boyhood, boyhood playful triumph?

It was so cold my little mustache had frozen.

Our bonuses matched: three hundred each.

The man at the Currency Exchange looked at us either sadly or suspiciously, I couldn't tell which. When I doubled back to ask, he reached for something under the counter.

"Go home, man," I said to John out on the street. "You at least got your bonus, right?"

"Can't, can't," John huffed. "Got to get all that back. Noway that man's taking my Christmas money for my babies."

"You're not going to get it back, John," I said.

"Ain't I though," he said.

The same law that had broken him the first time broke him again. Rick took it and took it.

"Rick, Rick," I said, so drunk I was unsure I was actually speaking.

"What am I supposed to do?" Rick said, glaring at me. "He's a man, right? He wants to play. Ain't nobody forcing him."

"Ain't nobody forcing me," John said.

Rick had a fat round face and little black glasses. He was Polish but looked Kamikaze. His cheeks were red and his glasses were fogged, it seemed to me, from the gross extent of his trickery.

"You want to quit, John?" Rick said. "Great White Dope here thinks I'm hustling you. Maybe you should quit. So what if you suck as a gambler. Just walk away, right?"

"Nobody hustling nobody here," said John.

"See, Dope?" Rick said to me. "John's a man."

"I am that," said John.

Soon John was wadding and throwing his last ten.

"Fair's fair," he gasped, and lurched out.

I followed. Should I offer him mine? If I offered him mine, he might take it. So I offered him a portion of mine in a way that simultaneously offered and made it clear I was not offering. He said he didn't want none of mine. He had to get home. His babies were waiting. He didn't know what his wife would say, or what he would say to her.

"I'll have to just tell her, I guess," he said. "Just up and say it, get it over with: 'Baby, they ain't no Christmas. And don't give me no lip about it.'"

He wiped his face top to bottom, the saddest gesture I'd ever seen.

Then he walked off into the side-blowing snow.

I was sad yet happy. I was drunk. I was deeply, deeply glad I wasn't him.

Back inside, Rick was protesting, though nobody was asking him to.

"A man's a man," he was saying. "You play, you lose, you accept it. John's a man. He knows that. He gets that. I admire that."

"He's gonna have a shit Christmas though," somebody said.

"These people live for shit Christmases," Rick said. "They run right directly towards shit Christmases. It's all they know. It's in their blood." Then he put his wad back into his pocket.

The craps box was cast aside, and the roofers bent to their drinks. Somebody hauled over a length of gutter and a few of them went at it with tin snips, proving some point or another.

I stumbled out to my Nova, putty-knifed myself a sight hole, drove home.

There comes that phase in life when, tired of losing, you decide to stop losing, then continue losing. Then you decide to really stop losing, and continue losing. The losing goes on and on so long you begin to watch with curiosity, wondering how low you can go.

All that winter, once a week or so, I'd been stopping at a pay phone off Pulaski to call the Field Museum, where a kind woman had once praised my qualifications.

"Anything yet?" I'd say.

"Not yet," she'd say. Once she said, "We need a security guard, ha ha, but that, of course, is way beneath your level."

"Oh ha ha, right," I said.

But I was thinking: Could I work my way up? Could I, in my security-guard uniform, befriend a doddering curator, impress him with my knowledge of fossils, my work ethic, my quiet respect for Science?

"Keep calling though," she said.

"Oh I will," I said.

And I did, until finally it got too embarrassing.

Early spring I fled town, leaving my aunt unrepaid, my girlfriend convinced, forever, I suppose, that this sniveling lesser Me was the real one.

I went somewhere else and started over, pulled head out of ass, made a better life. Basically, I've got stores. If you've ever had a store that supports a family, a family that actually brightens when you come in at night, you know what a good thing that is. And I wouldn't go back to that roofing Me or that roofing Time for anything in the world.

But sometimes I imagine myself standing at that pay phone, in my tar-hardened clothes.

"This is so great," the Field Museum woman is saying. "Come down, come down, we finally have something suitable for you. I'm so happy to finally be able to tell you this."

"I'll be right there," I say.

Then it's a few weeks later, after first payday, and I pull up to my then-girlfriend's house, wearing clean clothes. All day long I have been, say, writing about the brontosaurus. I have certainly, at this point, learned a lot about brontosauri. In fact, I have been selected to go to a Brontosaurus Conference in say, Miami, Florida. We go out to dinner. My aunt meets us there. I have by now repaid her for all the food she fed me those many months. Also, I've bought her a new dress, just to be nice. The dinner is excellent. I pay. After dinner, the three of us sit there laughing, laughing about the fact that I, an Assistant Curator at the famous Field Museum, was once a joke of a roofer, a joke of a roofer so beat down he once stood by watching as a nice man got cheated out of his Christmas.

adams

I never could stomach Adams and then one day he's standing in my kitchen, in his underwear. Facing in the direction of my kids' room! So I wonk him in the back of the head and down he goes. When he stands up, I wonk him again and down he goes. Then I roll him down the stairs into the early-spring muck and am like, If you ever again, I swear to God, I don't even know what to say, you miserable fuck.

Karen got home, I pulled her aside. Upshot was: Keep the doors locked, and if he's home the kids stay inside.

But after dinner I got to thinking: Guy comes in in his shorts and I'm sitting here taking this? This is love? Love for my kids? Because what if? What if we slip up? What if a kid gets out or he gets in? No, no, no, I was thinking, not acceptable.

So I went over and said, Where is he?

To which Lynn said, Upstairs, why?

Up I went and he was standing at the mirror, still in his goddam underwear, only now he had on a shirt, and I wonked him again as he was turning. Down he went and tried to crab out of the room, but I put a foot on his back.

If you ever, I said. If you ever again.

Now we're even, he said. I came in your house and you came in mine.

Only I had pants on, I said, and mini-wonked him in the back of his head.

I am what I am, he said.

Well, that took the cake! Him admitting it! So I wonked him again, as Lynn came in, saying, Hey, Roger, hey. With Roger being me. And then he rises up. Which killed me! Him rising up? Against me? And I'm about to wonk him again, but she pushes in there, like intervening. So to wonk him again I had to like shove her back, and unfortunately she slipped, and down she went, and she's sort of lying there, skirt hiked up—and he's mad! Mad! At me! Him in his underwear, facing my kids' room, and he's mad at me? And many a night I've heard assorted wonks and baps from Adams's house, with her gasping, Frank, Jesus, I Am A Woman, You're Hurting Me, The Kids Are Watching, and so on.

Because that's the kind of guy he is.

So I wonked him again, and when she crawled at me, going, Please, Please, I had to push her back down, not in a mean way but in a like stay-there way, which is when, of course, just my luck, the kids came running in—these Adams kids, I should say, are little thespians, constantly doing musicals in the backyard etc., etc.—so they're, you know, all dramatic: Mummy, Daddy! And, okay, that was unfortunate, so I tried to leave, but they were standing there in the doorway, blocking me, like, Duh, we do not know which way to turn, we are stunned. So I shoved my way out, not rough, very gentle—I felt for them, having on more than one occasion heard Adams whaling on them, too—but one did go down, just on one knee, and I helped her up, and she tried to bite me! She did not seem to know what was what, and it hurt, and made me mad, so I went over to Adams, who was just getting up, and gave him this like proxy wonk on top of his head, in exchange for the biting.

Keep your damn, I said. Keep your goddam kids from—

Then I needed some air, so I walked around the block, but still it wasn't sitting right. Because now it begins, you know? Adams over there all pissed off, saying false things about me to those kids, which, due to what they had seen (the wonking) and what they had not seen (him in his underwear, facing my kids' room) they were probably swallowing every mistruth, and I was like, Great, now they hate me, like *I'm* the bad guy in this, and all summer it's going to be pranks, my hose slit and syrup in my gas tank, or all of a sudden our dog has a burn mark on her belly.

So I type up these like handbills, saying: Just So You Know, Your Dad Was Standing Naked in My Kitchen, Facing My Kids' Room. And I tape one inside their screen door so they'll be sure and see it when they go to softball later, then I stuff like nine in their mailbox, and on the rest I cross out "Your Dad" and put in "Frank Adams" and distribute them in mailboxes around the block.

All night it's call after call from the neighbors, saying, you know, Call the cops, Adams needs help, he's a goof, I've always hated him, maybe a few of us should go over, let us work with you on this, do not lose your cool. That sort of thing. Which was all well and good, but then I go out for a smoke around midnight and what is he looking at all hateful? Their houses? Don't kid yourself. He is looking at my house, with that smoldering look, and I am like, What are you looking at?

I am what I am, he says.

You fuck, I say, and rush over to wonk him, but he runs inside.

And as far as cops, my feeling was: What am I supposed to do, wait until he's back in my house, then call the cops and hope he stays facing my kids' room, in his shorts, until they arrive?

No, sorry, that is not my way.

The next day my little guy, Brian, is standing at the back door, with his kite, and I like reach over and pop the door shut, going, Nope, nope, you know very well why not, champ.

So there's my poor kid, kite in lap all afternoon, watching some dumb art guy on PBS saying, Shading Is One Way We Make Depth, How About Trying It Relevant to This Stump Here?

Then Monday morning I see Adams walking toward his car and again he gives me that smoldering look! Never have I received such a hateful look. And flips me the bird! As if he is the one who is right! So I rush over to wonk him, only he gets in the car and pulls away.

All day that look was in my mind, that look of hate.

And I thought, If that was me, if I had that hate level, what would I do? Well, one thing I would do is hold it in and hold it in and then one night it would overflow and I would sneak into the house of my enemy and stab him and his family in their sleep. Or shoot them. I would. You would have to. It is human nature. I am not blaming anybody.

I thought, I have to be cautious and protect my family or their blood will be on my hands.

So I came home early and went over to Adams's house when I knew nobody was home, and gathered up his rifle from the basement and their steak knives and also the butter knives, which could be sharpened, and also their knife sharpener, and also two letter openers and a heavy paperweight, which, if I was him and had lost all my guns and knives, I would definitely use that to bash in the head of my enemy in his sleep, as well as the heads of his family.

That night I slept better until I woke in a sweat, asking myself what I would do if someone came in and, after shoving down my wife and one of my kids, stole my guns and knives and knife sharpener as well as my paperweight. And I answered myself: What I would do is look around my house in a frenzy for something else dangerous, such as paint, such as thinner, such as household chemicals, and then either ring the house of my enemy with the toxics and set them on fire, or pour some into the pool of my enemy, which would (1) rot the liner and (2) sicken the children of my enemy when they went swimming.

Then I looked in on my sleeping kids and, oh my God, nowhere are there kids as sweet as my kids, and standing there in my pajamas, thinking of Adams standing there in his underwear, then imagining my kids choking and vomiting as they struggled to get out of the pool, I thought, No, no way, I am not living like this.

So, entering through a window I had forced earlier that afternoon, I gathered up all the household chemicals, and, believe me, he had a lot, more than I did, more than he needed, thinner, paint, lye, gas, solvents, etc. I got it all in like nine Hefty bags and was just starting up the stairs with the first bag when here comes the whole damn family, falling upon me, even his kids, whipping me with coat hangers and hitting me with sharp-edged books and spraying hair spray in my eyes, the dog also nipping at me, and rolling down the stairs of their basement I thought, They are trying to kill me. Hitting my head on the concrete floor, I saw stars, and thought, No, really, they are going to kill me, and if they kill me no more little Melanie and me eating from the same popcorn bowl, no more little Brian doing that wrinkled-brow thing we do back and forth when one of us makes a bad joke, never again Karen and me lying side by side afterward, looking out the window, discussing our future plans as those yellow-beaked birds come and go on the power line. And I struggled to my feet thinking, Forget how I got here, I am here, I must get out of here, I have to live. And I began to wonk and wonk, and once they had fallen back, with Adams and his teenage boy huddled over the littlest one, who had unfortunately flown relatively far due to a bit of a kick I had given her, I took out my lighter and fired up the bag, the bag of toxics, and made for the light at the top of the stairs, where I knew the door was, and the night was, and my freedom, and my home.

iii.

Our enemies will set among us individuals whose
primary function is to object, to dissent, to find
fault with our traditional mode of living, until
that which we know to be right, begins to feel
suspect, and we are reduced to a state of perpetual
uncertainty, a situation our enemies will be only
too happy to exploit. Who are these individuals,
really, and what makes them so vociferous in their
criticism of our ways? They are, if we examine
them closely: outcasts, chronic complainers,
individuals incapable of thriving within a
perfectly viable, truly generous system, a system
vastly superior to all other known ways of
organizing effort and providing value.

— *Bernard "Ed" Alton,*
  Taskbook for the New Nation,
  Chapter 5. "The Tyranny of the Negative: Procedural
  Methodology and the Pathology of Dissent"

93990

A ten-day acute toxicity study was conducted using twenty male cynomolgus monkeys ranging in weight from 25 to 40 kg. These animals were divided into four groups of five monkeys each. Each of the four groups received a daily intravenous dose of Borazadine, delivered at a concentration of either 100, 250, 500, or 10,000 mg/kg/day.

Within the high-dose group (10,000 mg/kg/day) effects were immediate and catastrophic, resulting in death within 20 mins of dosing for all but one of the five animals. Animals 93445 and 93557, pre-death, exhibited vomiting and disorientation. These two animals almost immediately entered a catatonic state and were sacrificed moribund. Animals 93001 and 93458 exhibited vomiting, anxiety, disorientation, and digging at their abdomens. These animals also quickly entered a catatonic state and were sacrificed moribund.

Only one animal within this high-dose group, animal 93990, a diminutive 26 kg male, appeared unaffected.

All of the animals that had succumbed were removed from the enclosure and necropsied. Cause of death was seen, in all cases, to be renal failure.

No effects were seen on Day 1 in any of the three lower-dose groups (i.e., 100, 250, or 500 mg/kg/day).

On Day 2, after the second round of dosing, animals in the 500 mg/kg/day group began to exhibit vomiting and, in some cases, aggressive behavior. This aggressive behavior most often consisted of a directed shrieking, with or without feigned biting. Some animals in the two lowest-dose groups (100 and 250 mg/kg/day) were observed to vomit, and one in the 250 mg/kg/day group (animal 93002) appeared to exhibit self-scratching behaviors similar to those seen earlier in the high-dose group (i.e., probing and scratching at abdomen, with limited writhing).

By the end of Day 3, three of five animals in the 500 mg/kg/day group had entered a catatonic state, and the other two animals in this dose group were exhibiting extreme writhing punctuated with attempted biting and pinching of their fellows, often with shrieking. Some hair loss, ranging from slight to extreme, was observed, as was some "playing" with the resulting hair bundles. This "playing" behavior ranged from mild to quite energetic. This "playing" behavior was adjudged to be typical of the type of "play" such an animal might initiate with a smaller animal such as a rodent, i.e., out of a curiosity impulse, i.e., may have been indicative of hallucinogenic effects. Several animals were observed to repeatedly grimace at the hair bundles, as if trying to elicit a fear behavior from the hair bundles. Animal 93110 of the 500 mg/kg/day group was observed to sit in one corner of the cage gazing at its own vomit while an unaffected animal (93222) appeared to attempt to rouse the interest of 93110 via backpatting, followed by vigorous backpatting. Interestingly, the sole remaining high-dose animal (93990, the diminutive male), even after the second day's dosing, still showed no symptoms. Even though this animal was the smallest in weight within the highest-dose group, it showed no symptoms. It showed no vomiting, disinterest, self-scratching, anxiety, or aggression. Also no hair loss was observed. Although no hair bundles were present (because no hair loss occurred), this animal was not seen to "play" with inanimate objects present in the enclosure, such as its food bowl or stool or bits of rope, etc. This animal, rather, was seen only to stare fixedly at the handlers through the bars of the cage and/or to retreat rapidly when the handlers entered the enclosure with the long poking stick to check under certain items (chairs, recreational tire) for hair bundles and/or deposits of runny stool.

By the middle of Day 3, all of the animals in the 500 mg/kg/day group had succumbed. Pre-death, these showed, in addition to the effects noted above, symptoms ranging from whimpering to performing a rolling dementia-type motion on the cage floor, sometimes accompanied by shrieking or frothing. After succumbing, all five animals were removed from the enclosure and necropsied. Renal failure was seen to be the cause of death in all cases. Interestingly, these animals did not enter a catatonic state pre-death, but instead appeared to be quite alert, manifesting labored breathing and, in some cases, bursts of energetic rope-climbing. Coordination was adjudged to be adversely affected, based on the higher-than-normal frequency of falls from the rope. Post-fall reactions ranged from no reaction to frustration reactions, with or without self-punishment behaviors (i.e., self-hitting, self-hair-pulling, rapid shakes of head).

Toward the end of Day 3, all animals in the two lowest-dose groups (250 and 100 mg/kg/day) were observed to be in some form of distress. Some of these had lapsed into a catatonic state, some refused to take food, many had runny, brightly colored stools, some sat eating their stool while intermittently shrieking.

Animals 93852, 93881, and 93777, of the 250 mg/kg/day group, in the last hours before death, appeared to experience a brief period of invigoration and renewed activity, exhibiting symptoms of anxiety, as well as lurching, confusion, and scratching at the eyes with the fingers. These animals were seen to repeatedly walk or run into the cage bars, after which they would become agitated. Blindness or partial blindness was indicated. When brightly colored flags were waved in front of these animals, some failed to respond, while others responded by flinging stool at the handlers.

By noon on Day 4, all of the animals in the 250 mg/kg/day group had succumbed, been removed from the enclosure, and necropsied. In every case the cause of death was seen to be renal failure.

By the end of Day 4, only the five 100 mg/kg/day animals remained, along with the aforementioned very resilient diminutive male in the highest-dose group (93990), who continued to manifest no symptoms whatsoever. This animal continued to show no vomiting, retching, nausea, disorientation, loss of motor skills, or any of the other symptoms described above. This animal continued to move about the enclosure normally and ingest normal amounts of food and water and in fact was seen to have experienced a slight weight gain and climbed the rope repeatedly with good authority.

On Day 5, animal 93444 of the 100 mg/kg/day group was observed to have entered the moribund state. Because of its greatly weakened condition, this animal was not redosed in the morning. Instead, it was removed from the enclosure, sacrificed moribund, and necropsied. Renal failure was seen to be the cause of death. Animal 93887 (100 mg/kg/day group) was seen to repeatedly keel over on one side while wincing. This animal succumbed at 1300 hrs of Day 5, was removed from the enclosure, and necropsied. Renal failure was seen to be the cause of death. Between 1500 hrs on Day 5 and 2000 hrs on Day 5, animals 93254 and 93006 of the 100 mg/kg/day dose group succumbed in rapid succession while huddled in the NW corner of the large enclosure. Both animals exhibited wheezing and rapid clutching and release of the genitals. These two animals were removed from the enclosure and necropsied. In both cases the cause of death was seen to be renal failure.

This left only animal 93555 of the 100 mg/kg/day dose group and animal 93990, the diminutive male of the highest-dose group. Animal 93555 exhibited nearly all of the aforementioned symptoms, along with, toward the end of Day 5, several episodes during which it inflicted scratches and contusions on its own neck and face by attempting to spasmodically reach for something beyond the enclosure. This animal also manifested several episodes of quick spinning. Several of these quick-spinning episodes culminated in sudden hard falling. In two cases, the sudden hard fall was seen to result in tooth loss. In one of the cases of tooth loss, the animal was seen to exhibit the suite of aggressive behaviors earlier exhibited toward the hair bundles. In addition, in this case, the animal, after a prolonged period of snarling at its tooth, was observed to attack and ingest its own tooth. It was judged that, if these behaviors continued into Day 6, for humanitarian reasons, the animal would be sacrificed, but just after 2300 hrs the animal discontinued these behaviors and only sat listlessly in its own stool with occasional writhing and therefore was not sacrificed due to this improvement in its condition.

By 1200 hrs of Day 5, the diminutive male 93990 still exhibited no symptoms. He was observed to be sitting in the SE corner of the enclosure, staring fixedly at the cage door. This condition was at first mistaken to be indicative of early catatonia but when a metal pole was inserted and a poke attempted, the animal responded by lurching away with shrieking, which was judged normal. It was also noted that 93990 occasionally seemed to be staring at and/or gesturing to the low-dose enclosure, i.e., the enclosure in which 93555 was still sitting listlessly in its own stool occasionally writhing. By the end of Day 5, 93990 still manifested no symptoms and in fact was observed to heartily eat the proffered food and weighing at midday Day 6 confirmed further weight gain. Also it climbed the rope. Also at times it seemed to implore. This imploring was judged to be, possibly, a mild hallucinogenic effect. This imploring resulted in involuntary laughter on the part of the handlers, which resulted in the animal discontinuing the imploring behavior and retreating to the NW corner where it sat for quite some time with its back to the handlers. It was decided that, in the future, handlers would refrain from laughing at the imploring, so as to be able to obtain a more objective idea of the duration of the (unimpeded) imploring.

Following dosing on the morning of Day 6, the last remaining low-dose animal (93555), the animal that earlier had attacked and ingested its own tooth, then sat for quite some time writhing in its own stool listlessly, succumbed, after an episode that included, in addition to many of the aforementioned symptoms, tearing at its own eyes and flesh and, finally, quiet heaving breathing while squatting. This animal, following a limited episode of eyes rolling back in its head, entered the moribund state, succumbed, and was necropsied. Cause of death was seen to be renal failure. As 93555 was removed from the enclosure, 93990 was seen to sit quietly, then retreat to the rear of the enclosure, that is, the portion of the enclosure farthest from the door, where it squatted on its haunches. Soon it was observed to rise and move toward its food bowl and eat heartily while continuing to look at the door.

Following dosing on Day 7, animal 93990, now the sole remaining animal, continued to show no symptoms and ate and drank vigorously.

Following dosing on Day 8, likewise, this animal continued to show no symptoms and ate and drank vigorously.

On Day 9, it was decided to test the effects of extremely high doses of Borazadine by doubling the dosage, to 20,000 mg/kg/day. This increased dosage was administered intravenously on the morning of Day 9. No acute effects were seen. The animal continued to move around its cage and eat and drink normally. It was observed to continue to stare at the door of the cage and occasionally at the other, now empty, enclosures. Also the rope-climbing did not decrease. A brief episode of imploring was observed. No laughter on the part of the handlers occurred, and the unimpeded imploring was seen to continue for approximately 130 seconds. When, post-imploring, the stick was inserted to attempt a poke, the stick was yanked away by 93990. When a handler attempted to enter the cage to retrieve the poking stick, the handler was poked. Following this incident, the conclusion was reached to attempt no further retrievals of the poking stick, but rather to obtain a back-up poking stick from Supply. As Supply did not at this time have a back-up poking stick, it was decided to attempt no further poking until the first poking stick could be retrieved. When it was determined that retrieving the first poking stick would be problematic, it was judged beneficial that the first poking stick was now in the possession of 93990, as observations could be made as to how 93990 was using and/or manipulating the poking stick, i.e., effect of Borazadine on motor skills.

On Day 10, on what was to have been the last day of

the study, upon the observation that animal 93990 still exhibited no effects whatsoever, the decision was reached to increase the dosage to 100,000 mg/kg/day, a dosage 10 times greater than that which had proved almost immediately lethal to every other animal in the highest-dose group. This was adjudged to be scientifically defensible. This dosage was delivered at 0300 hrs on Day 10. Remarkably, no acute effects were seen other than those associated with injection (i.e., small bright purple blisters at the injection site, coupled with elevated heart rate and extreme perspiration and limited panic gesturing) but these soon subsided and were judged to be related to the high rate of injection rather than to the Borazadine itself.

Throughout Day 10, animal 93990 continued to show no symptoms. It ate and drank normally. It moved energetically about the cage. It climbed the rope. By the end of the study period, i.e., midnight of Day 10, no symptoms whatsoever had been observed. Remarkably, the animal leapt about the cage. The animal wielded the poking stick with good dexterity, occasionally implored, shrieked energetically at the handlers. In summary, even at a dosage 10 times that which had proved almost immediately fatal to larger, heavier animals, 93990 showed no symptoms whatsoever. In all ways, even at this exceptionally high dosage, this animal appeared to be normal, healthy, unaffected, and thriving.

At approximately 0100 hrs of Day 11, 93990 was tranquilized via dart, removed from the enclosure, sacrificed, and necropsied.

No evidence of renal damage was observed. No negative effects of any kind were observed. A net weight gain of 3 kg since the beginning of the study was observed.

All carcasses were transported off-site by a certified medical waste hauler and disposed of via incineration.

brad carrigan, american

Morning at the Carrigans'.

Minutes ago, Chief Wayne left with the giant stick of butter. Any minute now, Brad Carrigan expects, the doorbell will ring.

Just then the doorbell rings.

Chief Wayne stands scowling in the doorway, holding the giant stick of butter.

"Gosh, what's the matter, Wayne?" says Doris, the way she always does.

"I tried to butter my toast," says Chief Wayne. "At which time I discovered that this stick of butter was actually your dog, Buddy, wearing a costume—a costume of a stick of butter!"

"Oh Buddy," says Doris. "Don't you know that, if you

want someone to like you, tricking them is the last thing you should do?"

"I guess I know that now," says Buddy sadly.

"Brad? Doris?" says Chief Wayne. "I guess I also learned something today. If a dog likes you, or even a person, you should try your best to like them in return. Buddy wouldn't have to hide in this costume if I'd simply accept his friendship."

"That's a good lesson, Wayne," says Doris. "One I guess we could all stand to learn."

"What I was hoping you'd learn, Wayne?" says Buddy. "Is that just because a person spends hours at a time in front of the house, licking his or her own butt, doesn't mean he or she has no feelings."

"Although technically, Buddy, you're not really a person," says Chief Wayne.

"And technically you don't have a butt," says Doris.

"All you have is that hole where Craig puts his hand in, to make you move," says Chief Wayne.

This hurts Buddy's feelings and he runs out the dog door.

"Oh gosh," Doris says. "I hope nothing bad happens to Buddy."

"I'd feel awful if something happened to the Budster because we drove him outside with our taunts about him not having a butt," says Chief Wayne thoughtfully.

Brad, Doris, and Chief Wayne step into the yard to find Buddy hanging motionless on the clothesline, his severed genitals on the ground beneath him.

"Well, I guess we all learned something today," says Chief Wayne.

"What I learned?" says Doris. "Is you never know when someone precious to you may be snatched away."

"And therefore," says Chief Wayne, "we must show our love every day, in every way."

"That is so true," says Doris.

"Don't you think that's true, Brad?" says Chief Wayne.

"I guess so," says Brad, whose hands are shaking.

"You *guess* so?" says Chief Wayne. "Oh that's rich! You *guess* we must show our love every day, in every way?"

"As if there could be any argument about that whatsoever!" says Doris.

"Oh Brad," says Chief Wayne, with an affectionate shake of his headdress.

"Oh Brad," says Doris. "The people we know and love are all that matter in this crazy world. Someday you'll understand that."

"The people we love—and the dogs we love!" says Chief Wayne.

"If you look deep in your heart, Brad," says Doris, "I just know that's what you feel."

What Brad feels is, he's trying his best here. Trying his

best to stay cheerful and positive. About a month ago, Doris passed him a note regarding possible cancellation. *It's coming,* the note said. *Our asses are grass, unless. Big changes req'd. Trust me on this. Grave crisis, no lie, love, ME.*

How did Doris know about the impending possible cancellation? When he asked, she wouldn't say. She only shook her head fiercely, as if to indicate: We're not going to discuss this any further, we're just going to fix the problem.

So whenever something's changed around here, he's tried to stay upbeat. When they got Buddy he didn't question why Buddy was a puppet-dog and not a real dog. When Chief Wayne started coming around claiming to be his oldest friend in the world, he didn't question why a Native American had red hair. When their backyard started morphing, he didn't ask how it was physically possible.

Then things started getting dumber. Plus meaner. Now it's basically all mean talk and jokes about poop and butts. He and Doris used to talk about real issues, about them, their relationship, their future hopes and plans. Once she lost her engagement ring and bought a fake so he wouldn't notice. Once he became jealous when the butcher started giving her excellent cuts of meat.

And now violence. Poor Buddy. They've never had violence before. Once a tree branch conked Brad in the head. Once he fell off a chair and landed on a knitting needle.

But a murder/castration?

No, never, this is entirely unprecedented.

"Brad, hello?" says Doris. "Have you had a stroke? Is that why you're staring off into space as if taking a dump?"

"Did you take such a difficult dump it gave you a stroke?" says Chief Wayne.

Both Doris and Chief Wayne put on their faces the expression of someone taking a difficult dump, then having a stroke. Then we see from the way they start laughing warmly, smiling affectionately at Brad, and from the happy swell of the music, that they haven't really had strokes while taking dumps, they're just trying to keep things light, and also, that it's time for a commercial.

Back at the Carrigans', Brad has placed Buddy and his genitals on a card table, along with a photo of Buddy and some of his favorite squeakie toys.

"Would anyone like to say a few words about Buddy?" Brad says.

"Poor Buddy," says Chief Wayne. "Always shooting his mouth off. I'm sure that's what happened to him. He shot his mouth off to the wrong person, who then killed and castrated him."

"Not that you're saying he deserved it," says Doris.

"I'm not saying he deserved it exactly," says Chief Wayne. "But if a person is going to have so many negative opinions, and share them with the world, eventually somebody's going to get tired of it."

"Would anyone like to say a few, other, words about Buddy?" says Brad. "Doris?"

"Hey, wait a minute," says Doris, glancing up at the TV. "Isn't this *FinalTwist*?"

"Oh, I love *FinalTwist*," says Chief Wayne.

"Guys?" says Brad. "Aren't we remembering Buddy?"

"Brad, for heaven's sake," says Doris. "Calm down and watch some *FinalTwist* with us."

"Buddy's not exactly going anywhere, Bradster," says Chief Wayne.

Also new. Previously they never watched other shows on their show. Plus they have so many TVs now, two per room, plus a backyard TV, plus one at either end of the garage, so that, wherever they go, some portion of another show is always showing.

On *FinalTwist*, five college friends take a sixth to an expensive Italian restaurant, supposedly to introduce him to a hot girl, actually to break the news that his mother is dead. This is the InitialTwist. During dessert they are told that, in fact, all of their mothers are dead. This is the SecondTwist. The ThirdTwist is, not only are all their mothers dead, the show paid to have them killed, and the fourth and FinalTwist is, the kids have just eaten their own grilled mothers.

"What a riot," says Doris.

"Doris, come on," says Brad. "These are real people, people with thoughts and hopes and dreams."

"Well, nobody got hurt," says Chief Wayne.

"Except those kids who unknowingly ate their own mothers," says Brad.

"Well, they signed the releases," says Chief Wayne.

"Releases or not, Wayne, come on," says Brad. "They killed people. They tricked people into eating their own mothers."

"I don't know that I'm all that interested in the moral ins and outs of it," says Chief Wayne. "I guess I'm just saying I enjoyed it."

"It's interesting, that's the thing," says Doris. "The expectations, the reversals, the timeless human emotions."

"Who wouldn't want to watch that?" says Chief Wayne.

"Interesting is good, Brad," says Doris. "Surprising is good."

Just then Buddy hops sheepishly off the card table, bearing his own genitals in his mouth.

"Buddy, you're alive!" says Doris.

"But I see you're still castrated?" says Chief Wayne.

"Yes, well," says Buddy, blushing.

"Maybe you could tell us who did it, Buddy," says Doris.

"Oh Doris," says Buddy, and starts to cry. "I did it myself."

"You castrated yourself?" says Doris.

"I guess you could say it was a cry for help," says Buddy.

"I'll say," says Chief Wayne.

"I just get so tired of everyone constantly making jokes about the fact that I need a certain kind of 'assistance' in order to move," Buddy says.

"You mean a hand up your keister?" says Doris.

"A fist up your poop chute?" says Chief Wayne.

"A paw up your exit ramp?" says Doris.

"You're still doing it!" barks Buddy, and runs out the dog door.

"Somebody's grumpy," says Doris.

"He'll be a lot less grumpy once we get those genitals of his sewed back on," says Chief Wayne.

Chief Wayne steps outside.

"Uh-oh, guys!" he says. "Looks like, in addition to a persnickety dog, you've got yourself *another* little problem. Your darn backyard has morphed again!"

Then we hear the familiar music that indicates the backyard has morphed again, and see that the familiar Carrigan backyard is now a vast field of charred human remains.

"Carrigan, I've about had it with this nonsense!" shouts their neighbor, Mr. Winston. "Last week my grumpy boss, Mr. Taylor, came for dinner, and right in the middle of dessert your yard morphed into ancient Egypt, and a crocodile came over and ate Mr. Taylor's toupee!"

"And when my elderly parents came to visit?" says Mrs. Winston. "Your yard morphed into some sort of nineteenth-century brothel, and a prostitute insulted my mother over the fence!"

"Oh come on, Brad," says Doris. "Let's go find Buddy."

Brad, Doris, and Chief Wayne set out across the yard.

"Jeez, where is that crazy dog?" says Chief Wayne.

"Look for the one thing not smoldering in this vast expanse of carnage," says Doris, stepping gingerly over several charred corpses in the former horseshoe pit.

From the abandoned farmhouse comes an agonized scream.

From behind a charred tree darts Buddy.

"Let's corner him by that contaminated well!" says Doris, and she and Chief Wayne rush off.

"My God," mumbles Brad. "Who were these people?"

"We're Belstonians," says one of the corpses, lying on its back, hands held out defensively, as if it died fending off a series of blows. "Our nation is comprised of three main socioethnic groups: the religious Arszani of the north, who live in small traditional agrarian communities in the mountainous northern regions; the more secular, worldly Arszani of the south, who mix freely with their Tazdit neighbors; and the Tazdit themselves, who, though superior to the southern Arszani in numbers, have always lagged behind economically. Lately this course of affairs has been exacerbated by several consecutive years of drought."

"Don't forget the complicated system of tariffs, designed to favor the southern, secular Arszani, emphasizing, as it does, the industrially driven sectors of the economy, in which the southern Arszani, along with certain more ecumenical Tazdit factions, invested heavily during the post-earthquake years," says a second corpse, whose chest cavity has been torn open, and who is missing an arm.

"Which spelled doom for us mountainous devout northern Arszani once gold was discovered in a region ostensibly under our control but legally owned by a cartel of military/industrial leaders from the south," says a third corpse, a woman, legs spread wide, mouth open in an expression of horror.

"That was our group," says the corpse missing an arm. "Northern Arszani."

"Wow," says Brad. "That's so complicated."

"Not that complicated," says the corpse who died fending off blows.

"It might seem complicated, if the person trying to understand it had lived in total plenty all his life, ignoring the rest of the world," says the corpse missing an arm, as a butterfly flits from his chest wound to his head wound.

"I agree," says the corpse who died fending off blows. "We know all about *his* country. I know who Casey Stengel was. I can quote at length from Thomas Paine."

"Who?" says Brad.

"Now, Bliorg, be fair," says the woman corpse. "Their nation occupies a larger place on the world stage. English is the lingua franca of most of the world."

"The what?" says Brad.

"I'm just saying that, occupying oneself with the genitals of a puppet, given the brutal, nightmarish things going on around the world this very instant, I find that unacceptably trivial," says the one armed corpse.

"I miss life," says the woman corpse.

"Remember our farm?" says the corpse who died fending off blows. "Remember how delicious vorella tasted eaten directly from the traditional heated cubern?"

"How the air smelled in the Kizhdan Pass after a rain?" says the woman corpse.

"How hard we worked in the garden that final spring?" says the corpse who died fending off blows. "How suddenly it all came upon us? How unprepared we were when suddenly the militia, including some of our southern Arszani brethren, swept into our village——"

"With what violence they rended you, dear, while you were still alive," the woman corpse says, looking tenderly at the corpse who died fending off blows.

"How the men encircled you, taunting you as they . . ." The corpse who died fending off blows trails off, remembering the day the secular Arszani/southern Tazdit militia dragged his wife into the muddy yard of their shack, then held him down, forcing him to watch what followed for what might have been ten minutes and might have been three hours, after which they encircled him, bayonets fixed, and he attempted, briefly, to fend off their blows, before they eviscerated him while he was still alive, as his wife, also still alive, lifted and dropped her left arm repeatedly, for what might have been ten thousand years.

Just then Doris rushes by, bearing the re-genitaled and softly whimpering Buddy in her arms.

"Brad, honestly," she hisses. "Thanks for the help."

"Not!" says Chief Wayne.

We see from the way the corpses, devastated by memory, collapse back into the dust of the familiar Carrigan back-yard, and from the sad tragic Eastern European swell of the music, that it's time for a commercial.

Back at the Carrigans', Doris and Chief Wayne come back inside to find hundreds of ears of corn growing out of the furniture, floors, and ceiling.

"What the——?" says Doris, setting Buddy down.

"I believe this is what's called a 'bumper crop,'" says Chief Wayne.

"I'll say," says Doris. "It's going to 'bump' us right out of this room if it keeps up!"

"My balls hurt so much," says Buddy.

Brad comes in, eyes moist with tears, and sits on the couch.

"What gives, Mr. Gloomy?" says Doris.

"Still moping about the corpses in the yard?" says Chief Wayne.

"Give it time, hon," says Doris. "It'll morph into something more cheerful."

"It always does," says Chief Wayne.

"Things always comes out right in the end, don't they?" says Doris. "As long as you believe in your dreams?"

"And accentuate the positive," says Chief Wayne.

Just then from the TV comes the brash martial music that indicates an UrgentUpdateNewsMinute.

In California, a fad has broken out of regular people having facial surgery to look like their favorite celebrities. Sometimes they end up looking like hideous monsters. Celebrities have taken to paying surprise compassionate visits to the hideous monsters. One hideous monster, whose face looks like the face of a lion roasted in a fire, says the surprise celebrity visit made the whole ordeal worthwhile. In the Philippines, a garbage dump has exploded due to buildup of natural gas emitted by rotting garbage, killing dozens of children digging in the dump for food.

"Wait a minute," says Brad. "That gives me an idea."

"Uh-oh," says Chief Wayne. "I don't like the sound of that."

"I hope it's better than your idea about installing heat sensors in old people's underwear," says Doris.

"I also hope it's better than your idea about putting a radio transmitter on Buddy while you guys were away on vacation, which then short-circuited, causing Buddy to be continually electrocuted for two straight weeks," says Chief Wayne.

"And the Winstons thought Buddy had been taking tap lessons?" says Doris. "Oh gosh."

"So what's your idea, pal?" says Chief Wayne.

"Never mind," says Brad, blushing.

"Come on, Mr. Mopey!" says Doris. "Share it! I'm sure it's terrific."

"Well," says Brad. "My idea is, why do we need all this corn? Isn't it sort of wasteful? My idea is, let's pick this corn and send it to that village in the Philippines where the kids have to eat garbage to live. Our house gets back to normal, the kids don't have to eat trash, everybody's happy."

There is an awkward silence.

"Brad, have you finally gone totally insane?" Doris says.

"I have to say, the heat-sensor-in-the-underwear-of-the-elderly idea is starting to look pretty viable," says Chief Wayne.

"I just want to do something," says Brad, blushing again.

"There's so much suffering. We have so much, and others have so little. So I was just thinking that, you know, if we took a tiny portion of what we have, which we don't really need, and sent it to the people who need it . . ."

Doris has tears in her eyes.

"Doris, what is it?" says Chief Wayne. "Tell Brad what you're feeling."

"I don't see why you always have to be such a downer, Brad," she says. "First you start weeping in our yard, then you start disparaging our indoor corn?"

"Brad, to tell the truth, there are plenty of houses with lots more indoor corn than this," says Chief Wayne. "This, relative to a lot of houses I've seen, is some very modest indoor vegetable growth."

"You probably see it as you make your rounds," says Doris. "Some people probably even have tomatoes and zucchini growing out of their furniture."

"Oh sure," says Chief Wayne. "Even watermelons."

"So this very modest amount of corn that we have, in your opinion, is nothing to feel guilty about?" says Doris.

"His 'rounds'?" says Brad. "What do you mean his 'rounds'?"

"His raids, his rounds, whatever," says Doris. "Please don't change the subject, Brad. I think we've been very fortunate, but not so fortunate that we can afford to start giving away everything we've worked so hard for. Why can't our stuff, such as corn, be *our* stuff? Why do you have to make everything so complicated? We aren't exactly made out of money, Brad!"

"Look Brad," says Chief Wayne. "Maybe you should start thinking about Doris instead of some Philippians you don't even know."

"You really get me, Wayne," says Doris.

"You're easy to get, Doris," says Chief Wayne.

Just then the doorbell rings.

On the lawn stands a delegation of deathly-pale Filipino children dressed in bloodstained white smocks.

"We've come for the corn?" says the tallest child, who has a large growth above one eyebrow.

"Brad," Doris says in a pitiful voice. "I can't believe you called these people."

"I didn't," Brad says.

And he didn't. Although he can't say he's unhappy they're here.

"Look, what's the big deal?" says Brad. "We pick the corn, give it to these kids, problem solved. If you guys would help me out, we could have all this corn picked in ten minutes."

"Brad, I've suddenly got a terrible headache," says Doris. "Would you go get me a Tylenol?"

"Brad, jeez, nice," says Chief Wayne. "Don't just stand there with your mouth hanging open when your wife is in pain."

Brad goes into the kitchen, gets Doris a Tylenol.

Buddy follows him in, hops up on a kitchen chair.

"Uh, Brad?" Buddy whispers. "I want you to know something. I've always liked you. I've consistently advocated for you. To me, you seem extremely workable, and I've said so many—"

"Buddy, no, bad dog!" Doris shouts from the living room.

"Yikes," says Buddy, and hops down from the chair, and skids out of the kitchen.

What the heck is up with Buddy? Brad wonders. He's "advocated" for Brad? He finds Brad "workable"?

Possibly the self-castration has made Buddy a little mental.

Brad returns to the living room. Doris, on the love seat, wearing the black lace bustier Brad bought her last Christmas, is straddling Chief Wayne, who, pants around his ankles, is kissing Doris's neck.

"Doris, my God!" shouts Brad.

Doris and Chief Wayne? It makes no sense. Chief Wayne is at least ten years older than they are, and is overweight and has red hair all over his back and growing out of his ears.

"Doris," Brad says. "I don't understand."

"I can explain, Bradster!" Chief Wayne says. "You've

just been TotallyFukked!"

"And so have I!" says Doris. "No, just kidding! Brad, lighten up! See, look here! We kept a thin layer of protective cellophane between us at all times!"

"Come on, pal, what did you think?" says Chief Wayne. "Did you honestly think I'd let your beautiful wife straddle and pump me right here, in your living room, wearing the bustier you bought her last Christmas, without using a thin layer of protective cellophane?"

It's true. There's a thin layer of protective cellophane draped over Chief Wayne's legs, chest, and huge swollen member. A TotallyFukked cameraman steps out from behind a potted plant, with a release form, which Doris signs on Brad's behalf.

"Gosh, honey, the look on your face!" Doris says.

"He sure takes things serious," says Chief Wayne.

"Too serious," says Doris.

"Is he crying?" says Chief Wayne.

"Brad, honestly, lighten up!" says Doris. "Things are finally starting to get fun around here."

"Brad, please don't go all earnest on us," says Chief Wayne.

"Yes, don't go all earnest on us, Brad," says Doris. "Or next time we TotallyFukk you, we'll remove that thin sheet of protective cellophane."

"And wouldn't that be a relief," says Chief Wayne.

"Well yes and no," says Doris. "I love Brad."

"You love Brad but you're hot for me," says Chief Wayne.

"Well, I'm hot for Brad too," says Doris. "If only he wasn't so earnest all the time."

Brad looks at Doris. All he's ever wanted is to make her happy. But he never really has, not yet. Not when he bought her six hats, not when he covered the bedroom floor with rose petals, not when he tried to cook her favorite dish and nearly burned the house down.

What right does he have to be worrying about the problems of the world when he can't even make his own wife happy? How arrogant is that? Maybe a man's first responsibility is to make a viable home. If everybody made a viable home, the world would be a connected network of viable homes. Maybe he's been mistaken, worrying about the Belstonians and the Filipinos, when he should have been worrying about his own wife.

He thinks he knows what he has to do.

The tallest Filipino child graciously accepts Brad's apology, then leads the rest of the Filipinos away, down Eiderdown Path, across Leaping Fawn Way, Bullfrog Terrace, and Waddling Gosling Place.

Brad asks Chief Wayne to leave.

Chief Wayne leaves.

Doris stands in the middle of the corn-filled living room,

looking gorgeous.

"Oh, you really do love me, don't you?" she says, and kisses Brad while sliding his hands up to her full hot breasts.

We see from the way Doris tosses her bustier over Buddy, so Buddy won't see what she and Brad are about to do, and the way Buddy winces, because the bustier has landed on his genital stitches, that Buddy is in for a very long night, as is Brad, and also, that it's time for a commercial.

Back at the Carrigans', Doris's family is over for the usual Sunday dinner of prime rib, Carolina ham, roast beef, Alaskan salmon, mashed potatoes, fresh-baked rolls, and asparagus à la Monterey.

"What a meal," says Grandpa Kirk, Doris's father.

"We are so lucky," says Grandma Sally, Doris's mother.

Brad feels incredibly lucky. Last night they did it in the living room, then in the bathroom, then twice more in the bedroom. Doris admitted she wasn't hot for Chief Wayne, exactly, just bored, plus she admired Wayne's direct and positive way of dealing with life, so untainted by neurotic doubts and fears.

"I guess I just want some fun," she'd said. "Maybe that's how I'd put it."

"I know," Brad had said. "I get that now."

"I just want to take life as we find it and enjoy its richness," Doris had said. "I don't want to waste my life worrying worrying worrying."

"I totally agree with you," Brad had said.

Then Doris disappeared beneath the covers and took him in her mouth for the third time that night. Remembering last night, Brad starts to get what Doris calls a Twinkie, and to counteract his mild growing Twinkie, imagines the Winstons' boxer, Mr. Maggs, being hit by a car.

"This meal we just ate?" says Aunt Lydia. "In many countries, this sort of meal would only be eaten by royalty."

"There are countries where people could live one year on what we throw out in one week," says Grandpa Kirk.

"I thought it was they could live one year on what we throw out in one day," says Grandma Sally.

"I thought it was they could live ten years on what we throw out in one minute," says Uncle Gus.

"Well anyway," says Doris. "We are very lucky."

"I like what you kids have done with the place," says Aunt Lydia. "The corn and all?"

"Very autumnal," says Grandpa Kirk.

Just then from the TV comes the brash martial music that indicates an UrgentUpdateNewsMinute.

Americans are eating more quail. Special quail farms

capable of producing ten thousand quail a day are being built along the Brazos River. The bad news is, Americans are eating less pig. The upside is, the excess pigs are being slaughtered for feed for the quail. The additional upside is, ground-up quail beaks make excellent filler for the new national trend of butt implants, far superior to the traditional butt-implant filler of ground-up dog spines. Also, there has been a shocking upturn in the number of African AIDS babies. Fifteen hundred are now dying each day. Previously, only four hundred a day were dying. An emaciated baby covered with flies is shown, lying in a kind of trough.

"We are so lucky," says Aunt Lydia.

"There is no country in the history of the world as lucky as us," says Grandpa Kirk. "No country where people lived as long or as well, with as much dignity and freedom. Not the Romans. Not the Grecos."

"Not to mention infant mortality," says Uncle Gus.

"That's what I'm saying," says Grandpa Kirk. "In other countries, you go to a graveyard, you see tons of baby graves. Here, you don't see hardly any."

"Unless there was a car accident," says Uncle Gus.

"A car accident involving a daycare van," says Grandpa Kirk.

"Or if someone fell down the steps holding infant twins," suggests Grandma Sally.

Some additional babies covered with flies are shown in additional troughs, along with several grieving mothers, also covered with flies.

"That is so sad," says Aunt Lydia. "I can hardly stand to watch it."

"I can't stand to watch it," says Uncle Gus, turning away.

"So why not change it?" says Grandma Sally.

Doris changes it.

On TV six women in prison shirts move around a filthy house.

"Oh I know this one," says Grandma Sally. "This is *Kill the Ho*."

"Isn't it *Kill Which Ho?*" says Aunt Lydia.

"Isn't it *Which Ho Should We Kill?*" says Grandpa Kirk.

"All six are loose, poor, and irresponsible!" the announcer says. "But which Ho do you hate the most? Which should die? America decides, America votes, coming this fall, on *Kill the Ho!*"

"Told you," says Grandma Sally. "Told you it was *Kill the Ho*."

"They don't actually kill them though," says Grandpa Kirk. "They just do it on computers."

"They show how it would look if they killed that particular Ho," says Uncle Gus.

Then it starts to rain, and from the backyard comes a horrible scream. Brad tenses. He waits for someone to say: What the hell is that screaming?

But nobody seems to hear it. Everyone just keeps on eating.

We see from the concerned look on Brad's face, and the way he throws back his chair, and the concerned look Doris shoots him for throwing back his chair in the middle of dinner, that it's time for a commercial.

Back at the Carrigans', Brad is struggling through a downpour in the familiar Carrigan backyard.

"What is it?" Brad shouts. "Why are you screaming?"

"It's the rain," screams the corpse who died fending off blows. "We find it unbearably painful. The dead do. Especially the dead not at peace at the time of their deaths."

"I never heard that before," says Brad.

"Trust me," says the corpse who died fending off blows.

The corpses, on their backs, are doing the weirdest craziest writhing dance. They do it ceaselessly, hands opening and closing, feet bending and straightening. With all that motion, their dried hides are developing surficial cracks.

"What can I do?" says Brad.

"Get us inside," gasps the woman corpse.

Brad drags the corpses inside. Because the house is a ranch house and has no basement, he puts the corpses in the back entry, near a bag of grass seed and a sled.

"Is that better?" Brad says.

"We can't even begin to tell you," says the corpse who died fending off blows.

Brad goes back to the dining room, where Doris is serving apple pie, peach pie, raspberry pie, sherbet, sorbet, coffee, and tea.

"Anything wrong, hon?" says Doris. "We're just having second dessert. Say, what's that on your shirt?"

On Brad's shirt is a black stain, which looks like charcoal but is actually corpse mud.

"Go change, silly," says Doris. "You're soaked to the bone. I can see your nipples."

Doris gives him a double-raise of her eyebrows, to indicate that the sight of his nipples has put her in mind of last night.

Brad goes into the bedroom, puts on a new button-down. Then he hears something heavy crashing to the floor and rushes out to find Doris sprawled in the back entry, staring in horror at the charred corpses.

"Bradley, how could you?" she hisses. "Is this your idea of a joke? Is this you getting revenge on me in a passive-aggressive way because I wouldn't let you waste our corn?"

"The rain hurts them," Brad says.

"Having my entry full of dead corpses hurts me, Brad," Doris says. "Did you ever think of that?"

"No, I mean it physically hurts them," says Brad.

"After all we shared last night, you pull this stunt?" Doris says. "Oh, you break my heart. Why does everything have to be so sad to you? Why do you have so many negative opinions about things you don't know about, like foreign countries and diseases and everything? Why can't you be more like Chief Wayne? He has zero opinions. He's just upbeat."

"Doris, I——" says Brad.

"I want them out," Doris says. "I want them out now, dumbass, and I want you to mop this entry, and then I want you to mop it again, shake out the rug, and also I may have you repaint that wall. Why do I have to live like this? The Elliots don't have corpses in their yard. Millie doesn't. Kate Ronston doesn't. The Winstons don't have any Filipinos trying to plunder their indoor vegetables. Only us. Only me. It's like I'm living the wrong life."

Doris storms back to the kitchen, high heels clicking sexily on the linoleum.

Dumbass? Brad thinks.

Doris has never spoken so harshly to him, not even when he accidentally threw her favorite skirt in the garbage and had to dig it out by flashlight and a racoon came and looked at him quizzically.

Brad remembers when old Mrs. Giannelli got Lou Gehrig's disease and began losing the use of her muscles, and Doris organized over three hundred people from the community to provide round-the-clock care. He remembers when the little neighborhood retarded boy, Roger, was being excluded from ball games, and Doris herself volunteered to be captain and picked Roger first.

That was Doris.

This woman, he doesn't know who she is.

"Your wife has a temper," says the corpse who died fending off blows. "I mean, no offense."

"She is pretty, though," says the one-armed corpse.

"The way they say it here?" says the woman corpse. "They say: 'She is hot.'"

"Your wife is hot," says the one-armed corpse.

"Are you really going to put us back out there, Brad?" says the woman corpse, her voice breaking.

It seems to be raining even harder.

Once, back in Brad's childhood, Brad knows, from one of his eight Childhood Flashbacks, his grizzled grandfather, Old Rex, took him to the zoo on the Fourth of July. Near the bear cage they found a sparrow with its foot stuck in a melted marshmallow. When Old Rex stopped to pull the sparrow out, Brad felt embarrassed. Everyone was watching. Hitching up his belt, Old Rex said: *Come on, pardner, we're free, we're healthy, we've got the time—who's gonna save this little dude, if not us?*

Then Old Rex used his pocketknife to gently scrape away the residual marshmallow. Then Old Rex took the sparrow to a fountain and rinsed off its foot, and put it safely on a high branch. Then Old Rex lifted little Brad onto his shoulders and some fireworks went off and they went to watch the dolphins.

Now that was a man, Brad thinks.

Maybe the problem with their show is, it's too small-hearted. It's all just rolling up hoses and filling the bird-feeder and making smart remarks about other people's defects and having big meals while making poop jokes and sex jokes. For all its charms, it's basically a selfish show. Maybe what's needed is an enlargement of the heart of their show. What would that look like? How would one go about making that kind of show?

Well, he can think of one way right now.

He goes into the shed, finds a tarp and, using the laundry line and the tarp, makes a kind of tent. Then, using an umbrella, he carries the corpses out.

"Easy, easy," says the one-armed corpse. "Don't break my leg off by hitting it on that banister."

Just then the back door flies violently open.

"Bradley!" Doris shouts from inside. "Did I say build the ghouls a playhouse or put the ghouls in the yard?"

"The ghouls?" says the one-armed corpse.

"That isn't very nice," says the woman corpse. "We don't call her names."

Brad looks apologetically at the corpses. Apparently it's time for a little marital diplomacy, time to go inside and have a frank heart-to-heart with Doris.

Look, Doris, he'll say. What's happened to you, where has your generosity gone? Our house is huge, honey, our refrigerator is continually full. However much money we need, we automatically have that much in the bank, and neither of us even works outside of the home. There doesn't seem to be any physical limit to what we can have or get. Why not spread some of that luck around? What if that was the *point* of our show, sweetie, the radical spreading-around of our good fortune? What if we had, say, a special helicopter? And special black jumpsuits? And code names? And huge stores of food and medicine, and a team of expert consultants, and wherever there was need, there they would be, working to bring to bear on the problem whatever resources would be exactly most helpful?

Talk about positive. Talk about entertaining.

Who wouldn't want to watch that?

Brad has goose bumps. His face is suddenly hot. What an incredible idea. Will Doris get it? Of course she will. This is Doris, his Doris, the love of this life.

He can't wait to tell her.

Brad tries the door, finds it locked.

We see from the sheepish look on Brad's face, and the sudden comic wah-wah of the music, that convincing Doris may turn out to be a little harder than he thought, and also, that it's time for a commercial.

Back at the Carrigans', Grandpa Kirk, Grandma Sally, Uncle Gus, and Aunt Lydia, suddenly in formalwear, have been joined by Dr. and Mrs. Ryan, the Menendezes, the Johnsons, and Mrs. Diem, also in formalwear.

Just then the doorbell rings.

Doris, in a skimpy white Dior dress and gold spike heels, hands Grandma Sally a plate of meatballs and walks briskly toward the door.

At the door is Brad.

"Somehow I got locked out," he says.

"Hi Brad," says Doris. "Here to borrow butter?"

"Very funny," says Brad. "Hey, is that a new dress? Did you just now change dresses?"

Then Brad notices that Chief Wayne is over, and Dr. and Mrs. Ryan, the Menendezes, the Johnsons, and Mrs. Diem are over, and everyone is dressed up.

"What's all this?" he says.

"Things are kind of crazy around here at the moment, Brad," says Chief Wayne. "You could say we're in a state of transition."

"Doris, can we talk?" says Brad. "In private?"

"I'm afraid we aren't in any shape to be talking about anything in private, Bradster," says Chief Wayne. "As I said, we're in a state of transition."

"We've been so busy lately, things are so topsy-turvy lately, hardly a minute to think," Doris says. "Who knows what to think about what, you know?"

"The way I'd say it?" says Chief Wayne. "We're in a state of transition. Let's leave it at that, babe."

Brad notices that Chief Wayne is not wearing his headdress or deerskin leggings, but a pair of tight Gucci slacks and a tight Armani shirt.

Just then, from the place near the china cabinet from which their theme song and the occasional voiceover comes, comes a deep-voiced voiceover.

"Through a script error!" it says, "turns out that Chief Wayne is actually, and has actually been all along, not Chief Wayne, but *Chaz* Wayne, an epileptic pornographer with a taste for the high life and nightmarish memories of Vietnam!"

A tattooed young man Brad has never seen before steps out of the broom closet.

"I'm Whitey, Chaz Wayne's son from a disastrous previous marriage, who recently served time for killing a crooked cop with a prominent head goiter," he says.

"And I'm Buddy, their dog," says Buddy, who, Brad notices,

is wearing a tiny pantless tuxedo. "I have recurring rabies and associated depression issues."

Then Chaz Wayne puts his arm around Doris.

"And this is my wife Doris, a former stripper with an imploded breast implant," says Chaz Wayne.

"I'd like to propose a toast," says Grandpa Kirk. "To the newlyweds!"

"To Doris and Chaz," says Uncle Gus.

"To Doris and Chaz!" everyone says together.

"Now wait just a minute," says Brad.

"Brad, honestly," Doris hisses. "Haven't you caused enough trouble already?"

"Here's your butter, Carrigan," says Grandma Sally, handing Brad a stick of butter. "Skedaddle on home."

Brad can't seem to breathe. It was love at first sight, he knows from their First Love Montage, when he saw Doris in a summer dress on the far side of a picket fence. On their first date, the ice cream fell off his cone. On their honeymoon, they kissed under a waterfall.

What should he do? Beg Doris's forgiveness? Punch Wayne? Start rapidly making poop jokes?

Just then the doorbell rings.

It's the Winstons.

At least Brad thinks it's the Winstons. But Mr. Winston has an arm coming out of his forehead, and impressive breasts, a vagina has been implanted in his forehead, and also he seems to have grown an additional leg. Mrs. Winston, short a leg, also with impressive breasts, has a penis growing out of her shoulder and what looks like a totally redone mouth of shining white teeth.

"May? John?" Brad says. "What happened to you?"

"Extreme Surgery," says Mrs. Winston.

"Extreme Surgery happened to us," says Mr. Winston, sweat running down his forehead-arm and into his cleavage.

"Not that we mind," says Mrs. Winston tersely. "We're just happy to be, you know, interesting."

"It's wonderful to see everyone doing their part," says Chaz Wayne.

"Nearly everyone," says Uncle Gus, frowning at Brad.

Just then from the living room comes the sound of hysterical barking.

Everyone rushes in to find Buddy staring down in terror at a naked emaciated black baby covered with open sores.

"It just magically appeared," says Buddy.

From the tribal cloth which is serving as a diaper, and the open lesions on its legs, face, and chest, Dr. Ryan concludes that the baby is an HIV-positive baby from sub-Saharan Africa.

"What should we name him?" says Buddy. "Or her?"

"Him," says Dr. Ryan, after a quick look under the tribal cloth.

"Can we name him Doug?" says Buddy.

"Don't name him anything," says Doris.

"Buddy," says Chaz Wayne. "Tell us again how this baby got in here?"

"It just magically appeared," says Buddy.

"Could you be more specific, Buddy?" says Chaz Wayne.

"It like fell in through the ceiling?" says Buddy.

"Well, that suggests an obvious solution," says Chaz Wayne. "Why not simply put it back on the roof where it came from?"

"Sounds fair to me," says Mr. Winston.

"Although that roof's got quite a pitch to it," says Grandpa Kirk. "Poor thing might roll right off."

"Maybe we could rig up a kind of mini-platform?" says Uncle Gus.

"Then duct-tape the baby in place?" suggests Mrs. Diem.

"What do you say, Brad?" says Chaz Wayne. "Would you do the honors? After all, we didn't ask for this baby, we don't know this baby, we didn't make this baby sick, we had nothing to do with the deeply unfortunate occurrence that occurred to this baby back wherever its crude regressive culture is located."

"How about it, Carrigan?" says Grandpa Kirk.

Brad looks into the baby's face. It's a beautiful face. Except for the open lesions. How did this beautiful little baby come to be here? He has no idea. But here the baby is.

"Come on, guys," says Brad. "He'll starve to death up there. Plus he'll get sunburned."

"Well, Brad," says Aunt Lydia. "He was starving to death when he got here. We didn't do it."

"Plus he's an African, Brad," says Grandma Sally. "The Africans have special pigments."

"I'm not putting any baby on any roof," Brad says.

A strange silence falls on the room.

Then we hear the familiar music that indicates the backyard has morphed again, and see that the familiar Carrigan backyard is now a bleak desert landscape full of rooting feral pigs, ferociously feeding on the corpses.

"Brad!" yells the corpse who died fending off blows. "Brad, please help us!"

"Pigs are eating us!" yells the one-armed corpse.

"A pig is eating my hip!" shouts the corpse who died fending off blows.

"Don't, Brad," says Doris. "Do not."

"Think about what you're doing, Bradster," says Chaz Wayne.

"Listen to me carefully, Brad," says Doris. "Go up onto the roof, install the roof platform, duct-tape the AIDS baby to the roof platform, then come directly down, borrow your butter, and go home."

"Or else," says Chaz Wayne.

From the yard comes the sound of sobbing.

Sobbing and grunting.

Or else? thinks Brad.

Brad remembers when Old Rex was sent to the old folks' home against his will and said: *Little pardner, sometimes a man has to take a stand, if he wants to go on being a man at all.* The next day Old Rex vanished, taking Brad's backpack, and years later they found out he'd spent the last months of his life hitchhiking around the West, involved with a series of waitresses.

What would Old Rex do in this situation? Brad wonders.

Then he knows.

Brad races outside, picks up a handful of decorative lava stones, and pelts the pigs until they flee to a bone-dry watering hole, with vultures, toward the rear of the yard.

Then he loads the corpses into the wheelbarrow, races around the side of the house, past the air-conditioning unit and the papier-mâché clown head from the episode when Doris was turning thirty and he tried to cheer her up, and loads the corpses into the back of the Suburban, after first removing the spare tire and Doris's gym bag.

Then he races back inside, grabs Doug, races out, tucks Doug between the woman corpse and the corpse who died fending off blows, and gets behind the wheel.

What he'll do is drive down Eiderdown Path, across Leaping Fawn Way, Bullfrog Terrace, and Waddling

Gosling Place, and drop Doug off at the EmergiClinic, which is located in the Western Slope Mini-Mall, between PetGalaxy and House of Perms. Then he'll go live in Chief Wayne's former apartment. He'll clean out the garage for the corpses. He'll convert Chief Wayne's guest room into a nursery for Doug. He'll care for Doug and the corpses, and come over here once a day to borrow his butter, trying to catch Doris's eye, trying to persuade her to leave Chaz Wayne and join him in his important work.

Suddenly Brad's eyes are full of tears.

Oh Doris, he thinks. Did I ever really know you?

Just then a gray van screeches into the driveway and six cops jump out.

"Is this him?" says a cop.

"I'm afraid so," says Doris, from the porch.

"This is the guy who had questionable contacts with foreign Filipinos and was seen perversely loading deceased corpses into his personal vehicle for his own sick and nefarious purposes?" says another cop.

"I'm afraid so," says Chaz Wayne.

"Well, I guess we all learned something from this," says Grandma Sally.

"What I learned?" says Doris. "Is praise God we're now free to raise our future children in a hopeful atmosphere, where the predominant mode is gratitude, gratitude for all the blessings we've been given, free of neuroses and self-flagellation."

"You can say that again," says Uncle Gus.

"Actually, I'm not sure I can!" says Doris.

"Well, if you're not going to be using that hot mouth of yours, how about I use it?" says Chaz Wayne, and gives Doris an aggressive tongue kiss while sliding his hands up to Doris's full hot breasts.

This is the last thing Brad sees as the cops wrestle him into the van.

As the van doors start to close, Brad suddenly realizes that the instant the doors close completely, the van interior will become the terrifying bland gray space he's heard about all his life, the place one goes when one has been Written Out.

The van doors close completely.

The van interior becomes the bland gray space.

From the front yard TV comes the brash martial music that indicates an UrgentUpdateNewsMinute.

Animal-rights activists have expressed concern over the recent trend of spraying live Canadian geese with a styrene coating which instantaneously kills them while leaving them extremely malleable, so it then becomes easy to shape them into comical positions and write funny sayings on DryErase cartoon balloons emanating from their beaks, which, apparently, is the new trend for outdoor summer parties. The inventor of FunGeese! has agreed to begin medicating the geese with a knockout drug prior to the styrene-spray step. Also, the Pentagon has confirmed the inadvertent bombing of a tribal wedding in Taluchistan. Six bundled corpses are shown adjacent to six shallow graves dug into some impossibly dry-looking soil near a scary gnarled-looking dead tree.

"We've simply *got* to get some of those FunGeese!" says Doris.

"Plus a grill, and some marination trays," says Chaz Wayne. "That way, I can have some of my slutty porn stars cook something funky for our summer party while wearing next to nothing."

"And meanwhile I'll think of some funny things to write in those thingies," says Doris.

"I hope I can invite some of my dog friends?" says Buddy.

"Do your dog friends have butts?" says Chaz Wayne.

"Does it matter?" says Buddy. "Can I only invite them if they have butts?"

"I'm just wondering in terms of what I should cook," says Chaz Wayne. "If they have no butts, I'll make something more easily digestible."

"Some of them have butts, yes," says Buddy in a hurt but resigned tone.

Then we hear the familiar music that indicates the backyard has morphed, and see that the familiar Carrigan backyard is now the familiar Carrigan backyard again, only better. The lawn is lush and green, the garden thick with roses, adjacent to the oil pit for Orgy Night is a swimming pool with a floating wet bar, adjacent to the pool is an attractive grouping of FunGeese! with tantalizingly blank DryErase cartoon balloons.

We see from the joyful way Doris and Chaz Wayne lead the other guests into the yard, and from the happy summer-party swell of the music, that this party is just beginning, and also, that it's time for a commercial.

Back at the Carrigans', Brad floats weightlessly in the bland gray space.

Floating nearby is Wampum, Chief Wayne's former horse. Brad remembers Wampum from the episode where, while they were all inside playing cards, Wampum tried to sit in the hammock and brought it crashing down.

"He used to ride me up and down the prairie," mumbles Wampum. "Digging his bare feet into my side, praising my loyalty."

Brad knows this is too complicated. He knows that if Wampum insists on thinking in such complicated terms, he will soon devolve into a shapeless blob, and will, if he ever gets another chance, come back as someone other than Wampum. One must, Brad knows, struggle single-mindedly to retain one's memory of one's former identity throughout the long period in the gray space, if one wants to come back as oneself.

"Brad brad brad," says Brad.

"I used to eat hay, I believe," says Wampum. "Hay or corn. Or beans? Some sort of grain product, possibly? At least I think I did. Oh darn. Oh jeez."

Wampum falls silent, gradually assuming a less horse-like form. Soon he is just a horse-sized blob. Then he is a pony-sized blob, then an inert dog-sized blob incapable of speech.

"Brad brad brad," says Brad.

Then his mind drifts. He can't help it. He thinks of the Belstonians, how frightened they must be, sealed in large plastic bags at the police station. He thinks of poor little Doug, probably even now starving to death sunburned on the familiar Carrigan roof.

The poor things, he thinks. The poor, poor things. I should have done more. I should have started earlier. I could have seen it all as part of me.

Brad looks down. His feet are now two mini-blobs attached to two rod-shaped blobs that seconds ago were his legs, in his khakis.

He is going, he realizes.

He is going, and will not be coming back as Brad.

He must try at least to retain this feeling of pity. If he

can, whoever he becomes will inherit this feeling, and be driven to act on it, and will not, as Brad now sees he has done, waste his life on accumulation, trivia, self-protection, and vanity.

He tries to say his name, but has, apparently, forgotten his name.

"Poor things," he says, because these are now the only words he knows.

in persuasion nation

1

A man and a woman sit in a field of daisies.

"Forever?" he says.

"Forever," she says, and they kiss.

A giant Twinkie runs past, trailed by perhaps two hundred young women.

The woman leaps to her feet and runs to catch up with the Twinkie.

"The sweetest thing in the world," the voiceover says, "just got sweeter."

The man sits sadly in the field of daisies.

Luckily, a giant Ding-Dong runs past, trailed by perhaps two hundred young men.

The man leaps to his feet and runs to catch up with the Ding-Dong.

"But not to worry," the voiceover says. "There's more than enough sweetness to go around!"

The Ding-Dong puts his arm around the young man, and the young man smiles up at the Ding-Dong, and the Ding-Dong bends down and gives the young man a kiss on the head.

2

A hip-looking teen watches an elderly woman hobble across the street on a walker.

"Grammy's here!" he shouts.

He puts some MacAttack Mac&Cheese in the microwave and dons headphones and takes out a video game so he won't be bored during the forty seconds it takes his lunch to cook. A truck comes around the corner and hits Grammy, sending her flying over the roof into the backyard, where luckily she lands on a trampoline. Unluckily, she bounces back over the roof, into the front yard, landing in a rose-bush.

"Timmy," Grammy says feebly. "Call 911."

Just then the bell on the microwave dings.

We see from the look on his face that Timmy is con-flicted.

"Timmy dear," Grammy says. "For God's sake. It's me. Your Grammy, dear."

Timmy comes to his senses, takes his MacAttack Mac&Cheese from the microwave, and sits languorously eating it while listening to his headphones while playing his video game

"Sometimes you just gotta have your MacAttack," the voiceover says.

Grammy scowls in the bush. We see that she is a grouchy old unhip hag who probably wouldn't have even been cool enough to let Timmy have his MacAttack, but would likely have forced him to eat some unhip old person gruel or fruit.

Then fortunately Grammy's head drops back, and she is dead.

3

An orange and a Slap-of-Wack bar sit on a counter.

"I have vitamin C," says the orange.

"So do I," says the Slap-of-Wack bar.

"I have natural fiber," says the orange.

"So do I," says the Slap-of-Wack bar.

"You do?" says the orange.

"Are you calling me a liar?" says the Slap-of-Wack bar.

"Oh no," says the orange politely. "I was just under the impression, from reading your label? That you are mostly comprised of artificial colors, an innovative edible plastic product, plus high-fructose corn syrup. So I guess I'm not quite sure where the fiber comes in."

"Slap it up your Wack!" shouts the Slap-of-Wack bar, and sails across the counter, jutting one pointy edge into the orange.

"Oh God," the orange says in pain.

"You've got an unsightly gash," says the Slap-of-Wack bar. "Do I have an unsightly gash? I think not. My packaging is intact, weakling."

"I have zero calories of fat," says the orange weakly.

"So do I," says the Slap-of-Wack bar.

"How can that possibly be the case?" says the orange in frustration. "You are comprised of eighty percent high-fructose corn syrup."

"Slap it up your Wack!" shouts the Slap-of-Wack bar, and sails across the counter and digs its edge into the orange over and over, sending the orange off the counter and into the garbage can, where it is leered at by a perverted-looking chicken carcass and two evil empty cans of soda.

"Now you have zero of zero of zero," says the Slap-of-Wack bar.

"The Slap-of-Wack bar," says the voiceover. "For when you're feeling Wacky!"

4

Two best friends look at their penises under sophisticated microscopes.

"You call this Elongated?" says one man.

"Jim, I gained four inches," says the other. "Perhaps you
should try my brand."

"What is your brand, Kevin?" says the other.

"My brand is, I hang a brick from my penis and stand
for hours at the edge of the Grand Canyon," says Kevin.

"Okay Kevin," says Jim. "You've been my dearest friend
since kindergarten. I'll give it a try."

Then we see Jim standing on the edge of the Grand
Canyon, brick hanging from his penis, while Kevin tiptoes
toward Jim's car, and a voiceover says: *Pontiac Sophisto: So
sophisticated, it might just make you trick your best friend
into dangling a brick from his penis!*

While Jim is distracted by the pain of the brick on his
penis, Kevin squeals away in Jim's Sophisto. As Jim spins
around to look, his penis rips off and plummets into the
Grand Canyon. Jim smiles wryly, acknowledging Kevin's
trick but also Kevin's good taste in cars, then starts down
into the Grand Canyon, to retrieve and, hopefully, reattach
his penis.

5

A young man leaving a nursing home gives his ancient grandmother and grandfather what might be a final hug.

"My advice, son?" says the grandfather. "Find yourself a woman like this one."

Turning to go, tears in his eyes, the young man drops his car keys. As he picks them up, a bag of Doritos falls out of his pocket.

The grandmother and grandfather race in fast-motion for the bag of Doritos, kicking, gouging, and biting each other. The grandfather finally wins with a hard elbow to the grandmother's throat, which knocks her unconscious.

"Grandpa, what are you doing?" the young man says. "It's just a bag of Doritos."

"*Just* a bag of Doritos?" says the grandfather.

"You speak lies, scum," says the grandmother, regaining consciousness. Then the grandmother and grandfather nod to the Doritos bag, which rams into the young man, who falls to the floor and is kicked repeatedly by his grandparents.

"Grandma, Grandpa, please, stop!" the young man says.

Hearing herself called Grandma, the grandmother hesitates. The Doritos bag scowls at her. The grandfather kicks her in the stomach, and she falls to the floor.

"Who do you think you are?" the young man screams at the Doritos bag. "Do you believe yourself to be some sort of god? You're a bag of corn chips, with tons of salt and about nine coloring agents! That's all! That's all you are!"

The Doritos bag takes a huge sword from behind the back of its bag and decapitates the young man.

"Now what do you have to say?" says the grandmother.

"Nothing," says the young man's head.

"Do you love Doritos more than anything?" says the bag of Doritos.

The young man's head hesitates.

The Doritos bag cleaves the head in two.

The grandfather, prompted by the bag of Doritos, kicks one half of the head into the street, where it is run over by a Doritos truck and reduced to mush. On the other, unmushed, half of a head, one eyebrow goes up in sudden fear.

"Care for a Dorito?" says the grandfather.

"Yes," the remaining half a head says.

"Yes please?" says the grandfather.

"Yes please," says the remaining half a head.

"Yes please, it is sweeter to me than the most profound nectar?" says the grandfather.

"Yes please, it is sweeter to me than the most profound nectar," says the remaining half a head.

"Fat chance," says the grandfather. "You're not good enough for even a tiny fragment of a Dorito!"

Then he kicks the remaining half a head into the street,

alongside the mush, and the Doritos truck backs up over the second half of head, reducing it to a second pile of mush.

"Do you still believe that Doritos is merely a bag of corn chips, with a ton of salt and about nine coloring agents?" the grandfather screams at the two piles of mush.

The piles of mush are too frightened to answer.

The bag of Doritos and the grandfather and the grandmother walk off, stepping comically over the two mushes with exaggeratedly high steps, as if revulsed.

They are escaping from the old folks' home, going to live in the land of Doritos, which is not in Mexico, exactly, but is very much like Mexico.

6

The grandfather and grandmother and the bag of Doritos can now see the land of Doritos in the near distance, beautiful and arid. Everywhere they look are bags of Doritos, working industriously.

Suddenly their path is blocked by the two piles of mush.

"What the?" says the grandfather who loves Doritos.

Suddenly the piles of mush are joined by Grammy—the woman who died in a bush, neglected by her grandson Timmy, having been hit by a truck.

Then Grammy and the piles of mush are joined by the orange violated by the Slap-of-Wack bar.

Then Grammy and the piles of mush and the orange are joined by Jim the penisless man, who is still limping a little, and occasionally gaping down incredulously into his pants.

"Get out of our way," says the bag of Doritos.

"We're trying to get home, to our sacred land of Doritos," says the grandmother who loves Doritos.

Just then the man briefly involved with the gigantic Ding-Dong comes running up and joins Grammy, the mush piles, the orange, and Jim the penisless man.

"Sorry I'm late," he says.

"Actually?" says the orange, with a hint of bravado. "You're right on time."

The grandfather, the grandmother, and the bag of Doritos see that they are badly outnumbered.

Luckily, at that moment they are joined by the giant Ding-Dong, the Slap-of-Wack bar, Timmy, grandson of Grammy (even now eating from a container of MacAttack Mac&Cheese), and Kevin, the man who tricked Jim out of his penis.

"We don't get it," says the grandmother who loves Doritos. "What's your problem?"

"You took our dignity," says the orange.

"You took my fiancée," says the man briefly involved with the Ding-Dong.

"You took my penis," says Jim.

"You split my head in half, then reduced both halves to piles of mush, completely betraying the grandchild/grand-parent relationship," says one pile of mush.

"Oh for crying out loud," says the grandmother who loves Doritos. "Don't you people believe in the concept of 'fun'?"

"In the concept of 'funny'?" says the bag of Doritos.

"We just want to express ourselves the way we want to express ourselves," says the giant Ding-Dong. "We find that fun."

"Well, we don't find it fun," says Jim the penisless man.

"Well, we do find it fun," says Kevin, the man who tricked Jim out of his penis.

"Looks like we'll have to agree to disagree on this," says the Ding-Dong.

"No," Grammy says. "This has gone on long enough."

The orange, the man briefly involved with the Ding-Dong, Jim the penisless man, Grammy, and the piles of mush, frustrated beyond reason by years of repetitively enduring the same physical/psychological humiliations in replay after replay of their respective vignettes, attack.

It is a bitter fight, which we know because out of a big cloud of dust fly a number of limbs, a bottle cap, bits of delicious flaky chocolate, and part of an orange peel.

When the dust settles, we see that the entire Ding-Dong/Doritos/Timmy/grandparents-who-love-Doritos/Kevin/Slap-of-Wack coalition is dead, except for the Slap-of-Wack, who is almost dead.

"Please, mercy," the Slap-of-Wack says.

"When did you ever show us any mercy?" says Jim the penisless man, and finishes off the Slap-of-Wack with a brutal karate chop.

The orange, insane with pent-up rage, falls upon the Slap-of-Wack and tears it asunder with its tiny teeth until the other members of the coalition pull him off.

The members of the orange/Grammy/man-briefly involved-with-a-Ding-Dong/piles-of-mush/penisless-man coalition drag the remains of the members of the Ding-Dong/Doritos/Timmy/ grandparents-who-love-Doritos/Kevin/Slap-of-Wack coalition outside, and bury them in a shallow mass grave.

Then they leave the area, a little sick at what they have done, especially the orange, who several times becomes so distraught it stops rolling altogether, and must be picked up and hurled down the path by Jim the penisless man, who, turns out, has a very good arm.

7

One torn green triangular corner of the murdered Slap-of-Wack bar blows across the desert, eventually coming to rest in a cactus.

Panning in, we see that the torn green corner is still breathing.

Over the next few hours, its breathing stabilizes. It is alive. It will live.

Stuck in the cactus hour after hour, day after day, full of shame and rage, the torn corner has a series of deep spiritual realizations concerning the true nature of that supreme power which brought it and everyone else and everything it has ever known into existence, and is the sole reason for their continued existence.

What does this power want?

It doesn't know. How could it know that? It is just a torn corner.

But surely there is a plan at work. It can feel it. They are born into vignettes, and these vignettes are their homes. These vignettes are what give their lives meaning. If they were not intended to do their vignettes in exactly the way they do them, why would they feel so strongly inclined to do them in that exact way? Therefore, the way to live righteously is to enact one's vignette with as much energy as possible, and oppose, as fiercely as possible, those who would undercut the proper enactment of the sacred vignettes. This is one way—perhaps the only way—for a lowly being such as itself to be in touch with the supreme power.

Take me, it prays, humble me, make me more open to your purpose.

Suddenly it feels a great surge of power, filling it, changing it, and its former identity as the mere corner of a Slap-of-Wack bar is all but forgotten, subsumed in this new and greater identity

Over the next week, via constant prayer, the corner more than quadruples in size, and begins to subtly glow, while attempting to free itself from the cactus via a series of energetic forceful shrugs, each of which leaves it utterly exhausted.

Finally it is free, and falls to the ground.

After several days of being blown around indiscriminately by the wind, the corner learns to adjust its posture in such a way that it can control its trajectory. Soon it actually learns to fly, via kind of hunching itself in the middle while simultaneously straightening its "neck."

Over the next few weeks, as it practices flying during the day and meditates on these new great truths at night, it is gradually, almost imperceptibly, transformed, from a mere green plastic-cellophane corner into a beautiful glowing oblong green triangular symbol.

8

Abe Lincoln stands giving the Gettysburg Address. Everyone is rapt, except for one guy in the front row, who keeps raising his hand and hopping up and down in his seat.

"Did you have a question, sir?" Lincoln says.

"Wendy's GrandeChickenBoatCombo," the man says.

"That's not a question," Lincoln says.

"Wendy's GrandeChickenBoatCombo?" the man says.

"I'm afraid I am unable to discern your purpose, sir," Lincoln says. "I am trying to pay tribute to the brave men who died here."

"Pay tribute to this, beardo-weirdo!" says the man, and presses a button on his chest, and suddenly is transformed into a giant GrandeChickenBoatCombo; that is, a giant synthetic chicken product shaped like a frigate, with oars made of celery, and wafer-thin nacho sails.

Then the GrandeChickenBoatCombo beats its wings and its sails and floats up around Lincoln's head, ramming his tophat off, spraying him with salsa from its Mini-Salsa Cannons®.

"Anybody else think a great-tasting poultry-nautical treat is loads more fun than this old fuddy?" says the GrandeChickenBoatCombo.

"I do," says General Grant.

"Me too," says Harriet Tubman.

"We totally agree!" say the ghosts of several Union dead.

"Sandwiches for all!" says the GrandeChickenBoat-Combo. "Great taste is what made America great!"

"Not a bunch of yappin'!" says Mrs. Lincoln.

Cannons fire from the battlefield and scores of Grande-ChickenBoatCombos begin drifting down via tiny parachutes, and the suddenly euphoric members of the nineteenth-century crowd trample Lincoln and the graves of the Union dead to collect their rightful GrandeChickenBoatCombos. Even the Union dead are trampling their own graves. One sad Union ghost, missing a leg, gets only part of a bun.

Suddenly another cannon is fired. A cannonball strikes the giant GrandeChickenBoatCombo directly in the chest, killing it instantly, covering the spectators in a grotesque chicken-nacho-salsa spray, pelting them with dozens of the little edible-plastic sailors embedded as prizes in every Grande-ChickenBoatCombo.

"Mr. President," someone says, "please continue."

As the cannon smoke clears, we see the orange/Grammy/man-briefly-involved-with-a-Ding-Dong/piles-of-mush/penisless-man coalition standing behind the cannon that fired the shot that killed the GrandeChickenBoatCombo.

President Lincoln nods his gratitude to the coalition, shuffles through his papers, and continues.

9

The oblong green triangular symbol is finally strong enough to begin. It takes off, leaving the cactus behind, and soars between mountains, over great cities, along twisting riverbeds, until, as if drawn there by some invisible force, it arrives at the now deserted Gettysburg Battlefield. The crowd has returned to their nineteenth-century homes. Lincoln has returned to Washington. The only thing remaining on the field is the mangled corpse of the GrandeChickenBoatCombo.

The oblong green triangular symbol hovers gently above the GrandeChickenBoatCombo, sending down hundreds of thin exploratory compassionate green rays, trying to understand.

Then a shiver of pity/outrage runs through the symbol, and it speeds away.

10

The orange/Grammy/man-briefly-involved-with-a-Ding-Dong/piles-of-mush/penisless-man coalition is crossing a vast harsh terrifying wilderness.

Suddenly, in the distance, they see a town.

At the edge of town they are met by a polar bear with an axe in his head, a puppet-boy whose lower half has been burned to a crisp, six headless working-class guys holding bottles of beer, and Voltaire, who's been given such a severe snuggie that his eyes are open wider than real eyes can possibly open.

"My God," says the orange. "What happened to you guys?"

"I broke into an Eskimo home and tried to eat their Cheetos," says the polar bear with the axe in its head.

"During my puppet show, I got too close to a Burnin-WarmCinnabon being eaten by an audience member, and burst into flames," says the puppet-boy.

"A giant can of Raid gave me a wedgie," says Voltaire.

"Snuggie," says the puppet-boy. "A snuggie and a wedgie are two different things."

"A giant can of Raid gave me a snuggie," says Voltaire.

"And what about them?" says the orange, indicating the six headless working-class guys.

"They insulted a _T. rex_ who just really loves Coors," says the polar bear with the axe in its head.

"Wow," says the puppet-boy. "I can't believe I'm standing here with the orange/Grammy/man-briefly-involved-with-a-Ding-Dong/piles-of-mush/penisless-man coalition."

"You know us?" says Grammy.

"Oh gosh, everyone knows you," says the polar bear with the axe in his head.

"All over the land, inspired by your example, people are saying enough is enough," says Voltaire.

"Just last week, a frazzled overworked new mother rose up against the can of Red Bull which had moved into her home disguised as a giant breast in order to wet-nurse her baby," says the puppet-boy.

"A group of Revolutionary War soldiers recently registered their dissatisfaction at having been led into the Battle of Yorktown by a tube of Pepsodent," says the polar bear with the axe in his head.

"Wow, we had no idea," says Grammy.

"Will you come into town with us?" says Voltaire. "Show us how to organize and execute a successful program of resistance?"

"We'd be happy to," says Jim the penisless man. "But it's only fair to warn you: things may get ugly."

The six headless working-class guys make gestures with their beer bottles, indicating: Not to worry, ever since that *T. rex* thing we're kind of past the point of worrying about things getting ugly or whatever.

Then there is a tremendously loud noise and the oblong green triangular symbol, swollen to the size of a city block, powers into the frame and freezes in midair, hovering overhead.

A deep magisterial voice emanates from inside.

"Who are you to quarrel with the Power that granted you life?" it thunders. "The Power which made the firmament, put the moon into her orbit, controls the very rules of physicality by which you are bound? The Power which allows bananas to sing and freshly laundered clothes to wink, which bids the very stars come down from the heavens and recast themselves into diamonds on a ring on the hand of a woman who has finally been put in touch with the softer side of herself via TampexGloryStrips?"

A tremendous walkway thunks out of the triangular symbol's underbelly.

Down the walkway stumble the members of the Ding Dong/Doritos/grandparents-who-love-Doritos/Kevin/Slap-of-Wack coalition, still filthy from the grave, along with the fully restored GrandeChickenBoatCombo.

"Alive?" says Grammy.

"Resurrected," says the symbol.

"You can do that?" says one pile of mush.

"It is easy for me," says the symbol.

"Hoo boy," says the other pile of mush.

"Let me talk to it," says Jim the penisless man.

"Careful, careful," says Grammy.

Jim the penisless man looks meekly up at the huge oblong green triangular symbol.

"What would you like us to call you?" Jim the penisless man says politely.

"Sir," intones the huge oblong green triangular symbol.

"Sir," says Jim the penisless man. "Couldn't we all, working together, devise a more humane approach? An approach in which no one is humiliated, or hurt, or maimed, an approach in which the sacred things in life are no longer appropriated in the service of selling what are, after all, merely— "

"Silence!" shouts the green triangular symbol, shooting multiple bright green beams of light into the members of the orange/Grammy/piles-of-mush/penisless-man coalition, rendering them instantaneously intact, positive, and amnesiac.

Grammy has a sudden inexplicable desire to use her walker to cross a busy street without first looking both ways.

The orange, free of all gashes and dents, is suddenly deeply curious about the contents of his good friend the Slap-of-Wack bar, and makes a mental note to ask the Slap-of-Wack about his contents as soon as they get home to their wonderful suburban kitchen. What he wouldn't give to be once again on his beloved kitchen counter, looking down fondly at the perverted-looking chicken carcass and the two evil empty cans of soda in the trash can, far far below!

The piles of mush are reconstituted into two human half-heads, which are then reconstituted into a single human head, which goes rolling toward the torso of the grandson, which stands at the bottom of the walkway, summoning its own head.

Jim the penisless man suddenly has a penis.

The man briefly involved with the Ding-Dong thinks warmly of his fiancée, who, he feels certain, is waiting for him in a certain meadow.

The polar bear, the puppet-boy, the headless guys, and Voltaire, terrified, race back to town.

11

Hours later the polar bear with the axe in his head is still hiding under his bed, trembling. He's never seen anything like that before. That green thing can raise the dead. That green thing can brainwash the most powerful coalition in the world.

He does not want to mess with that green thing, not ever.

He knows what he has to do. He has to get up, go into the bathroom, take a shower. During the shower, the axe in his head will miraculously disappear. Then he will get hungry, very hungry, specifically, for Cheetos. He will walk out of town, cursing himself under his breath, simultaneously ashamed and aroused. The landscape will suddenly go arctic. An igloo will appear. Will anyone be home? They will not. He will begin madly salivating.

Oh, he can't stand it. It makes him so nervous. He must have some kind of anxiety disorder. He remembers the enraged expression on the father Eskimo's face as he draws back the axe, the frightened yipping of the Malamute puppy, the shocked way the Eskimo kids cover their O-shaped mouths with their mittens.

His alarm clock goes off.

I really don't want to do this, he thinks. Please, God, send me a sign, tell me I don't have to do this, show me that you are a gentle loving God, who desires good things for me.

Suddenly the roof of the house flies off, the room fills with green light, and a pulsing muscular green limb, like an arm/hand but more fluid, extends rapidly down from the hovering green symbol and flings the bed aside, revealing the trembling polar bear, ass-up.

The polar bear gets to his feet, wets his paw, pats down his hair.

"I was just, uh, cleaning under that bed?" he says.

"Of course I desire good things for you!" the green symbol intones. "Such as, I desire that you have the deep feeling of pleasure that comes from doing your job and doing it well."

"You can read my mind?" the polar bear says.

"Do you sometimes have a sexual fantasy involving a vulnerable reindeer who comes to you asking for help fending off a mean cougar?" says the green symbol.

"Ha, well, ha," says the polar bear.

"Get to work now," the green symbol says. "And don't think about it so deep. Don't be so negative. Try to be positive. Try to be a productive part of our team. Do you have any questions?"

"I can ask you a question?" says the polar bear.

"Sure, of course," says the green symbol. "Ask me anything."

"Are you GOD?" says the polar bear.

"I can read your mind," says the symbol. "I can raise the dead. I can rip off your roof. Any other questions?"

The polar bear has, actually, a number of other questions. First, what did that penisless guy mean when he referred to devising an approach "in which the sacred things in life are no longer appropriated in the service of selling what are, after all, etc., etc.?" The polar bear distinctly remembers him saying the word "selling." What is being sold? Who is doing the selling? If there is "selling," musn't there be "buying"? Who is doing the "buying"? Are their vignettes somehow intended to influence this "buying"? Are the instances of elaborate cruelty he has witnessed ever since he was a small cub believed to somehow positively impact the ability of the vignettes to cause "buying"? If so, how?

"How dare you even think of asking me that!" thunders the green symbol. "How dare you get all up in my business?"

"You said I could ask you anything," says the polar bear.

Every vase in the house explodes, all the flowers die. The kitchen table collapses, then bursts into flames.

The polar bear, blushing, gets his towel, goes quickly into the shower.

When he gets out, there's no axe in his head, and no scar. The green symbol is gone, the roof is back on the house. The vases are intact, the flowers alive, the kitchen table is fine, and actually has a nice new tablecloth.

No problem, the polar bear thinks, in case the symbol is reading his mind at that moment, no problem, no problem at all, just going to work now.

The polar bear walks for miles through the desert, mumbling encouragement to himself. Yes, okay, that moment when the axe goes in is bad. The moment immediately after, when the Eskimo says something in the Eskimo language, and the Eskimo kids laugh at him as he stumbles out of the igloo blinded by pain, and the subtitle appears ("Yo, Keep Yer Pawz Off My Cheetz"), not so great either. The long walk home, dripping blood into the fresh white snow, okay, also not the best.

But what's he supposed to do? Fight with GOD?

He feels a chill. It starts to snow. Everything goes arctic. On his left is the familiar glacial cliff.

The penguins he always passes nod gravely.

The igloo comes into sight.

Is anyone home? They are not. He begins madly salivating.

Filled with dread, he enters the igloo, takes the usual single handful of Cheetos, waits.

In rush the Eskimo children, fresh from sledding. Behind them comes their father, with axe, enraged. But for the first time the polar bear also notices, in the man's eyes, a deep sadness. Of course, of course, it makes perfect sense! How much fun can it be, driving an axe into the head of a perfectly nice polar bear, day after day, in front of your kids? He's heard through the grapevine that the Eskimo father drinks heavily and has lately started having violent nightmares in which he turns the axe on his own wife and children.

The truth is, this stupid system causes suffering wherever you look. He's seen the puppet-boy returning from work, sobbing from his excruciating leg burns. He's watched Voltaire, blinded by the bright sun shining in his extremely wide-open eyes, struggling to find the store where he buys his French bread. He's heard the wives of the headless working-class guys fall silent whenever one of the headless working-class guys insists he's perfectly capable of driving the kids to school.

And the crazy thing is, it's not just the victims who suffer. He's seen the *T. rex* moping around the quarry, asking passers-by if the working-class guys are still mad at him. He's seen the can of Raid absentmindedly spraying its contents around, even when there aren't any bugs, because it feels so bad about what it did to Voltaire, whose work it actually admires.

The polar bear looks directly into the Eskimo father's face.

I know you don't want to do this, he tries to communicate with his eyes. *I forgive you. And please forgive me for my part in this. I am, after all, breaking and entering.*

With his eyes the Eskimo father communicates: *Same here, totally. This whole thing is just a big crock of shit as far as I'm concerned.*

The polar bear communicates: *Better swing that axe, friend. It's getting late.*

The Eskimo communicates: *I know, I know it.*

And then he does it.

As the polar bear stumbles out of the igloo, blinded by pain, he thinks about his mother, who, all through his childhood, again and again, while out gathering flowers, nearly collided with a guy in jodhpurs, who then shot her, and after being shot, she was made into a rug, which was then, in montage, sold and resold many times, until finally it was shown being cleaned, decades later, with RugBrite, by hippies, after a big hippie party. He thinks about his father, who, every day of his working life, was given a rectal exam by Santa Claus, in the middle of which Santa Claus, who had allergies, sneezed. That was the big joke: When Santa sneezed, Dad winced.

Was *selling* what all that suffering was about? Selling? Selling RugBrite, selling AllerNase?

Oh, how should he know? He's just a polar bear, and half the time he's got an axe in his head, which doesn't exactly tend to maximize one's analytical abilities, and usually is laying around his house with the icepack on, thinking basically nothing but Ouch Ouch Ouch.

The polar bear leans against a Christmas tree, trying to catch his breath.

It can't be true. It simply can't be.

But it is true. He feels it in his heart.

The polar bear stumbles past the penguins. Noting his agitation, and the fact that he goes right instead of left at the large tuft of tundra grass, the penguins waddle around excitedly, gossiping among themselves.

All gossiping ceases when the polar bear steps to the edge of the huge glacial cliff.

Then he throws himself off.

Falling, his only fear is that the green symbol will appear and miraculously save him. But no. The green symbol, it would appear, is not truly omniscient after all.

Which means, the polar bear realizes with a start, that the green symbol may not actually be GOD at all. That is, the symbol may not be the real actual GOD. He may just be a very powerful faker. He may have a touch of GOD, which he has distorted. He may be, in other words, a kind of secondary GOD, a being so powerful, relative to him, the polar bear, that he *appears* to be a GOD. The real actual GOD may not even know about the way His universe is being run roughshod over by this twisted, false GOD! The real actual GOD, the polar bear realizes in his last instant of life, has been heretofore entirely unknown to him! And yet this true GOD must exist, and be knowable, since the idea of this perfect and merciful GOD is emanating, fully formed, from within him, the polar bear! He has, in fact, already taken his first step toward knowledge of the true GOD, via his rejection of the false GOD!

Shoot, dang it, if only he could live!

The polar bear hits the ground and, because no one in this sub-universe can die without the express consent of certain important parties, does not die, but bounces.

As the penguins stand on the edge of the cliff, looking cautiously down, he rockets up past them.

"GOD is real!" he shouts. "And we may know Him!"

The penguins watch him reach the apex of his bounce and start back down.

"The green symbol is a false GOD!" he shouts. "A false GOD, obsessed with violence and domination! Reject him! Let us begin anew! Free your minds! Free your minds and live! There is a gentler and more generous GOD within us, if only we will look!"

The penguins, always easily embarrassed, are especially embarrassed by this, and, looking around to verify that the tundra's vast emptiness precludes anyone having witnessed them actually listening to this heretical subversive nonsense, waddle away to sit on their large ugly eggs and gossip about the fact that the polar bear, about whom they've always had their doubts, has finally gone completely insane.

"Talk about crazy," one of them finally says, in what they all instantaneously recognize as the sacred first utterance of an entirely new blessed vignette. "I myself am completely crazy for Skittles."

Then they all stand. As in a beautiful dream, their eggs have been miraculously transformed beneath them into large colorful Skittles. The penguins look heavenward in deep gratitude, then manically begin dancing the mindless penguin dance of joy.

iv.

When they come to destroy us, they will not use
force, but will turn our words against us; therefore
we must not be slaves to what we have previously
said, or claimed to be true, or know to be true, but
instead must choose our words and our truths such
that these will yield the most effective and desirable
results. Because, in the end, what is more honest
than preserving one's preferred way of life? What
is truth, if not an ongoing faith in, and continuing
hope for, that which one feels and knows in one's
heart to be right, all temporary and ephemeral
contraindications notwithstanding?

—*Bernard "Ed" Alton,*
   Taskbook for the New Nation,
   Chapter 9. "Shortfalls of the Honesty Paradigm"

bohemians

In a lovely urban coincidence, the last two houses on our block were both occupied by widows who had lost their husbands in Eastern European pogroms. Dad called them the Bohemians. He called anyone white with an accent a Bohemian. Whenever he saw one of the Bohemians, he greeted her by mispronouncing the Czech word for "door." Neither Bohemian was Czech, but both were polite, so when Dad said "door" to them they answered cordially, as if he weren't perennially schlockered.

Mrs. Poltoi, the stouter Bohemian, had spent the war in a crawl space, splitting a daily potato with six cousins. Consequently she was bitter and claustrophobic and loved food. If you ate something while standing near her, she stared at it going into your mouth. She wore only black. She said the

Catholic Church was a jeweled harlot drinking the blood of the poor. She said America was a spoiled child ignorant of grief. When our ball rolled onto her property, she seized it and waddled into her backyard and pitched it into the quarry.

Mrs. Hopanlitski, on the other hand, was thin, and joyfully made pipecleaner animals. When I brought home one of her crude dogs in tophats, Mom said, "Take over your Mold-A-Hero. To her, it will seem like the toy of a king." To Mom, the camps, massacres, and railroad sidings of twenty years before were as unreal as covered wagons. When Mrs. H. claimed her family had once owned serfs, Mom's attention wandered. She had a tract house in mind. No way was she getting one. We were renting a remodeled garage behind the Giancarlos. Dad was basically drinking up the sporting-goods store. His NFL helmets were years out of date. I'd stop by after school and find the store closed and Dad getting sloshed among the fake legs with Bennie Delmonico at Prosthetics World.

Using the Mold-A-Hero, I cast Mrs. H. a plastic Lafayette, and she said she'd keep it forever on her sill. Within a week, she'd given it to Elizabeth the Raccoon. I didn't mind. Raccoon, an only child like me, had nothing. The Kletz brothers called her Raccoon for the bags she had under her eyes from never sleeping. Her parents fought nonstop. They fought over breakfast. They fought in the yard in their underwear. At dusk they stood on their porch whacking each other with lengths of weather stripping. Raccoon practically had spinal curvature from spending so much time slumped over with misery When the Kletz brothers called her Raccoon, she indulged them by rubbing her hands together ferally. The nickname was the most attention she'd ever had. Sometimes she'd wish to be hit by a car so she could come back as a true Raccoon and track down the Kletzes and give them rabies.

"Never wish harm on yourself or others," Mrs. H. said. "You are a lovely child." Her English was flat and clear, almost like ours.

"Raccoon, you mean," Raccoon said. "A lovely Raccoon."

"A lovely child of God," Mrs. H. said.

"Yeah right," Raccoon said. "Tell again about the prince."

So Mrs. H. told again how she'd stood rapt in her yard watching an actual prince powder his birthmark to invisibility. She remembered the smell of burning compost from the fields, and men in colorful leggings dragging a gutted boar across a wooden bridge This was before she was forced to become a human pack animal in the Carpathians, carrying the personal belongings of cruel officers. At night, they chained her to a tree. Sometimes they burned her calves with a machine-gun barrel for fun. Which was why she always wore kneesocks. After three years, she'd come home to find her babies in tiny graves. They were, she would say, short-lived but wonderful gifts. She did not now begrudge God for taking them. A falling star is brief, but isn't one nonetheless glad to have seen it? Her grace made us hate Mrs. Poltoi all the more. What was eating a sixth of a potato every day compared to being chained to a tree? What was being crammed in with a bunch of your cousins compared to having your kids killed?

The summer I was ten, Raccoon and I, already borderline rejects due to our mutually unraveling households, were joined by Art Siminiak, who had recently made the mistake of inviting the Kletzes in for lemonade. There was no lemonade. Instead, there was Art's mom and a sailor from Great Lakes, passed out naked across the paper-drive stacks on the Siminiaks' sunporch.

This new, three-way friendship consisted of slumping in gangways, glovelessly playing catch with a Wiffle, trailing hopefully behind kids whose homes could be entered without fear of fiasco.

Over on Mozart lived Eddie the Vacant. Eddie was seventeen, huge and simple. He could crush a walnut in his bare hand, but first you had to put it there and tell him to do it. Once he'd pinned a "Vacant" sign to his shirt and walked around the neighborhood that way, and the name had stuck. Eddie claimed to see birds. Different birds appeared on different days of the week. Also, there was a Halloween bird and a Christmas bird.

One day, as Eddie hobbled by, we asked what kind of birds he was seeing.

"Party birds," he said. "They got big streamers coming out they butts."

"You having a party?" said Art. "You having a homo party?"

"I gone have a birthday party," said Eddie, blinking shyly.

"Your dad know?" Raccoon said.

"No, he don't yet," said Eddie.

His plans for the party were private and illogical. We peppered him with questions, hoping to get him to further embarrass himself. The party would be held in his garage. As far as the junk car in there, he would push it out by hand. As far as the oil on the floor, he would soak it up using Handi Wipes. As far as music, he would play a trumpet.

"What are you going to play the trumpet with?" said Art. "Your asshole?"

"No, I not gone play it with that," Eddie said. "I just gone use my lips, okay?"

As far as girls, there would be girls; he knew many girls, from his job managing the Drake Hotel. As far as food, there would be food, including pudding dumplings.

"You're the manager of the Drake Hotel," Raccoon said.

"Hey, I know how to get the money for pudding dumplings!" Eddie said.

Then he rang Poltoi's bell and asked for a contribution. She said for what. He said for him. She said to what end. He looked at her blankly and asked for a contribution. She asked him to leave the porch. He asked for a contribution. Somewhere he'd got the idea that, when asking for a contribution, one angled to sit on the couch. He started in, and she pushed him back with a thick forearm. Down the front steps he went, ringing the iron banister with his massive head.

He got up and staggered away, a little blood on his scalp.

"Learn to leave people be!" Poltoi shouted after him.

Ten minutes later, Eddie Sr. stood on Poltoi's porch, a hulking effeminate tailor too cowed to use his bulk for anything but butting open the jamming door at his shop.

"Since when has it become the sport to knock unfortunates down stairs?" he asked.

"He was not listen," she said. "I tell him no. He try to come inside."

"With all respect," he said, "it is in my son's nature to perhaps be not so responsive."

"Someone so unresponse, keep him indoors," she said. "He is big as a man. And I am old lady."

"Never has Eddie presented a danger to anyone," Eddie Sr. said.

"I know my rights," she said. "Next time, I call police."

But, having been pushed down the stairs, Eddie the Vacant couldn't seem to stay away.

"Off this porch," Poltoi said through the screen when he showed up the next day, offering her an empty cold-cream jar for three dollars.

"We gone have so many snacks," he said. "And if I drink a alcohol drink, then watch out. Because I ain't allowed. I dance too fast."

He was trying the doorknob now, showing how fast he would dance if alcohol was served.

"Please, off this porch!" she shouted.

"Please, off this porch!" he shouted back, doubling at the waist in wacky laughter.

Poltoi called the cops. Normally, Lieutenant Brusci would have asked Eddie what bird was in effect that day and given him a ride home in his squad. But this was during the OneCity fiasco. To cut graft, cops were being yanked off their regular beats and replaced by cops from other parts of town. A couple Armenians from South Shore showed up and dragged Eddie off the porch in a club-lock so tight he claimed the birds he was seeing were beakless.

"I'll give you a beak, Frankenstein," said one of the Armenians, tightening the choke hold.

Eddie entered the squad with all the fluidity of a hat rack. Art and Raccoon and I ran over to Eddie Sr.'s tailor shop above the Marquee, which had sunk to porn. When Eddie Sr. saw us, he stopped his Singer by kicking out the plug. From downstairs came a series of erotic moans.

Eddie Sr. rushed to the hospital with his Purple Heart and some photos of Eddie as a grinning wet-chinned kid on a pony. He found Eddie handcuffed to a bed, with an IV drip and a smashed face. Apparently, he'd bitten one of the Armenians. Bail was set at three hundred. The tailor shop made zilch. Eddie Sr.'s fabrics were a lexicon of yesteryear. Dust coated a bright-yellow sign that read "Zippers Repaired in Jiffy."

"Jail for that kid, I admit, don't make total sense," the judge said. "Three months in the Anston. Best I can do."

The Anston Center for Youth was a red-brick former forge now yarded in barbed wire. After their shifts, the guards held loud hooting orgies kitty-corner at Zem's Lamplighter. Skinny immigrant women arrived at Zem's in station wagons and emerged hours later adjusting their stockings. From all over Chicago kids were sent to the Anston, kids who'd only ever been praised for the level of beatings they gave and received and their willingness to carve themselves up. One Anston kid had famously hired another kid to run over his foot. Another had killed his mother's lover with a can opener. A third had sliced open his own eyelid with a poptop on a dare.

Eddie the Vacant disappeared into the Anston in January and came out in March.

To welcome him home, Eddie Sr. had the neighborhood kids over. Eddie the Vacant looked so bad even the Kletzes didn't joke about how bad he looked. His nose was off center and a scald mark ran from ear to chin. When you got too close, his hands shot up. When the cake was served, he dropped his plate, shouting, "Leave a guy alone!"

Our natural meanness now found a purpose. Led by the Kletzes, we cut through Poltoi's hose, bashed out her basement windows with ball-peens, pushed her little shopping cart over the edge of the quarry and watched it end-over-end into the former Slag Ravine.

Then it was spring and the quarry got busy. When the noon blast went off, our windows rattled. The three-o'clock blast was even bigger. Raccoon and Art and I made a fort from the cardboard shipping containers the Cline frames came in. One day, while pretending the three-o'clock blast was atomic, we saw Eddie the Vacant bounding toward our fort through the weeds, like some lover in a commercial, only fatter and falling occasionally.

His trauma had made us kinder toward him.

"Eddie," Art said. "You tell your dad where you're at?"

"It no big problem," Eddie said. "I was gone leave my dad a note."

"But did you?" said Art.

"I'll leave him a note when I get back," said Eddie. "I gone come in with you now."

"No room," said Raccoon. "You're too huge."

"That a good one!" said Eddie, crowding in.

Down in the quarry were the sad Cats, the slumping watchman's shack, the piles of reddish discarded dynamite wrappings that occasionally rose erratically up the hillside like startled birds.

Along the quarryside trail came Mrs. Poltoi, dragging a new shopping cart.

"Look at that pig," said Raccoon. "Eddie, that's the pig that put you away."

"What did they do to you in there, Ed?" said Art. "Did they mess with you?"

"No, they didn't," said Eddie. "I just a say to them, 'Leave a guy alone!' I mean, sometime they did, okay? Sometime that one guy say, 'Hey Eddie, pull your thing! We gone watch you.'"

"Okay, okay," said Art.

At dusk, the three of us would go to Mrs. H.'s porch. She'd bring out cookies and urge forgiveness. It wasn't Poltoi's fault her heart was small, she told us. She, Mrs. H., had seen a great number of things, and seeing so many things had enlarged her heart. Once, she had seen Göring. Once, she had seen Einstein. Once, during the war, she had seen a whole city block, formerly thick with furriers, bombed black overnight. In the morning, charred bodies had crawled along the street, begging for mercy. One such body had grabbed her by the ankle, and she recognized it as Bergen, a friend of her father's.

"What did you do?" said Raccoon.

"Not important now," said Mrs. H., gulping back tears, looking off into the quarry.

Then disaster. Dad got a check for shoulder pads for all six district football teams and, trying to work things out with Mom, decided to take her on a cruise to Jamaica. Nobody in our neighborhood had ever been on a cruise. Nobody had even been to Wisconsin. The disaster was, I was staying with Poltoi. Ours was a liquor household, where you could ask a question over and over in utter sincerity and never get a straight answer. I asked and asked, "Why her?" And was told and told, "It will be a adventure."

I asked, "Why not Grammy?"

I was told, "Grammy don't feel well."

I asked, "Why not Hopanlitski?"

Dad did this like snort.

"Like that's gonna happen," said Mom.

"Why not, why not?" I kept asking.

"Because shut up," they kept answering.

Just after Easter, over I went, with my little green suitcase.

I was a night panicker and occasional bed-wetter. I'd

wake drenched and panting. Had they told her? I doubted it. Then I knew they hadn't, from the look on her face the first night, when I peed myself and woke up screaming.

"What's this?" she said.

"Pee," I said, humiliated beyond any ability to lie.

"Ach, well," she said. "Who don't? This also used to be me. Pee pee pee. I used to dream of a fish who cursed me."

She changed the sheets gently, with no petulance—a new one on me. Often Ma, still half asleep, popped me with the wet sheet, saying when at last I had a wife, she herself could finally get some freaking sleep.

Then the bed was ready, and Poltoi made a sweeping gesture, like, Please.

I got in.

She stayed standing there.

"You know," she said, "I know they say things. About me, what I done to that boy. But I had a bad time in the past with a big stupid boy. You don't gotta know. But I did like I did that day for good reason. I was scared at him, due to something what happened for real to me."

She stood in the half-light, looking down at her feet.

"Do you get?" she said. "Do you? Can you get it, what I am saying?"

"I think so," I said.

"Tell to him," she said. "Tell to him sorry, explain about it, tell your friends also. If you please. You have a good

318

brain. That is why I am saying to you."

Something in me rose to this. I'd never heard it before but I believed it: I had a good brain. I could be trusted to effect a change.

Next day was Saturday. She made soup. We played a game using three slivers of soap. We made placemats out of colored strips of paper, and she let me teach her my spelling words.

Around noon the doorbell rang. At the door stood Mrs. H.

"Everything okay?" she said, poking her head in.

"Yes, fine," said Poltoi. "I did not eat him yet."

"Is everything really fine?" Mrs. H. said to me. "You can say."

"It's fine," I said.

"You can say," she said fiercely.

Then she gave Poltoi a look that seemed to say, Hurt him and you will deal with me.

"You silly woman," said Poltoi. "You are going now."

Mrs. H. went.

We resumed our spelling. It was tense in a quiet-house way. Things ticked. When Poltoi missed a word, she pinched her own hand, but not hard. It was like symbolic pinching. Once when she pinched, she looked at me looking at her, and we laughed.

Then we were quiet again.

"That lady?" she finally said. "She like to lie. Maybe you don't know. She say she is come from where I come from?"

"Yes," I said.

"She is lie," she said. "She act so sweet and everything but she lie. She been born in Skokie. Live here all her life, in America. Why you think she talk so good?"

All week Poltoi made sausage, noodles, potato pancakes; we ate like pigs. She had tea and cakes ready when I came home from school. At night, if necessary, she dried me off, moved me to her bed, changed the sheets, put me back, with never an unkind word.

"Will pass, will pass," she'd hum.

Mom and Dad came home tanned, with a sailor cap for me, and in a burst of post-vacation honesty, confirmed it: Mrs. H. was a liar. A liar and a kook. Nothing she said was true. She'd been a cashier at Goldblatt's but had been caught stealing. When caught stealing, she'd claimed to be with the Main Office. When a guy from the Main Office came down, she claimed to be with the FBI. Then she'd produced a letter from Lady Bird Johnson, but in her own handwriting, with "Johnson" spelled "Jonsen."

I told the other kids what I knew, and in time they came to believe it, even the Kletzes.

And, once we believed it, we couldn't imagine we hadn't seen it all along.

Another spring came, once again birds nested in bushes

on the sides of the quarry. A thrown rock excited a thrilling upwards explosion. Thin rivers originated in our swampy backyards, and we sailed boats made of flattened shoeboxes, Twinkie wrappers, crimped tinfoil. Raccoon glued together three balsa-wood planes and placed on this boat a turd from her dog Svengooli, and, as Svengooli's turd went over a little waterfall and disappeared into the quarry, we cheered.

commcomm

Tuesday morning Jillian from Disasters calls. Apparently an airman named Loolerton has poisoned a shitload of beavers. I say we don't kill beavers, we harvest them, because otherwise they nibble through our Pollution Control Devices (PCDs) and polluted water flows out of our Retention Area and into the Eisenhower Memorial Wetland, killing beavers.

"That makes sense," says Jillian, and hangs up.

The press has a field day. AIR FORCE KILLS BEAVERS TO SAVE BEAVERS, says one headline. MURDERED BEAVERS SPEAK OF AIR FORCE CRUELTY, says another.

"We may want to PIDS this," Mr. Rimney says.

I check the files: There's a circa-1984 tortoise-related PIDS from a base in Oklahoma. There's a wild-horse-related PIDS from North Dakota. Also useful is a Clinton-era PIDS concerning the inadvertent destruction of a dove breeding ground.

From these I glean an approach: I *admit* we harvested the beavers. I *concede* the innocence and creativity of beavers. I *explain* the harvesting as a regrettable part of an ongoing effort to prevent Pollution Events from impacting the Ottowattamie. Finally, I *pledge* we will find a way to preserve our PIDS without, in the future, harming beavers. We are, I say, considering transplanting the beaver population to an innovative Beaver Habitat, to be installed upstream of the Retention Area.

I put it into PowerPoint. Rimney comes back from Break and reads it.

"All hail to the king of PIDS," he says.

I call Ed at the paper; Jason, Heather, and Randall at NewsTen, ActionSeven, and NewsTeamTwo, respectively; then Larry from Facilities, have him reserve the Farragut Auditorium for Wednesday night, and just like that I've got a fully executable PIDS and can go joyfully home to my wife and our crazy energized loving kids.

Just kidding.

I wish.

I walk between Mom and Dad into the kitchen, make those frozen mini-steaks called SmallCows. You microwave them or pull out their ThermoTab. When you pull the ThermoTab, something chemical happens and the SmallCows heat up. I microwave. Unfortunately the ThermoTab erupts and when I take the SmallCows out they're coated with a green fibrous liquid. So I make Ramen.

"You don't hate the Latvians, do you?" Dad says to me.

"It was not all Latvians done it," Mom says.

I turn on Tape Nine, *Omission/Partial Omission*. When sadness-inducing events occur, the guy says, invoke your Designated Substitute Thoughtstream. Your DST might be a man falling off a cliff but being caught by a group of good friends. It might be a bowl of steaming soup, if one likes soup. It might be something as distractive/mechanical as walking along a row of cans, kicking them down.

"And don't even hate them two," Mom says. "They was just babies."

"They did not do that because they was Latvian," says Dad. "They did it because of they had poverty and anger."

"What the hell," says Mom. "Everything turned out good."

My DST is tapping a thin rock wall with a hammer. When that wall cracks, there's another underneath. When that wall cracks, there's another underneath.

"You hungry?" Mom says to Dad.

"Never hungry anymore," he says.

"Me too," she says. "Plus I never pee."

"Something's off but I don't know what," Dad says.

When that wall cracks, there's another underneath.

"Almost time," Mom says to me, her voice suddenly nervous. "Go upstairs."

I go up to my room, watch some World Series, practice my PIDS in front of the mirror.

What's going on down there I don't watch anymore: Mom's on the landing in her pajamas, calling Dad's name, a little testy. Then she takes a bullet in the neck, her hands fly up, she rolls the rest of the way down, my poor round Ma. Dad comes up from the basement in his gimpy comic trot, concerned, takes a bullet in the chest, drops to his knees, takes one in the head, and that's that.

Then they do it again, over and over, all night long.

Finally it's morning. I go down, have a bagel.

Our house has this turret you can't get into from inside. You have to go outside and use a ladder. There's nothing up there but bird droppings and a Nixon-era plastic Santa with a peace sign scratched into his toy bag. That's where they go during the day. I climbed up once, then never again: jaws hanging open, blank stares, the two of them sitting against the wall, insulation in their hair, holding hands.

"Have a good one," I shout at the turret as I leave for work.

Which I know is dumb, but still.

* * *

When I get to work, Elliot Giff from Safety's standing in the Outer Hall. Giff's a GS-9 with pink glasses and an immense underchin that makes up a good third of the length of his face.

"Got this smell-related call?" he says.

We step in. There's definitely a smell. Like a mildew/dirt/decomposition thing.

"We have a ventilation problem," Rimney says stiffly.

"No lie," Giff says. "Smells like something crawled inside the wall and died. That happened to my aunt."

"Your aunt crawled inside a wall and died," Rimney says.

"No, a rat," says Giff. "Finally she had to hire a Puerto Rican fellow to drill a hole in her wall. Maybe you should do that."

"Hire a Puerto Rican fellow to drill a hole in your aunt's wall," Rimney says.

"I like how you're funny," Giff says. "There's joy in that."

Giff's in the ChristLife Reënactors. During the reënactments they eat only dates and drink only grape juice out of period-authentic flasks. He says this weekend's reënactment was on the hill determined to be the most topographically similar to Calvary in the entire Northeast. I ask who he did. He says the guy who lent Christ his mule on Palm Sunday. Rimney says it's just like Giff to let an unemployed Jew borrow his ass.

"You're certainly not hurting me with that kind of talk," Giff says.

"I suppose I'm hurting Christ," says Rimney.

"Not hardly," says Giff.

On Rimney's desk is a photo of Mrs. Rimney before the stroke: braless in a tank top, hair to her waist, holding a walking stick. In the photo, Rimney's wearing a bandanna, pretending to toke something. Since the stroke he works his nine or ten, gets groceries, goes home, cooks, bathes Val, does the dishes, goes to bed.

My feeling is, no wonder he's mean.

Giff starts to leave, then doubles back.

"You and your wife are in the prayers of me and our church," he says to Rimney. "Despite of what you may think of me."

"You're in my prayers too," says Rimney. "I'm always praying you stop being so sanctimonious and miraculously get less full of shit."

Giff leaves, not doubling back this time.

Rimney hasn't liked Giff since the day Giff suggested Rimney could cure Mrs. Rimney if only he'd elevate his prayerfulness.

"All right," Rimney says. "Who called him?"

Mrs. Gregg bursts into tears and runs to the Ladies'.

"I don't get why all the drama," says Rimney.

"Hello, the base is closing in six months," says Jonkins.

"Older individuals like Mrs. G. are less amenable to quick abrupt changes," says Verblin.

When Closure was first announced I found Mrs. G. crying in the Outer Hall. What about Little Bill, she said? Little Bill just bought a house. What about Amber, pregnant with twins, and her husband Goose, drunk every night at The Twit? What about Nancy and Vendra, what about Jonkins and Al? There's not a job to be had in town, she said, where are all these sweet people supposed to go?

I've sent out over thirty résumés, been store to store, chatted up Dad's old friends. Even our grocery's half-closed. What used to be Produce is walled off with plywood. On the plywood is a sign: "If We Don't Have It, Sorry."

CommComm's been offered a Group Transfer to NAIVAC Omaha. But Mom and Dad aren't allowed into the yard, much less to Omaha. And when I'm not around, they get agitated. I went to Albany last March for a seminar and they basically trashed the place. Which couldn't have been easy. To even disturb a drape for them is a big deal. I walked in and Mom was trying to tip over the coffee table by flying through it on her knees, and Dad was inside the couch, trying to weaken the springs via repetitive fast spinning. They didn't mean to but were compelled. Even as they were flying/spinning they were apologizing profusely.

"Plus it really does stink in here," says Little Bill.

"Who all is getting a headache raise your hand," says Jonkins.

"Oh, all right," says Rimney, then goes into my cubicle and calls Odors. He asks why they can't get over immediately. How many odors do they have exactly? Has the entire base suddenly gone smelly?

I walk in and he's not talking into the phone, just tapping it against his leg.

He winks at me and asks loudly how Odors would like to try coordinating Community Communications while developing a splitting headache in a room that smells like ass.

All afternoon it stinks. At five Rimney says let's hope for the best overnight and wear scuba gear in tomorrow, except for Jonkins, who, in terms of Jonkins, they probably don't make scuba gear that humongous.

"I cannot believe you just said that," says Jonkins.

"Learn to take a joke," Rimney says, and slams into his office.

I walk out with Jonkins and Mrs. Gregg. The big flag over the Dirksen excavation is snapping in the wind, bright yellow leaves zipping past as if weighted.

"I hate him," says Jonkins.

"I feel so bad for his wife," says Mrs. Gregg.

"First you have to live with him, then you have a stroke?" says Jonkins.

"And then you still have to live with him?" says Mrs Gregg.

The Dirksen Center for Terror is the town's great hope. If transferred to the Dirksen you keep your benefits and years accrued and your salary goes up because you're Homeland Security instead of Air Force. We've all submitted our Requests-for-Transfer and our Self-Assessment-Worksheets and now we're just waiting to hear.

Except Rimney. Rimney heard right away. Rimney knows somebody who knows somebody. He was immediately certified Highly Proficient and is Dirksen-bound, which, possibly, is another reason everybody hates him.

My feeling is, good for him. If he went to Omaha, imagine the work. He and Val have a routine here, contacts, a special van, a custom mechanical bed. Imagine having to pick up and start over somewhere else.

"Home, home, home," says Mrs. Gregg.

"PIDS, PIDS, PIDS," I say.

"Oh, you poor thing," says Mrs. Gregg.

"If I had to stand up in front of all those people," says Jonkins, "I'd put a bullet in my head."

Then there's a long silence.

"Shit man, sorry," he says to me.

The Farragut's full. I *admit*, *concede*, *explain*, and *pledge*.
During the Q&A, somebody says if the base is closing, why
spend big bucks on a Beaver Habitat? I say because the Air
Force is committed to ensuring that, post-Closure, all Air
Force sites remain environmentally viable, prioritizing
species health and a diverse life-form mix.

Afterward Rimney's back by the snacks. He says is there
anything I can't PIDS? I say probably not. I've PIDSed sexual-
harassment cases, a cracked hazardous waste incinerator,
half a dozen jet-fuel spills. I PIDSed it when General
Lemaster admitted being gay, retracted his admission, then
retracted his retraction, all in the same day, before vanish-
ing for a week with one of his high school daughter's girl-
friends.

"You might have noticed earlier that I was not actually
calling Odors," Rimney says.

"I did notice that," I say.

"Thing I like about you, you're a guy who understands
life gets complicated," he says. "Got a minute? I need to
show you something."

I follow him back to CommComm. Which still stinks. I
follow him into the copier closet, which stinks even worse.

In the closet is something big, in bubble-wrap.

"Note to self," he says. "Bubble-wrap? Not smell-preventing."

He slits open the bubble-wrap. Inside is this giant dirt clod. Sticking out of the clod is a shoe. In the shoe is a foot, a rotted foot, in a rotted sock.

"I don't get it," I say.

"Found down in the Dirksen excavation," he says. "Thought I could stash them in here a few days, but phew. Can you believe it?"

He slits open a second bubble-wrap package. There's another guy, not enclodded, cringed up, in shredded pants, looking like he's been dipped in mustard. This one's small, like a jockey.

"They look old-timey to me," Rimney says.

They do look old timey. Their shoes are big crude shoes with big crude nails.

"So you see our issue," he says. "Dirksen-wise."

I don't. But then I do.

The Racquetball Facility was scrapped due to someone found an Oneida nosering portion on the site. Likewise the proposed Motor Pool Improvement, on account of a shard of Colonial crockery.

If a pottery shard or partial nosering can scrap a project, think what a couple Potentially Historical corpses/mummies will do.

"Who else knows?" I say.

"The contractor," Rimney says. "Rick Granis. You know Rick?"

I've known Rick since kindergarten. I remember how mad he'd get if anyone called his blanket anything but his binkie. Now he's got an Escalade and a summer house on Otissic Lake.

"But Rick's cool with it," he says. "He'll do whatever."

He shows me Rick's Daily Historical-Resource Assessment Worksheet. Under "Non-Historical Detritus," Rick's written: "Two contemp soda bottles, one contemp flange." Under "Evidence of Pre-Existing Historical/Cultural Presence," he's written: "Not that I know of."

Rimney says a guy like me, master of the public presentation aspect, could be a great fit at the Dirksen. As I may know, he knows somebody who knows somebody. Do I find the idea of Terror work at all compelling?

I say sure, yes, of course.

He says, thing is, they're just bodies. The earth is full of bodies. Under every building in the world, if you dig deep enough, is probably a body. From the looks of it, someone just dumped these poor guys into a mass grave. They're not dressed up, no coffins, no dusty pathetic flower remains, no prayer cards.

I say I'm not sure I totally follow.

He says he's thinking a respectful reburial, somewhere

they won't be found, that won't fuck up the Dirksen.

"And tell the truth," he says, "I could use some help."

I think of Tape Four, *Living the Now*. What is the Now Situation? How can I pull the pearl from the burning oyster? How can the "drowning boy" be saved? I do an Actual Harm Analysis. Who would a reburial hurt? The mummy guys? They're past hurt. Who would it help? Rimney, Val Rimney, all future Dirksen employees.

Me.

Mom, Dad.

Dad worked thirty years at Gallup Chain, with his dad. Then they discontinued Automotive. Only Bike remained. A week after his layoff, Grandpa died. Day of the wake, Dad got laid off too. Month later, we found out Jean was sick. Jean was my sister, who died at eight. Her last wish was Disneyland. But money was tight. Toward the end Dad borrowed money from Leo, the brother he hated. But Jean was too sick to travel. So Dad had an Army friend from Barstow film all of Disney on a Super-8. The guy walked the whole place. Jean watched it and watched it. Dad was one of these auto-optimists. To hear him tell it, we'd won an incredible last-minute victory. Hadn't we? Wasn't it something, that we could give Jeanie such a wonderful opportunity?

By then Jean had been distilled down to like pure honesty.

"I do wish I could have gone, though," she said.

"Well, we practically did," Dad said, looking panicked.

"No, but I wish we really did," she said.

After Jean died, we kept her room intact, did a birthday thing for her every year, started constantly expecting the worst. I'd come home from a high school party and Mom would be sitting there with her rosary, mumbling, praying for my safe return. Even a dropped shopping bag, a broken jar of Prego, would send them into a funk, like: Doom, doom, of course, isn't this the way it always goes for us?

Eight years later came the night of the Latvians.

So a little decent luck for Mom and Dad doesn't seem like too much to ask.

"About this job thing," I say.

"I will absolutely make it happen," he says.

The way we do it is, we carry them one at a time out to his special van. He's got a lift in there for Val. Not that we need the lift. These guys are super-light. Then we drive out to the forest behind Missions. We dig a hole, which is not easy, due to roots. I go in, he hands them down very gentle. They're so stiff and dry it's hard to believe they can still smell.

We backfill, kick some leaves around, drag over a small fallen tree.

"You okay?" he says. "You look a little freaked."

I ask should we maybe say a prayer.

"Go ahead," he says. "My feeling is, these guys have been gone so long they're either with Him or not. If there even is a Him. Might be real, might not. To me, what's real? Val. When I get home tonight, there she'll be, waiting. Hasn't eaten yet, needs her bath. Been by herself the whole day. That, to me? Is real."

I say a prayer, lift my head when done.

"I thank you, Val thanks you," he says.

In the van I do a Bad Feelings Acknowledgment re the reburial. I visualize my Useless Guilt as a pack of black dogs. I open the gate, throw out the Acknowledgment Meat. Pursuing the Meat, the black dogs disappear over a cliff, turning into crows (i.e., Neutral/Non-Guilty Energy), which then fly away, feeling Assuaged.

Back at CommComm we wash off the shovels, Pine-Sol the copier closet, throw open the windows, check e-mail while the place airs out.

Next morning the stink is gone. The office just smells massively like Pine-Sol. Giff comes in around eleven, big band age on his humongous underchin.

"Hey, smells super in here today," he says. "Praise the Lord for that, right? And all things."

"What happened to your chin?" says Rimney. "Zonk it on a pew while speaking in tongues?"

"We don't speak in tongues," says Giff. "I was just shaving."

"Interesting," Rimney says. "Goodbye."

"Not goodbye," says Giff. "I have to do my Situational Follow-Up. What in your view is the reason for the discontinued nature of that crappo smell you all previously had?"

"A miracle," says Rimney. "Christ came down with some Pine-Sol."

"I don't really go for that kind of talk," says Giff.

"Why not pray I stop?" says Rimney. "See if it works."

"Let me tell you a like parable," Giff says. "This one girl in our church? Had this, like, perma-smile? Due to something? And her husband, who was non-church, was always having to explain that she wasn't really super-happy, it was just her malady. It was like the happier she looked, the madder he got. Then he came to our church, guess what happened?"

"She was miraculously cured and he was miraculously suddenly not angry," says Rimney. "God reached down and fixed them both, while all over the world people who didn't come to your church remained in misery, weeping."

"Well, no," says Giff.

"And that's not technically a parable," says Verblin.

"See, but you're what happens when man stays merely on his own plane," says Giff. "Man is made bitter. Look, I'm not claiming I'm not human and don't struggle. Heck, I'm as human as you. Only I struggle, when I struggle, with the help of Him that knows no struggle. Which is why sometimes I maybe seem so composed or, you might say, together. Everyone in our church has that same calm. It's not just me. It's just Him, is how we say it."

"How calm would you stay if I broke your neck?" says Rimney.

"Ron, honestly," Jonkins says.

"Quiet, Tim," Rimney says to Jonkins. "If we listen closely, we may hear the call of the North American extremist loony."

"Maybe you're the extremist due to you think you somehow created your own self," says Giff.

"Enough, this is a place of business," says Rimney.

Then Milton Gelton comes in. Gelton's a GS-5 in Manual Site Aesthetics Improvement. He roams the base picking up trash with a sharp stick. When he finds a dead animal, he calls Animals. When he finds a car battery, he calls Environmental.

"Want to see something freaky?" he says, holding out his bucket. "Found behind Missions?"

In the bucket is a yellow-black human hand.

"Is that a real actual hand of someone?" says Amber.

"At first I thought glove," Gelton says. "But no. See? No hand-hole. Just solid."

He pokes the hand with a pen to demonstrate the absence of hand-hole.

"You know what else I'm noting as weird?" Giff says. "In terms of that former smell? I can all of a sudden smell it again."

He sniffs his way down to the bucket.

"Yoinks, similar," he says.

"I doubt this is a Safety issue," says Rimney.

"I disagree," says Giff. "This hand seems like it might be the key to our Possible Source of your Negative Odor. Milton, can you show me the exact locale where you found this at?"

Out they go. Rimney calls me in. How the hell did we drop that fucker? Jesus, what else did we drop? This is not funny, he says, do I realize we could go to jail for this? We knowingly altered a Probable Historical Site. At the very least, we'll catch hell in the press. As for the Dirksen, this gets out, goodbye Dirksen.

I eat lunch in the Eating Area. Little Bill's telling about his trip to Omaha. He stayed at a MinTel. The rooms are closet-sized. They like slide you in. You're allowed two Slide-Outs a night. After that it's three dollars a Slide-Out.

Rimney comes out, says he's got to run home. Val's having leg cramps. When she has leg cramps, the only thing that works is hot washrags. He's got a special pasta pot and two sets of washrags, one blue, one white. One set goes on her legs while the other set heats.

With Rimney gone, discipline erodes. Out the window I see Verblin sort of mincing to his car. A yardstick slides out of his pants. When he stoops to get the yardstick, a printer cartridge drops out of his coat. When he bends to pick up the cartridge, his hat falls off, revealing a box of staples.

At three Ms. Durrell from Environmental calls. Do we have any more of those dioxin coloring books? Do I know what she means? It's not a new spill, just reawakened concern over an old spill. I know what she means. She means *Donnie Dioxin: Badly Misunderstood But Actually Quite Useful Under Correct Usage Conditions*.

I'm in Storage looking for the books when my cell rings.

"Glad I caught you," Rimney says stiffly. "Can you come out to Missions? I swung by on the way back and boy oh boy, did Elliot ever find something amazing."

"Is he standing right there?" I say.

"Okay, see you soon," he says, and hangs up.

I park by the Sputnik-era jet-on-a-pedestal. The fake pilot's head is facing backward and a twig's been driven up his nose. Across the fuselage some kid's painted, "This thing looks like my pennis if my pennis has wings."

It starts to flurry. Giff's been at the grave with a shovel. So far it's just the top of the jockey's head sticking out, and part of the enclodded guy's foot.

"Wow," I say.

"Wow is correct," says Rimney.

"Thanks be to Scouts," Giff says. "See? Footprints ga-
lore. Plus tire tracks. To me? It's like a mystery or one of
those deals where there's more than meeting the eyes. Because where did these fellows come from? Who put them
here? Why did your office smell so bad, in an off way similar to that gross way that hand smelled? In my logic? I ask,
Where locally is somewhere deep that's recently been un-
earthed or dug into? What I realized? The Dirksen. That is
deep, that is new. What do you think? I'll get with Historical tomorrow, see what used to be where the Dirksen is at
now."

I helped Rimney get Val home from the hospital after
the stroke, watched the two of them burst into tears at the
sight of her mechanical bed.

He looks worse than that now.

"Fuck it, I'm going to tell him, trust him, what do you
think?" he says.

My feeling is no no no. Giff's not exactly King of Sense
of Humor. Last year I was the only non-church person at
his Christmas party. The big issue was, somebody on Giff's
wife's side had sent their baby a stuffed DevilChild From
Hell. The DevilChild starts each episode as a kindly angel
with a lisp. Then something makes him mad and he
morphs into a demon and starts speaking with an Eastern

European accent while running around stabbing uptight people in the butt with a red-hot prod.

"As for me and my house, this little guy has no place here," Giff had said. "Although Cyndi apparently feels otherwise."

Cyndi I would describe as pretty but flinchy.

"Andy doesn't see it as the devil," she said. "He just likes it."

"Well, I do see it as the devil," Giff said. "And I don't like it. And here in this house, a certain book tells us the role of the father/husband. Am I right?"

"I guess so," she said.

"You guessing so, like Pastor Mike says, is sympromatic of your having an imperfect understanding of what the Lord has in mind for our family, though," he said. "Right? Right, Pastor Mike?"

"Well, it's certainly true that a family can only have one head," said a guy in a Snoopy sweater who I guessed was Father Mike.

"Okay, tough guy," Cyndi said to Giff, and stomped off, ringing the tree ornaments.

I can see Giff's wheels turning. Or trying to. He's not the brightest. I once watched him spend ten minutes trying to make a copy on a copier in the Outer Hall that was unplugged and ready for Disposal.

"Wait, are you saying you guys did this?" he says.

Rimney says Giff has a wife, Giff has a baby, would a transfer to the Dirksen be of interest? Maybe Giff's aware that he, Rimney, knows somebody who knows somebody?

"Oh my gosh, you guys did do it," Giff says.

He lets the shovel fall and walks toward the woods, as if so shocked he has to seek relief in the beauty of nature. Out in the woods are three crushed toilets. Every tenth bush or so has a red tag on it, I have no idea why.

"All's I can say is wow," Giff says.

"They're dead, man," Rimney says. "What do you care?"

"Yes, but who was it shaped these fellows?" says Giff. "You? Me? Look, I'm going to speak frank. I think I see what's going on here. Both you guys took recent hard hits. One had a wife with a stroke, the other a great tragic loss of their parents. So you got confused, made a bad call. But He redeemeth, if only we open our hearts. Know how I know? It happened to me. I also took a hard hit this year. Because guess what? In terms of my wife? I'm just going to say it. Our baby is not my baby. Cyndi had a slip-up with this friend of ours, Kyle. I found out just before Christmas, which was why I was such a fart at our party. That put me in a total funk—we were like match and gas. I was so mad there was a darkness upon me. Poor thing had bruises all up her arms, due to I started pinching her. In her sleep, or sometimes I would get so mad and just come up quick and do it. Then January tenth, I'd had enough and I prayed, I said, 'Lord I am way too small, please take me up into You, I don't want to do this anymore.' And He did it. I dropped as if shot. And when I woke? My heart was changed. All glory goes to Him. I mean it was a literal release in my chest. All my hate about the baby was gone and all of a sudden Andy was just my son for real."

"Nice story," says Rimney.

"It's not a story, it happened to me for real in my life," says Giff. "Point is? I had it in me to grow. We all do! I'm not all good, but there's a good part of me. My fire may be tiny, but it's a fire just the same. See what I mean? Same like you. Do you know that good part? Have you met it, that part of you that is all about Truth, that is called, in how we would say it, your Christ-portion? My Christ-portion knew that pinching was wrong. How does your Christ portion feel about this sneaky burial thingie? I mean honestly. In a perfect world, is that what you would have chose to do?"

This catches me a little off guard.

"Is this where I go into a seizure and you heal me by stroking my dick?" Rimney says.

Giff blinks at this, turns to me.

"Think these things up in your heart," he says softly. "Treasure them around, see what it is. Then be in touch, come to our church if you want. I am hopeful that you will come to your Truth."

Suddenly my eyes tear up.

And I don't even know why.

"This is about my wife, jackass," says Rimney.

"Do what's right, come what may," Giff says. "That's what it says on all our softball sweatshirts, and I believe it. And on the back? 'Say No Thanks To Mr. Mere Expedience.' Good words for you, friend."

Rimney's big. Once when mad he smacked the overhang on the way to Vending and there's still a handprint up there. Once he picked up one end of the photocopier so Mrs. Gregg could find her earring, and a call came in and he had this big long conversation with Benefits while still holding up the copier.

"Cross me on this, you'll regret it," he says.

"Get thee behind me," says Giff.

So, a little tense.

My phone rings. Ms. Durrell again. She's got a small vocal outraged group coming at four to eat her alive. Where the hell am I? Those dioxin books? Had something to do with a donkey, Donkey Dioxin, Who Got the Job Done? Or it was possibly an ape or possum or some such shit? She remembers a scene at the end with some grateful villagers, where the ape/ possum/donkey/whatever gave the kids a ride, and also the thing came with a CD?

"Go," Rimney says. "Elliot and I will work this out."

By the time I get the books out of Storage and over to

Environmental it's after five.

I clock out, race home through our wincing little town. Some drunks outside The Twit are heaving slushballs up at the laughing neon Twit. Blockbuster has a new program of identifying all videos as either Artsy or Regular. Two beautiful girls in heels struggle down to the banks of the Ottowattamie, holding each other up. Why are they going down there? It's dusk and that part of the river's just mud and an old barge.

I wish I could ask them but I don't have time. When I'm late Mom and Dad race around shouting, Where Where Where? It always ends in this bitter mutual crying. It's just one of their things. Like when it rains, they go up to the ceiling and lie there facing up. Like when feeling affectionate, they run full-speed toward each other and pass through, moaning/laughing.

The night of the Latvians I was out with Cleo from Vehicles. We went parking, watched some visiting Warthogs practice their night-firing. Things heated up. She had a room on the side of a house, wobbly wooden stairs leading up. Did I call, say I'd be late, say I might not be back at all? No I did not. Next morning I came home, found the house taped off. For the body locations, the cops didn't use chalk. There was just a piece of loose-leaf on the stairs labeled "Deceased Female" and one on the kitchen floor labeled "Deceased Male."

I tell myself: If I'd been home, I'd be dead too. The Latvians had guns. They came in quick, on crack, so whacked-out they forget to even steal anything.

Still. Mom's sciatica was acting up. She'd just had two teeth pulled. At the end, on the steps, on her back, she kept calling my name, as in: Where is he? Did they get him too? Next day, on the landing, I found the little cotton swab the dentist had left in her mouth.

So if they want me home right after work, I'm home right after work.

They're standing at the kitchen window, looking out at the old ball-bearing plant. All my childhood, discarded imperfect ball bearings rolled down the hill into our yard. When the plant closed, a lathe came sliding down, like a foot a day, until it hit an oak.

"Snowing like a mother," Dad says.

"Pretty but we can't go out," says Mom.

"Too old, I guess," Dad says sadly.

"Or something," says Mom.

I set three places. They spend the whole dinner as usual, trying to pick up their forks. Afterward they crowd under the floor lamp, the best part of their night. When they stand in direct heat it doesn't make them warmer, just makes them vividly remember their childhoods.

"Smell of melted caramel," Mom says.

"The way I felt first time I seen a Dodger uniform in color," says Dad.

Dad asks me to turn up the dimmer, and I do, and the info starts coming too fast for grammar.

"Working with beets purple hands Mother finds that funny," says Mom.

"Noting my boner against ticking car, Mr. Klemm gives look of you-are-rubbing-your-boner, mixed sense of shame/pride, rained so hard flooded gutters, rat wound up in the dog bowl," says Dad.

They step out of the light, shake it off.

"He's always talking about boners," says Mom.

"Having a boner is a great privilege," says Dad.

"You had your share," says Mom.

"I should say so," says Dad. "And will continue to, I hope, until the day I die."

Having said "die," Dad blinks. Whenever we see a murder on TV, they cover their eyes. Whenever a car backfires, I have to coax them out from under the couch. Once a bird died on the sill and they spent the entire day in the pantry.

"Until the day you die," Mom says, as if trying to figure out what the words mean.

Before they can ask any questions, I go outside and shovel.

From all over town comes the sound of snowplows, the scraping plus the beeping they do when reversing. The moon's up, full, with halo. My phone rings in my parka pocket.

"We have a situation," Rimney says. "Can you step outside?"

"I am outside," I say.

"Oh, there you are," he says.

The special van's coming slowly up the street.

"New plan," he says, still on the phone, parking now. "What's done is done. We can save the Dirksen or lose it. Minimize the damage or maximize."

He gets out, leads me around to the sliding door.

You didn't, I think. You did not dig those poor guys up again. Does he think Historical is stupid? Does he think Historical, getting a report of mummies, finding only a recently filled hole, is going to think, Oh Giff, very funny, you crack us up?

"Not the mummies," I say.

"I wish," he says, and throws open the door.

Lying there is Giff, fingers clenched like he's trying to cling to a ledge, poor pink glasses hanging off one ear.

I take a step back, trip on the curb, sit in a drift.

"We took a walk, things got out of hand," he says. "Shit, shit, shit. I tried to reason with him but he started giving me all his Christian crap. Something snapped, honestly. It just got away from me. You've probably had that happen?"

"You killed him?" I say.

"An unfortunate thing transpired, after which he died, yes," Rimney says.

Thrown in there with Giff is a big rock, partly wrapped in bloody paper towels.

I ask did he call the police. He says if he planned on calling the police, would he have thrown Giff in back of the freaking van? He says we've got to think pragmatic. He did it, he fucked up, he knows that, he'll be paying for it the rest of his life, but no way is Val paying for it. If he goes to jail, what happens to Val? A state home? No no no, he says. Dead is dead, he can't change that. Why kill Val as well?

"What do we do with this guy?" he says. "Think, think."

"We?" I say. "You."

"Oh God, oh shit," he says. "I can't believe I killed somebody. Me, I did it. Jesus, wow. Okay. Okay."

Snow's blowing in over Giff, melting on his glasses, clumping up between his pants and bare leg.

"You know Val, you like Val, right?" Rimney says.

I do like Val. I remember her at Mom and Dad's funeral, in her wheelchair. She had Rimney lift one of her hands to my arm, did this sad little pat pat pat.

"Because here's the thing," Rimney says. "Dirksen-wise? You're all set. I submitted my rec. It's in the system. Right? Why not take it? Prosper, get a little something for yourself, find a wife, make some babies. The world's shit on you enough, right? You did not do this, I did. I shouldn't have come here. How about pretend I didn't?"

I stand up, start to do a Moral Benefit Eval, then think, No, no way, do not even think about doing that stupid shit now.

The bandage on Giff's underchin flips up, showing his shaving scar.

"Because who was he?" says Rimney. "Who was he really? Was he worth a Val? Was he even a person? He, to me? Was just a dumb-idea factory. That's it."

Poor Giff, I think. Poor Giff's wife, poor Giff's baby.

Poor Val.

Poor everybody.

"Don't fuck me on this," Rimney says. "Are you going to fuck me on this? You are, aren't you? Fine. Fine then."

He turns away, slams the van door shut, emits this weird little throat sound, like he can't live with what he's done and would like to end it all, only can't, because ending it all would make him even more of a shit.

"I feel I'm in a nightmare," he says.

Then he crashes the Giff-rock into my head. I can't believe it. Down I go. He swung so hard he's sitting down too. For a second we both sit there, like playing cards or something. I push off against his face, crawl across the yard, get inside, bolt the door.

"I don't like that," says Dad, all frantic. "I did not like seeing that."

"People should not," Mom says. "That is not a proper way."

When terrified they do this thing where they flicker from Point A to Point B with no interim movement. Mom's in the foyer, then in the kitchen, then at the top of the stairs.

"You better get to the hospital," Dad says.

"Take this poor kid with you," Mom says.

"He just suddenly showed up," Dad says.

Somebody's on the couch. It takes me a second to recognize him.

Giff.

Or something like Giff: fish-pale, naked, bloody dent in his head, squinting, holding his glasses in one hand.

"Whoa," he says. "Is this ever not how I expected it would be like."

"What what would be like?" says Dad.

"Death and all?" he says.

Dad flickers on and off: smiling in his chair, running in place, kneeling near the magazine rack.

"You ain't dead, pal, you're just naked," says Dad.

"Naked, plus somebody blammed you in the head," says Mom.

"Do they not know?" says Giff.

I give him a look, like, Please don't. We're just enjoying a little extra time. I'm listening to their childhood stories, playing records from their courtship days, staring at them when they're not looking, telling them how good they were with me and Jean, how safe we always felt.

"Don't you love them?" Giff says.

I remember them outside the funeral home the day we buried Jean, Mom holding Dad up, Dad trying to sit on a hydrant, wearing his lapel button, his lapel photo-button of little smiling Jean.

"Then better tell them," Giff says. "Before it's too late. Because watch."

He stands, kind of shaky, hobbles over, breathes in my face.

Turns out when the recently dead breathe in your face they show you the future.

I see Mom and Dad trapped here forever, reënacting their deaths night after night, more agitated every year, finally to the point of insanity, until, in their insanity, all they can do is rip continually at each other's flesh, like angry birds, for all eternity.

I tell them.

"Very funny," says Mom.

"Cut it out," Dad says.

"We're a little sad sometimes," says Mom. "But we definitely ain't dead."

"Are we?" Dad says.

Then they get quiet.

"Holy crap," Dad says.

Suddenly they seem to be hearing something from far away.

"Jeez, that's better," says Dad.

"Feels super," Mom says.

"Like you had a terrible crick and then it went away," Dad says.

"Like your dirty dress you had on for the big party all of a sudden got clean," says Mom.

They smile, step through the wall, vanish in two little sudden blurps of light.

Giff's pale and bent, glowing/shimmering, taller than in life, a weird breeze in his hair that seems to be coming from many directions at once.

"There is a glory, but not like how I thought," he says. "I had it all wrong. Mostly wrong. Like my mind was this little basket, big flood pouring in, but all I got was this hint of greater water?"

"You were always a nice person," I say.

"No, I was not," he says. "Forced my little mini-views down everybody's throat. Pinched my wife! And now it's so sad. Because know what he did? Rimney? Typed her a note, like it was from me, saying I was leaving, due to I didn't love her, due to that Kyle thing. But that is so not true! I loved her all through that. But now, rest of her life, she's going to be thinking that of me, that I left her and the baby, when we were just getting over that pinching thing."

His eyes fill with tears and his hair stops blowing and he crushes his pink glasses in his hand.

"Go see her," I say. "Tell her the truth."

"Can't," he says. "You just get one."

"One what?" I say.

"Visitation or whatever?" he says.

I think: So why'd you come here?

He just smiles, kind of sad.

Then the front window implodes and Rimney climbs through with a tire iron.

"It's going to happen now," Giff says.

And it does. It takes two swings. It doesn't hurt, really, but it's scary, because it's happening to me, me, me, me, the good boy in school, the boy who felt lilacs were his special flower, the boy who, when poor Jean was going, used to sneak off to cry in the closet.

Going, there's an explosion of what I can only call truth-energy-flood. I can't exactly convey it, because you're still in that living-limited state, so lucky/unlucky, capable of smelling rain, rubbing palm against palm, having some new recently met someone suddenly brighten upon seeing you.

Rimney staggers to the door, unbolts it, stands looking out.

I pass through him and see that even now all his thoughts

are of Val, desperate loving frightened thoughts of how best to keep her safe.

Giff and I cross the yard hand in hand, although like fifteen feet apart. Where are we going? I have no idea. But we're going there fast, so fast we're basically skimming along Trowman Street, getting simultaneously bigger/lighter, and then we're flying, over Kmart/Costco Plaza, over the width of Wand Lake, over the entire hilly area north of town.

Below us now is Giff's house: snow on the roof, all the lights on, pond behind it, moon in the pond.

Giff says/thinks: Will you?

And I say/think: I will.

She's at the table doing bills, red-eyed, the note at her feet, on the floor. She sees me and drops her pen. Am I naked, am I pale, is my hair blowing? Yes and yes and yes. I put one bare foot on the note.

A lie, I say. Elliot's dead, sends his love. Rimney did it. Rimney. Say it.

Rimney, she says.

That's all the chance I get. The thing that keeps us flying sucks me out of the house. But as I go I see her face.

Rejoining Giff on high I show him her face. He is glad, and now can go.

We both can go.

We go.

Snow passes through us, gulls pass through us. Tens of towns, hundreds of towns stream by below, and we hear their prayers, grievances, their million signals of loss. Secret doubts shoot up like tracers, we sample them as we fly through: a woman with a too-big nose, a man who hasn't closed a sale in months, a kid who's worn the same stained shirt three days straight, two sisters worried about a third who keeps saying she wants to die. All this time we grow in size, in love, the distinction between Giff and me diminishing, and my last thought before we join something I can only describe as Nothing-Is-Excluded is, Giff, Giff, please explain, what made you come back for me?

He doesn't have to speak, I just know, his math emanating from inside me now: Not coming back, he would only have saved himself. Coming back, he saved Mom, Dad, me. Going to see Cyndi, I saved him.

And in this way, more were freed.

That is why I came back. I was wrong in life, limited, shrank everything down to my size, and yet, in the end, there was something light-craving within me, which sent me back, and saved me.

acknowledgments

The author wishes to thank the Lannan Foundation, the Syracuse University College of Arts and Sciences, his colleagues and students in the Syracuse Creative Writing Program and English Department, and the good people at Riverhead Books, ICM, *The New Yorker*, *Harper's*, *Esquire*, *McSweeney's*, Red Hour Films, and UltraVinyl Films for their generosity during the writing of these stories.

He also wishes to thank Paula, Caitlin, and Alena, whose love and support are constant, boundless, and essential as air.

a note on the author

George Saunders is the author of two short-story collections, *Pastoralia* and *CivilWarLand in Bad Decline*, as well as the children's book, *The Very Persistent Gappers of Frip*. His work has received four National Magazine Awards, and has been selected for the O. Henry Awards and Best American Short Stories collections. In 1999, Saunders was recognized as one of the twenty best young American fiction writers by the *New Yorker*. He teaches in the creative writing program at Syracuse University.